The Seed Apple

A Novel by

SHELDON GREENE

ISBN: 1523612568
ISBN 13: 9781523612567

CHAPTERS

1

INSIDE OUT

Canyon Springs, California, wasn't anything like I thought it would be, but nothing is. Take my vision of America before I arrived in 1947, something between the Lone Ranger and Al Capone salvaged from two old movies. As for California, I had pictured a sun hot enough to fry an egg, oranges growing on trees, and endless flowing rivers of cars. The last thing I had expected to find were Jewish Indians and the disturbing coincidence of grey eyes.

It was dry, so dry that I could feel my skin shrinking almost as soon as I stepped out of the plane. I took a deep breath and imagined the bronchitis retreating into the damp basement of my lungs. For once in my life I felt like sending Dr. Zucker a thank-you note with my check. It was Dr. Zucker who, having treated me for chronic bronchitis two times a week for two straight months, suggested a dry climate with the confession,

"Even medicine has its limits." Coming from him I had to pay attention, for he believes in medicine as the American Legion believes in the flag.

I went inside the airport building and got a second shock-- it was as cold as the inside of a beer cooler, just as damp as back home in Bolton, Pennsylvania, in January, and my bronchitis triumphantly advanced. They've got it backwards, I thought, the winter is inside the buildings and the central heat is out- side. No wonder they said things were strange in California. It was a good thing I was still wearing my tweed jacket, or I'd have gotten a chill. Fortunately, the airlines took only a few minutes to deliver my new plaid suitcase, and I was back out into the heat again, boarding a refrigerator with wheels to the town center in search of the El Paseo Motel.

There I was, suitcase in hand, feeling as out of place as I had 35 years before, the first day I landed in America, gawking at people in their bright neoprene outfits (there are so many names for plastic clothing I can't keep track of them, perhaps it's not neoprene), and craning my neck at the inverted giant mops that line the streets, instead of shade elms.

The more I looked at the outlandish clothes the more the natives looked back, at least until I realized just what was so curious about me: not the tweed jacket. No, it was that I had forgotten to remove my rubbers from my shoes. Why, I might just as well have been carrying an open umbrella. I noticed the rubbers about the same time that I saw the sign down the street that advertised the El Paseo Motel.

The brochure had claimed it was historic, but except for the plaque declaring it to be on the site of the first hotel in

Canyon Springs, it was all pasteboard stucco and curtain wall aluminum and glass, an undistinguished compound, prison-like, surrounding a kidney-shaped turquoise swimming pool. I had an upstairs room, looking over some gravel-covered roofs, television aerials and cooling units. The bed sagged a little but no worse than the one at home. At least the cooler wasn't turned on and the aluminum windows opened onto a balcony to let in the dry air. I puttered around the room, deliberately taking my time. After all, I had a whole month to do nothing but unpack.

In truth, I was already feeling lonely and homesick; I'm just not the kind of person who comes into a strange place, sits down and starts a conversation with the person next to me. I'm more the type that other people like to talk to.

Nevertheless, stiffening my lip, I put myself into those bright green Bahama shorts, the striped nylon short sleeve shirt and the fishnet baseball cap with the fish on the front, the rubber sandals from Hong Kong, and looked at myself in the full-length mirror. Not Cary Grant, but not altogether unattractive either; a little round-shouldered, tall and on the spare side. With my long face, wide-set blue eyes, knife-thin beaked nose, I looked more Prussian than Jewish, an irony that never gave me much comfort. I ran my hand over the greying stubble of my beard rejecting a shave. After all I wasn't on my way to an interview. The survey completed, I grabbed a book and an oversize towel and went downstairs to the poolside.

I spread the towel on an empty lounge chair and sat down next to a friendly-looking man and a woman about my age. There I was, feeling and looking like a mushroom frying in a sun so bright that even my pores were squinting. I didn't get a page into my book before my neighbors introduced themselves--Dan and Thelma Boop from Anaheim, California. I had never before met anyone named Boop and wondered if it was common to California but I held off asking. Dan had risen to the highest bureaucratic rank in the postal service and, according to him, he would have been the postmaster if he hadn't been a card-carrying Libertarian. This I initially took to be membership in the local Friends of the Library, an interest which should have had nothing to do with his capacity to move the mail from here to there.

Obviously, I had misunderstood him. For the next hour, I sat next to a prickly plant listening to a condemnation of government intervention in just about everything from the regulation of the size of almonds to the shape of toilet seats. Through this monologue his wife sipped what looked to be a drink made with ice and lime, and looked alternatively pie-eyed and apologetic. When he finally left off in the middle of a theory of the disappearance of the state to get another beer, Thelma said, "I hope he's not boring you, Sam."

"Mendel," I corrected her.

"He's as bad as those Jehovah's Witnesses when it comes to the Libertarian thing. You'd better move over there into the shade, Mr. Mendel, next to Sarah Cavanaugh. You're not used to the desert sun." To prove it she poked the skin of my arm the way my mother used to poke a roast chicken.

She was right; my stomach was already the color of a boiled Armour wiener. I hastily moved into the shade next to a woman who was wearing a full-length canary yellow kimono and a wide-brimmed straw hat, and who was, to my satisfaction, engrossed in what looked like a textbook.

Thelma followed me. "Sarah?" she said. The woman next to me took no apparent note of her. "Sarah?" Thelma repeated as to a sleeping person. "Come out of that book and meet a new guest." This time the woman responded, peering up from under her hat, and I got a first look at those disturbing grey eyes.

If she was bothered -- and I'm sure she was, I would have been if someone had pulled me out of the private world of an engrossing book -- she showed no sign of it, as she gazed at Thelma Boop. I liked the reaction, this first impression of the woman. There was shyness, warmth and intelligence in her eyes as she turned from Thelma to me.

Our eyes met, her open grey and my pale blue eyes met and got reacquainted, for these were eyes that I knew, at least had known and not forgotten. They were old friends, those grey eyes; old, old friends come from far away, come from the other side even, and the awareness of the fact caught in my throat and made me blink. All of this, she saw.

What of the rest of her? There is more to a person than the eyes, although there's not much more that's more important than the eyes, especially in the beginning. She hadn't said a word and neither had I, but I saw that we could be, perhaps even would be, friends. I had forgotten all about Thelma.

"This is Mr. Mendel."

"Just Mendel. Mendel Traig."

She smiled. She had full lips and her teeth were large and yellow, probably from smoking.

"Where are you from, not from here?" she asked. Her voice was smoky, soft and husky for a woman.

"Bolton, Pennsylvania."

"I've been there." She had a very crisp way of talking; she pronounced each syllable, unlike many Americans who swallow the ends of words. "You've gotten quite a burn," she said. "Do you have something for it?"

"No, but I can get something later at the drugstore."

Her curiosity satisfied, or perhaps her duty to be polite discharged, she went back to her book. Thelma gave me a wink and returned to her husband, the would-be postmaster general.

The pool caught my eyes. Two boys under twelve, mirror images of each other, were keeping a red and white beach ball in the air, jumping, splashing, screaming and laughing, nearly drowning a flabby man who was doing the side stroke with an extinguished cigar clamped in his teeth.

I decided to cool off and went to the edge, descending step by step. The water was cold compared to the air, and I inched my way, feeling the ice creep up my loins to the most sensitive place, after which it didn't seem to matter, and plunged in feeling the chill winch up my spine, and the water seep into my sinus (what would Dr. Zucker say?). I did a noisy lap or two, gasping for air like an asthmatic, and finally ended clinging to the side and thinking how out of shape I was. Maybe I should take up jogging, or tennis after my bronchitis went away, I thought.

I dragged myself up the ladder shaking my head to get the water out of my ears. My companion of only a few minutes had disappeared, no doubt a rejection of my drowning-man swimming stroke. Not knowing whether I would ever see her again and actually caring--those grey eyes--I retreated into my book; some spy novel.

After only twenty pages, I put the book down, watched the afternoon shadows grow, and found myself wondering what this Sarah Cavanaugh was doing down here - where she came from, and when I would next see her. Hunger, true to its nature, interrupted this speculation, and I found myself reading a little hand-out magazine which listed in rivaling superlatives all of the local restaurants, complete with a little map.

For a small town, there were a lot of cuisines to choose from, ranging from two or three Chinese regions to the cooking of Mexico, with Yugoslavia somewhere in between. There was even a place that served something called "turf and surf" that had to be sod boiled in sea water, possibly one of those organic vegetarian dishes. I decided on a delicatessen. If the Jewish food wasn't up to the standard of New York, at least I would approach the other nationalities with caution. And if the food was too bad, I could always buy some sardines and cheese, maybe some salami, and heat up some tea on the water heater that was suspended on the bathroom wall of my room.

First a little nap -- the jet lag was taking its toll -- then a shower to get the chlorine off my tender skin, and away I went wearing what might have been the flag of Jamaica.

The Lox Box was noisy with conversation and smelled of creamed herring, fat, and corned beef. It's a good thing I had brought my book along, because there was a long line of tourists ahead of me. I managed to read a few pages in the line and was soon seated, studying the foot-long glossy menu,, and suspicious that there was a limerick writer rather than a cook in the kitchen. Something made me look up and I saw near the door, toward the back of the line, a familiar pair of grey eyes observing me with level curiosity. Without a thought I raised my hand and gestured to her. She smiled, and approached me a happy expectant smile on her face. At the time I wasn't sure whether the smile was for me or for the empty chair opposite me. Her indigo silk dress was belted at the waist and blossomed from a small waist over and around wide hips. She was well proportioned but had picked up some extra layers over the years.

She sat down and said in that husky now breathless voice, "I didn't mean to be rude this afternoon, but I had a telephone call to make."

"Don't apologize." She gave me a look that said she didn't intend to apologize, she did just what she wanted to do, but that didn't keep her from considering other people's feelings. "Is this place any good?" I asked.

"It's not Cantors." She saw the name meant nothing to me and added, "It's a place in L.A. I forgot you're from Pennsylvania and wouldn't know Cantors. The corned beef's not bad."

With a name like Cavanaugh she probably wasn't Jewish, I thought, but in a city like Los Angeles maybe everyone is a little Jewish, so I took her advice and ordered a corned beef sandwich, some bean and barley soup, and some Russian tea cakes with tea. After turning me toward the traditional deli fare, she had a salad without dressing, saying as she grazed in a matter-of-fact way, "I'm trying to lose a few pounds."

The corned beef was acceptable, but it took a long time in coming, and in the meantime we got a little acquainted. Not that I gave her the "third degree," as they say, although no one ever told me what the first two degrees were. No, I just sat there enjoying the company, feeling the tug of the string that connected those grey eyes to something inside me. And she talked a little, not continuously, and not sparingly either. Eventually, she told me what she was doing in Canyon Springs besides losing weight and not even in response to a question of mine, not directly at least. I told her that I had just come and would be in Canyon Springs for a month, and she replied that she too would be here for a month on an assignment. She was, of all things, a metallurgical engineer concerned mostly with stress, working for a company called Alumaloy. They had a contract to supply some new light metal for a tower in the desert, something to do with government communications. While she was in the area she had decided to enroll in something I had never heard of, a "fat farm" she called it, looking a little self-deprecating for the first time.

"It must be the place where they got this corned beef," I said. "Seriously, what's a fat farm?"

"The opposite of what it sounds like. It's a place where they help you lose weight. Actually, I finished last week."

Towers in the desert and paying money to starve were just what Nudelman and Estelle, my friends in Bolton, would expect in California. To be honest, I didn't really care what Sarah talked about. My interest at that moment was in her. I had to admit that she would do well to lose a few pounds, but at her age and -given her overall appearance of neatness, confidence and proportion - she seemed to be too concerned about it. Had she lived in Bolton, she might not have cared so much, but who knows what's important to a woman with a big job in the manufacturing business. I thought of my two lady companions back home, neither had what you would describe as an ideal figure. Estelle Cantor was always dieting, so she said. Certainly if they could have combined their physical assets the result might have been startling. Whatever their physical shortcomings, it was more who they were that appealed to me.

There Sarah was, telling me a few anecdotes about her diet, looking at the remains of the tea cake with well-controlled longing while I found myself savoring it, dragging out its consumption and for once getting pleasure out of the fact that at 48 I still weighed no more than 147 pounds no matter how much cake I ate. It struck me that I was being mean, so I stuffed the last piece into my mouth and suggested we walk back to the hotel.

"I'd be glad to, but I can't," she said. "I've got my car outside. I've got to go out to the tower site for a few moments to take a reading on the instruments."

"So I'll see you around the pool, maybe," and I stood up feeling a return of the initial loneliness.

She must have seen my disappointment, for she said, "You can come with me if you've nothing better to do. It's a nice ride. I'll even put the top down."

"Don't tell me you drive a sports car. Now I know I'm in California."

"Then you'll come along?"

I nodded, thinking, what would Zuckerman say to me if I didn't? He likes fast cars and the experience would fill a postcard.

This Sarah Cavanaugh was a fast driver, not that I was scared. The car, so she told me, was quite safe; something maroon with an Italian name, like a movie director, all leather and wood inside. I've always thought that leather chairs and polished wood belonged in a library rather than a car but what do I know.

We rode out of the town, into the open desert. The sun had set behind the jagged mountains; there was a trace of its warmth left behind in the colors, but mostly the promise of a cool night in the pellucid sky above the horizon. The air felt good blowing around my head, and it was scented with something unfamiliar, delicate, yet aromatic that might have gone into pipe tobacco.

Beside me Sarah the engineer, her eyes attentive, shifted the wooden gear knob, saying nothing to me and I, not wanting to intrude on her pleasure, said nothing in return.

Sharing the silence, we rode on and for the first time I understood a little of what my ancestors must have felt when alone they faced nightfall in the desert; a suspended stillness, a brightened sky ripped open by the black jagged hills. It was no wonder that some of them talked to God out there, or thought that they did, for if God wanted to have a chat with one of us I couldn't think of a better place.

And that thought was in my mind when I saw the tower, rising in silhouette from the crown of a hill like a hand with a finger pointing at something in the sky. Then Sarah spoke for the first time, "That's the tower."

We drove closer, climbed a narrow road which branched left and ascended the hill on which the tower stood. There were no signs to tell you what it was or who was doing it, or for that matter, why. There were no workers, no machinery, nothing that identified the construction with work in process. As for the tower itself, from the ground looking up it was hard to tell exactly what it would become. In the semi-light of pendant nightfall, it was a web of greyish metal as wide as an office building at the base and tapering generally upward, at a slight angle.

She stopped the car, reached behind her seat and pulled out a light with a square battery attached to it. Then she got out of the car and walked toward the base, leaving me to do as I chose. Usually looking through holes in a fence at construction doesn't appeal to me. Maybe it was the semi-darkness, the lack of manifest function of the structure which attracted me to it, pulled me out of the car and prompted me to go inside its frame.

I didn't follow in her tracks. She had gone over to a wooden box and was looking at something like a water meter. I went under the frame, which was raised on four metal piers. Once inside I could just make out other shapes. It was like one of those Russian dolls with other dolls inside, for it seemed to contain a smaller metal tower, although in the darkness it was hard to see. Sarah joined me and moved the cone of light from her torch from point to point, giving me a fragmentary view of the shape within a shape.

"What is it, a tower within a tower?" I asked.

"Exactly. An older one."

"The whole thing looks like there's no work going on."

"It was started four years ago," she explained. "But some group got an injunction and since then it's been tied up in the courts."

"Is the court battle still going on?"

"The builders won an appeal. Work will start again this week, but there are still some legal complications. But don't ask me to explain them. I'm just down here to evaluate the existing structure."

We went through the base of the inside tower only to see still another shape, this one of rough stone no more than twenty feet high.

"I suppose there's something inside that one as well?" I asked.

"I really don't know, but that was part of the legal fuss. It's a sacred place to the local Indians, and they don't want people mucking about on their holy site. But that's not the whole thing."

"This must be very old then."

"Someone told me it's three thousand years old, maybe the oldest thing built by man in the United States, and with some interesting pictographs on it." We were about to turn and go back to the car when we heard the neighing of a horse coming from the other side of the stone platform, followed by the sound of feet scraping on stone and the clatter of horses' hooves. Two people on horseback came around the stone platform and rode straight at us. Sarah flashed the light at them and the horses, one brown and the other white, veered out under the tower frame and disappeared over the side of the hill. The clatter of their hooves receded as the horses scrambled down a rough slope. We turned and walked out from under the outer tower to the rim of the hill, but by the time we could see over the edge, they were already on the desert floor and galloping in different directions.

"Who do you think it was?" I asked.

"Maybe some of the people who don't want the project completed. It could have been Indians. Did you get a look at them?"

"There wasn't much light, but one of them looked like a girl. I thought that there was long hair blowing behind her back as she rode off, but these days you can't be sure even about that."

As we rode back across the now dark desert, I asked her, "Why is the tower leaning like that, isn't it going to fall over?"

"No, that's part of the design, it's unique and unorthodox. Sort of like one of those stunted trees that grow on windy mountains -- it leans into the wind. That's one of the things I'm supposed to be looking at."

"I guess if the leaning tower of Pisa has been standing all of these years, why not a leaning tower of Canyon Springs. Anything is possible in California, that's what they told me before I came. I've been here less than one day, and I already see they were right. It should attract the tourists. What do they want to do, put one of those revolving restaurants on top?"

"They do. Part of the way up at least, but I think it's basically for communication."

"Who will they communicate with?"

"Nuclear submarines, apparently in case of war. Conventional broadcasting as well, when they're not pushing the doomsday button."

"Why is it out here in the desert?"

"It's the rock. You probably didn't notice in the dark, but the top of that hill is a solid rock, one that apparently goes down several thousand feet into the ground. Taken together, what will be above ground and what is below ground, it's supposed to be the best stationary antenna for transmitting and receiving radio signals in the world."

"Who knows, maybe that's why the first platform was important to the Indians. Maybe they were communicating with something out there."

"Not my department," she said. We fell into silence again, and I watched the lights of the town glow brighter. And to think that only a few hours ago I was worried about being bored.

As we pulled into the parking lot on the side of the motel, I was beginning to really understand what they meant by jet lag. I was, despite the afternoon's nap, feeling like I couldn't stay awake. So we said good night in the patio of the motel and shook hands. She thanked me for coming along with her, and I thanked her for the opportunity. She was returning to L.A. early in the morning, but would be back Monday or Tuesday and might see me around the pool.

"So fine," I said, offering to walk her to her door.

"No," she answered. "I'll manage alone, but thanks for the offer anyway." And up we went, by the same stairs only to find that we were right next to each other. It was good night again and each to our rooms.

I took another shower to get the dust of the desert off of me and realized when the water hit me that I'd forgotten about

the sunburn remedy. Oh well, I thought, by now it's too late
to do any good. It came to me that I might ask her for some,
but knocking on the door of a strange woman in the middle
of the evening was the last thing I was prepared to do. Suffer,
Mendel. If it's the biggest problem you have on this trip, you'll
be lucky, I told myself. I fell asleep quickly enough, feeling the
cool sheets on my hot skin, and I dreamed that I was climbing
a tower into the clouds following someone. I woke out of the
dream afraid of something indefinable, my heart beating fast,
and it was a long time before I could sleep again.

2

AN ENCHANTED GARDEN

Only the second day and I was already loose in the ends, as the saying goes. All I really had to do was cure my bronchitis, and the dry air was taking care of that. Even my sunburn was tolerable. My only task on that entire Friday was to find out where the synagogue was. I could at least pick up one loose strand of my usual life by attending Sabbath services that evening. Who knows, I might even meet someone to talk to.

As it turned out, the only synagogue listed in the Yellow Pages was on the other side of town. I asked the desk clerk if there was one closer, nothing fancy, even one without air conditioning would do, but he barely even knew what a synagogue was. He did volunteer the information that the Masonic Temple was in Indio and the Odd Fellows met every Friday night for a chili feed.

Doing nothing took up the whole day. I was glad I hadn't chosen inactivity as a vocation. I had time from my hands down to my feet. At length, having eaten something, I was on my way across town to the synagogue when I saw a withered old man wearing cowboy boots and carrying a blue velvet bag. He was going in the opposite direction. Without a thought I turned around and followed him like Alice in pursuit of the March hare, and that in retrospect is not a bad metaphor, considering what occurred.

It was, of course, the blue velvet bag embroidered with a yellow Star of David that attracted me. Without that I would never have given him a second glance. There was nothing on his wrinkled shiny bronze face with the straight white hair peeking out of the dusty black cowboy hat that suggested even a couple of ounces of Jewish blood. He looked just like one of those Charles Curtis pictures of an old Indian.

Should I talk to him, ask him if he is going where I think he is going or should I simply follow him? I had the notion that if I spoke to him he would just walk away from me. With that thought, irrational and born of shyness, I trailed him at a distance of half a block. Judging by his pace he was in a hurry and, although I was taller, I had to walk fast to keep up with him. After a few blocks he turned down a side street and I expected him to turn into some bougainvillea-hung courtyard at the end of which was some anonymous storeroom synagogue. Instead, he headed toward the tasteless two-story glass facade of the Canyon Springs Spa.

To my relief, he kept on walking right past it until, crossing a street, he came to what looked like an authentic replica of a Mexican plaster wall capped with a triple row of faded, fluted tile, and embraced by old blood red bougainvillea. The wall was long in both directions and surrounded one of those large, undeveloped blocks that incongruously alternate like the squares of a chessboard with modern landscaped theme developments. At the time I had no idea of the reason for the strange pattern of development, but I eventually found out. Rising over the wall was what looked like a tropical forest.

The man went up to a recessed wooden door near the center of one course of the wall. Without waiting, without knocking, he opened the door and went inside. I hesitated at the juncture of two courses of the wall and wondered what to do next. After all, the place was private, mysterious, it could be anything; there could be vicious dogs behind the wall or a mental institution.

Still uncertain, I walked closer and examined the door. It was made of weathered thick slats of wood, with a wrought iron latch, very old-looking, and there wasn't so much as a nameplate. I had three options: go inside, try to reach the synagogue on the other side of town (too late for that), or return to the hotel and forget the service. Did Joshua hesitate when he reached the walls of Jericho, I thought? He did not, and neither would I.

Summoning my courage, and with an ear cocked for watchdogs, I opened the door and walked into the Garden of Eden. A path curved away, under all sorts of tropical trees with fruits and flowers that I had never before seen. In contrast to the surrounding desert, it was cooler and even humid, but not uncomfortably so. The air was moist and laden with tropical scents resembling honeysuckle and cinnamon. An oasis! More than an oasis, for there was in the location and variety of the trees, shrubs and low plants bordering the path, a subtle hint of design.

I walked down the path ogling the flora. An arbor of branches of the tallest trees closing over it, the path meandered carrying no hint of where it would lead, yet always revealing a fresh surprise: a few moss-covered stones, a trickle of water from an unknown source, a tree of pendant-white trumpet flowers, another festooned with ripe mango-like fruit.

Enchanted I walked on not even caring where I was going. Ahead I saw a thinning of growth and a gate flanked by thick stands of bamboo. In the same instant two human forms flashed across the path, one behind the other, moving quickly through the aperture between the foliage. One was male, the second female, and they were young. That much was obvious, for they were both nude from their longish brown hair to their flying feet.

I stopped in my tracks unsure whether I should continue, a little fearful of what might lie behind the gate. But my curiosity overrode my timidity as it usually does, and I continued, at the same time peering into the screen of foliage for another fleeting glimpse of them.

As I approached the gate, I half-expected the man I was following to greet me and say, welcome, Mr. Traig, we were expecting you, but nothing like that happens in real life. I hesitated and looked over the gate, prepared to move quickly in the opposite direction if need be.

What I saw was a two-story Spanish adobe house. Long wooden balconies ran all around the second story, overhung by a tile roof. Like the outside wall, the structure might have been hundreds of years old by the look of it. In the center of the building, partially enclosed by its two wings, was a brick patio with a stone fountain and, to the left of the fountain, a row of benches of plain wood without backs, facing what looked to be a portable ark the place in which the Torah scroll is kept.

Four men were standing near the benches, casually talking. I recognized the man who I had followed. Two others were about as old as him and similarly dressed. The fourth was in his early twenties. What was this place? The Jewish Home for the Aged, one of those planned retirement centers I had read about, or was it simply the home of some rich person with a taste for horticulture and seclusion? Whatever it was, a service was going to be held and I knew I would be welcome.

I opened the gate and stepped into the open, and four heads turned at once in my direction. Not sure what their reaction would be, I hesitated for a moment at least until I saw the youngest of the group smile and even beckon to me with a gesture of his arm. Now what, I asked myself. They must be expecting someone besides the Sabbath. The older men watched me approach for an instant, then turned back to their conversation, but the young man continued to watch me with an expectant expression, much as if he had me on a line and was reeling me in. When I had come to within a few paces of the group, he nodded after looking down at the velvet bag which I too carried. Then he turned and trotted around the corner of the house and out of sight, leaving me alone with the three others who continued to converse in a language made up exclusively of vowels.

I simply stood there, waiting. Besides the sunset, which marks the beginning of the Sabbath, the service was still lacking a _minyan_, the required minimum seven worshippers. Judging by the weakened light the sun would soon leave the sky, although between the trees and the house I couldn't see the horizon.

As I looked up, I saw someone who could, and who appeared to be doing just that. Up on the roof was a platform on which a man was standing, facing west. He was looking at the horizon through an instrument, a kind of phonograph turntable on a pole. Also on the platform, somewhat behind him, was another pole, this one hung with a small metal disk, a gong perhaps. At my distance I couldn't make out the details of his features. He was neither fat nor thin, neither tall nor short. His dress, like his form, was undistinguished: a pair of loose-fitting black pants and a white shirt. Only his hair was singular: a wavy copper red.

I was just about to turn away from him when, without turning his head, he shouted, "She's coming," and at that moment something did come, though it wasn't the Sabbath, not yet. Instead I heard the thud and clatter of a fast-moving horse and on it, the young man who had disappeared around the house.

"Good Sabbath," he shouted to the man on the roof.

"You're not leaving?" The man looked down at him for a moment. The one on the horse replied only by urging his mount into a trot back around the wing of the house. I heard the pace quicken and gradually dissipate. Here was one Jew who would be riding on the Sabbath.

I turned and saw that the three old men were now seated on the benches wrapped in their prayer shawls, though not the white silk kind I was used to. These were brightly striped and looked more like Indian ponchos. When I could no longer hear the horse, the man on the roof shouted, "The bride arrives!" and he struck the gong. Before the sound had died, three more men and two women came around the other wing of the house, pacing to the rhythm of a leather covered drum.

Before too long the man on the roof came out of the house and the celebration of the coming of the Sabbath began. What I saw then I had never seen before. Not that it was unfamiliar, for it wasn't. It was like listening to a dialect of your own language. There were chants which sounded like Hebrew, but not always. There were words which I understood, and yet many were strange to me. And there was music, delicate, beautiful music with a little flute, half the size of a piccolo, and a small harp with not more than ten strings, as well as the drum.

How can I describe it in words? A collage of fragments of all the sacred music I had ever heard. There was discord, a complex drumming, a reckless Benedictine chant, the undulation of Indian music, a vine of Hebraic melody. Add the sigh of a gentle wind, the murmur of a brook in the fall, the joy that one feels when a loved one returns, yes, the latter most of all.

I had assumed that the man on the roof would lead the ceremony, but he didn't. The whole of it came off as smoothly as breathing. It was as if they had done it so many times that it was second nature to them, but at the same time there was no feeling of somnolence. No, they were experiencing it as if it were for the first time and this, of all that I saw, impressed me the most. Someone who listens to music a great deal would understand; it was in the tone, in the nuance, in the way they moved, in the lively expression on their faces, in their eye contact. As I watched, I understood why it was that the celebration began precisely at sundown--the coming represented a personal visit.

When it was over, I didn't know what to expect. As yet, no one had said anything to me, and I assumed that the only reason the young man had welcomed me was that he was looking for someone to replace him. I half-expected them to ignore me, to simply go into the house leaving me standing in the patio. I was wrong. All of them gathered around me with the same expression that I had seen on their faces during the ceremony, and they said to me, "Welcome." They said it with such sincerity, and I felt the warmth of it. It was as if I were the surrogate for the Sabbath Bride. The man who had been on the roof simply took me by the arm, as he would an old friend, and led me inside the house to a dining room where a table had been laid with bowls and platters of food. It wasn't what I was used to by the look of it.

He poured wine into a ceramic sky blue goblet, said the blessing, and this I understood. He did the same with the bread, not a braided *challah*, but a flat yellowish pancake. He passed the wine around, and we each took a sip. Likewise we had a morsel of bread, and the people began filling their plates.

Only then did he introduce himself, "Arin Binyan," he said, and gave me his hand.

I told him my name, and we looked at each other. Like me, like my new friend Sarah, he was an observer. While he was studying me I got a closer look at him, at the builder of the tower, although at the time I didn't know it, didn't know, couldn't imagine anything of what I was to learn of him. All that I could see to look at him was that his skin was the color of the American Indian, that tanned bronze look that sunbathers covet, combined with classic Semitic features: a longish face, high prominent cheekbones, deep-set dark eyes and a thin curving nose above a delicate bow-shaped mouth and sharp chin, not to mention the incongruous burning bush on his head.

He was neither Indian nor Semite, he was both. At the time I imagined that some Jewish peddler had come out west in the last century, found himself a Native American wife, settled down, became prosperous and started a family. I was only off by three thousand years.

What he was thinking about me I have no idea, but it was clear that something of the same process was going on in his head. With this thought I smiled, and as if he had come to the same conclusion, he too smiled, and I think nodded as if in silent agreement. It was the kind of nod that sometimes occurs between two strangers on the street, but was more intense. He gestured toward the table and said, "Please, eat."

"I'm sorry, but I've already eaten."

Looking disappointed, he said, "Do me the honor of having something at least. It is a custom. The guest must eat something."

Do me the honor, I repeated to myself, an antique formalism. He had a trace of an accent to go with the curious turn of speech, as though he, like me, had grown up speaking a different language.

"Of course," I said. He handed me a plate which, like the ones on the table, was of handmade pottery, and I took a little of the food. This is not the time for a culinary review, and I'm not qualified to give one. It is enough to say that it tasted good, and had ingredients that were strange to my palate, except for the cake which tasted of bitter almond, honey and vanilla, reminding me of one of Estelle Cantor's favorites.

So far, I've said nothing of the others. As with Arin, they came up and introduced themselves, threw in some small talk, but not one of them asked me anything of a personal nature. If only somebody had prolonged the conversation beyond "Nice day," I might have been prompted to ask some of the questions that were literally strangling me. But I held back, afraid to say the wrong thing, like asking someone who had spent the better part of a day baking a cake where she had bought it. I resolved for the moment to act as though I knew as much as they did.

Arin's wife, Miriam, offered me more food. She was slender, with black straight hair streaked here and there with grey, and a broad flat Eskimo face. After eating, the others took their leave, and I thought it best to do the same. Arin, looking very tired, walked me to the door. He shook my hand, looked into my eyes with warmth weakened by his fatigue, and asked me to come back the next day. I thanked him for the invitation, and he repeated it.

I turned to leave, and he handed me a pocket flashlight saying, "The path is dark. This will take you out and bring you back again." I took the light and was glad to have it.

The ceremony, its rituals both familiar and strange, lingered like the smell of a gardenia. And what of the man, Arin Binyan? Was he an eccentric, a cult figure -- I had heard that there were such people in California -- a heretic who had concocted his own mishmash religion? Before falling asleep, I resolved to return and find out more. The second day, like the first, was not what I had expected. I fell into a real Sabbath sleep that night, a profound sleep that let me know what the world must have been like when there was only a void.

3

MYSTORY

The third day, the Sabbath, was like the day before. The late winter sun was warm when it touched the skin, yet withdrawn and more detached, confident in its monopoly of a pristine blue sky. My adaptation to the desert resort life was quicker than I would have imagined. My small but colorful wardrobe no longer caused me to wince. I looked in the mirror and saw that the angry burn was already fading toward a tan, and my pale blue eyes in contrast to my skin looked brighter and more lively. I even went for a swim in the pool before breakfast, no longer inching down the steps, although I was still hesitant to jump right in. Without stopping, I swam three laps and pulled myself out over the side, breathing heavily but observing that my bronchitis was beginning to recede. Recognizing my improved health, I even had a twinge of guilt over a month's absence from my job as Administrator of the Synagogue and Center when a week might have been sufficient

The sun, the sight of the ragged mountains rising so abruptly from the desert floor quickly pushed that feeling to the back of my mind. I found myself looking over the low roofs of the horizontal, sometimes drab, stucco buildings at the steep fluted mountain wall, looking up to the saw-toothed edge where it meets the sky in a collision of brilliant white light, and thinking that I'd never been in the presence of a landscape of this scale...not to demean the gentle rolling terrain of Western Pennsylvania.

Every day I try to learn something about myself. This day I reaffirmed my basic conservatism, for back I went to the same restaurant where I had eaten breakfast the day before, even buying a copy of the local newspaper to read over my poached egg and rye bread toast. I've never lost the particular fondness for rye bread--although the rye bread of reality can't match the rye bread of my memory, always fresh and fragrant from my mother's oven. Still, this wasn't bad rye bread, flown in daily from Los Angeles, the New Jerusalem.

Halfway through the poached egg I saw, on page four of the first section of the local newspaper, an article with a picture of the tower. The tower was the first surprise but not the last in the article. As Sarah had said, work was resuming on the first stage this week after a five year delay due to litigation filed by the Halibut League, an environmental group, and the Anasazi Indian tribe, which considered the project a desecration of their sacred high place. As for the tower, the article explained that when completed, it would

both beam low frequency signals to nuclear submarines anywhere in the world, and serve as a worldwide Christian radio transmitter and restaurant. At the time, the connection
between the two, if any, eluded me. The developer of the
project, Arin Binyan, refused comment on the rumor that he
was threatened with yet another lawsuit. I doubled back on
that paragraph in the article. It was indeed Arin Binyan, I
hadn't been mistaken. The name was odd, and it stuck in my
mind. Yet it was hardly imaginable that the spiritual man
I had met, a man of another century, I wasn't sure which
century, would also be the developer of an innovative communications tower and tourist attraction. People always surprise me; they often have sides to their nature which don't
show, like Jacob Shatz, who dresses in loud suits and tells
foul jokes at the wrong time, but who is an authority on the
harpsichord music of Scarlatti.

Now I *had* to return to the house. So return I did, with a
mixture of anticipation and apprehension, the latter born of
a shyness that I've never totally overcome, the former flowing from my incurable, and often vexatious, curiosity. I was
shown into a low-ceilinged, long room by an elderly Indian-
looking woman. The room was furnished with dark Spanish-
style furniture, the floor was handmade tile polished by years
of use, and the ceiling had rough-hewn black timbers running
its width every five feet. At the far end were French doors
beyond which was a patio and the garden.

Binyan was standing with his back to me looking out of
these French doors. Hearing me, he turned and approached,
his hand extended, an open, welcoming expression on his face.

He came close, and I saw that the fatigue of the night before was gone, although perhaps it was just that his mood was
lighter.

"I hoped that you would return, Mr. Traig." He took my
hand and held it fast, not shaking it, simply holding it as if he
wanted to keep me there with him. Perhaps he did, for there is
sometimes a bond which grows out of anonymity. Two people
meet for the first time. They sense a potential for understanding, pursue it without restraint, and mutual friendship can de-
velop even in a few hours. As I looked into his large, opaque,
but sensitive eyes, I had the feeling that we could be just such
precocious friends. We looked at each other with appreciation
of one another's imagined yet unknown qualities.

"Would you like a tour of the house?"

"Very much."

"Then come with me. It's an easy way of getting acquainted."

We went first down a long tiled gallery to his study. He
called it his work room, but it looked more like a stage set
for Faust; there was the same ponderous medieval furniture, a
massive oak library table, shelves running to the ceiling load-
ed with books, much like in my own apartment except that,
where my books were printed in this century, many of his were
bound in leather and looked like they were hundreds of years
old.

I wanted to go further. Books are my obsession, and I
would have been content to remain in this room for the rest of
my vacation. My intuition was right. He and I had something
in common.

"Did you collect these books?"

"No. It was my great-great-grandfather."

I took this in with envy and awe. My eyes wandered from the dark oak shelves to a table on which stood an architect's model of the tower. He went to it and scrutinized it much as a sculptor might study his own work, with a mixture of pride and criticism of its flaws.

I asked him how much of it had been completed.

"You know about the tower?"

"I read about it," I said and went on to tell him about my having met Sarah Cavanaugh.

He hesitated for a moment then he pointed to a platform close to the bottom. "Just here, but before the end of the month, we'll have the central pylon installed."

"And how high will that be?"

"Seven hundred feet, about one third the ultimate height." He pointed inside the structure to a column. "You see that tube inside, running part way up the center like a smoke stack? That's the spine of the next stage. This quadrilinear extension goes the rest of the way."

I stepped back and gazed at what to me resembled a drunken version of the Eiffel Tower. "I don't know about such things, but it looks quite remarkable. Who designed it?"

"I did. With my son." The last he added with a lower, more subdued tone.

"Was that your son, the one on the horse?"

"Yes, but he's not the designer. He's still in college. It was my other son." Somehow the tone of his voice, and the abrupt remoteness in his eyes, kept me from asking more questions, and I turned instead back to the books.

"Where did your great-great-grandfather come from, the one that collected the books, I mean?" I asked only to change the subject. It was a natural question for me, since everyone comes from somewhere else, except for the Indians, and even they came from Siberia.

"He came from here."

"You mean the United States?"

"I mean right here in Binyan Valley."

"You mean he was born here?"

"And his father before him."

But for his appearance I might have thought that he was simply upgrading his family history. Only the Indians were here then, or so I supposed. Maybe he really was an Indian, a convert to Judaism. Yes, that had to be it. That would explain his wife's looks. He must have gotten rich selling off some of the reservation land to hotels and developers. There was always an explanation. "Are you of Indian stock, then?"

Then he told me something of his family's history, and when I expressed both incredulity and interest he guided me to the shelf with the journals. I riffled through the pages of one and he said, "Most people aren't interested anymore. There are other diversions." He looked a bit sour, then brightened and added, "You seem to be a scholarly sort of man, Mr. Traig."

"Call me Mendel."

"Then I am Arin." He saw my eyes ranging around the shelves and said, "Look around, fondle the books. Most of them will be glad to get some attention from someone who cares about them."

"You talk about them as if they are alive."

"They are." He looked up at me, his eyes wide. "Don't you agree?"

"Yes, yes," I said, as excited as a child in a toy store with a rich uncle.

The shelf in front of me held some twenty volumes of various sizes, all bound in stiff faded leather. Some had titles in Hebrew, some gave no hint of their contents other than by the appearance of age. I picked one off the shelf at random, a hand-written manuscript. Arin walked up behind me and looked over my shoulder, saying, "Now that one is particularly rare. It's Abulaffiah's, *Book of Enoch*." I put the book back on the shelf, handling it with the respect it deserved, and turned to him, wonder in my eyes.

"It's so strange to find a library like this here in the desert. Of course, it's a good place to preserve them, but I would expect it to be in a city, near a university."

"One thing about the desert is its surprises. It's like a quiet person; it takes some patience to understand it." Taking me by the elbow, he said, "Come over here, and I will show you the proof of Solomon's expedition." We were walking toward a cabinet when the nude people in the garden came to mind, and I said, "While we're talking about the fascinating history of your family, let me ask you about something really strange that I saw in the garden."

"What was that?"

"Nude..." I managed to get only the first word out when the door opened and Miriam entered. She nodded and smiled at me, then, looking at Arin, she said, "Windel is here. He drove down from Los Angeles."

He looked up and shook his head. "Tell him I never talk business on the Sabbath. In all these years he should know that by now."

"Then see him as a guest, Arin."

He smiled at her and looked at me. "You can see who the wise one is in the family. Tell him I'll be down in a moment." Then, looking apologetic, he said to me, "Excuse me, please. I'll come back as soon as I can. In the meantime, the library is at your disposal." As an afterthought on the way to the door, he added, "Over on that shelf near the door you'll see a grey notebook that might interest you in light of what we were talking about. Solomon's voyage, we'll save for another time." And with that he closed the heavy wood door behind him, leaving me alone in the center of the room, feeling myself being scrutinized if not judged by all those ancient books. Even the sun was probing me, for I could feel its warm touch on my back.

I stood there like the proverbial donkey caught between two piles of hay, unable to decide where to start, when my eye was caught by the notebook that he had mentioned, standing out on the shelf, the only green clothbound volume among the leather bindings. With expectation I went over to it, picked it up and held it in my hand, savoring the anticipation of its contents. I always get that feeling in varying degrees with a new book, but I can't recall excitement like I felt that day as I walked over to a stout oak armchair at the table, sat down and opened the folio to the first page. It was old, possibly one hundred years old, judging by the paper, the ink faded to brown in places, and the penmanship, vertical, open, even

ostentatious. At the top of the first page was written in bolder
script, "Translation from the Hebrew of Extant Portion of the
Journal of Malachi Binyan. Gabriel Cardozo, 1768, translated
into English, Boaz Binyan, 1909" I began to read.

THE JOURNAL OF ABRAHAM BINYAN
(As originally translated by Gabriel Cardozo in 1768
English translation by Boaz Binyan in 1909)

"I, Abraham Binyan, master builder of the Binyani, now having reached my 89th year in God's grace, have set my hand
to the final task of recording for my children and their children that part of my life which I recall and which has meaning to them. There is much of my life that I remember in my
late years that causes me to reflect, even to speculate on what
might have happened had I done something different. It is
one of the tasks of the old person to wait for that meeting with
the dark spirit and another to relive and experience again the
pain and the joy of a life lived.

"I have lived here in this oasis in this lonely dry valley,
months away from any settlement other than the simple
native encampments, for 35 years. A house has been built
of ample proportions, of mud brick with walls a full arm's
length in width. The water is sweet and springs out of the
ground year round. Virtually every species of tree, plant
and flower that we carried with us from Yucatan flourishes
in this new Garden of Eden. My children are grown, have
reached maturity, and like old trees have fallen, leaving behind their children, now also grown. About me, before
my fading eyes, I see their children, and in them I see not

only the image of my offspring but the memory of my own childhood in another place. Seeing this, I am comforted with the notion that like the trees which we have planted, brought to this vast land by our forebear from the land beyond the sea of the rising sun as seeds, my seed will sprout again and again on this soil so long as men shall live, so long as this sacred earth shall give them sustenance. As I sit with the children about me, I have but one task, to impregnate them with the long and distinguished history of our tribe, the Master Builders, and to impress on them the duty to teach it to each generation, for those who know not their seed, know not themselves, and those who know not themselves are as animals of the field.

"My forebears have inscribed their history before me. Some remains, some has been lost to us like the Book of Moses. All that we have of them is what our ancestor, Jakov, remembered after he crossed the endless sea in a boat manned by Phoenician and Israelite seafarers at the time of a king called Shlomo (Solomon).

"To begin my story, I must look back in memory to our home and lands in Yucatan that nurtured our people for generations after Yakov mixed his blood with Xuya, a princess of the Mayans. It was the year I completed work on the latest face of the Temple of the Rain God, Chac Mool. We had fully 2,000 measures of land given over to maize, peppers, and other foods, cultivated by five hundred peasants who lived on the land in small villages of mud and thatch. We were not demanding of more than our share, and they lived much the same as if we were not even among them, but in those times the easy master and the hard master suffered the same fate. Drought, declining fertility of the soil, and disease are not just, they visit every home.

"In good times a man tills his land and is content. In hard times he is not glad, and when he is beaten with the stick of oppression, taxed and worked to the point of desperation, no ruler can sleep quietly. Such were the circumstances before we left. The peasants had been bled in ceaseless wars, but the sons of the warrior princes had forgotten the austerity of their fathers, had grown fat and self-indulgent, preferring the banquet table and the bed to the management of empire. This they left to the priests, who expanded their supervision of the growth cycle (they studied the heavens and told the farmers when to plant) into an incessant and perpetual program of construction of larger and more elaborate ceremonial platforms to the Gods, ostensibly to ensure the coming harvest, but temples only expand the power of the priestly class. Each peasant was required to give one month of each year in labor to temple building, while the wealthy contributed precious stones or gold instead of labor. The peasants accepted this duty with resignation, until the crops began to fail, and disease struck them down like a whirlwind lashing a field. A few of their leaders saw that the priests no longer served, they ruled without function, and all over the land peasants anointed the holy places with the blood of the priests.

"When it was clear to us that life no longer held out purpose or promise, we made plans to find a place where the farmer's stick still dug a clean straight furrow, and the corn still yielded its promise. But how and where? To the north were other peoples, who spoke strange tongues, harsh warrior people. Perhaps they too had need of master builders. I could exchange my services for a home and land, as had been done long ago by my ancestors. What we could take with us we would, including those peasants who, like us, were willing to take risks and face uncertainties. Before making final plans I went to see the old prince in Uxmal. He received me formally, a sign of deference, seated cross-legged on a mat, wearing a high and elaborate headdress composed of quetzal feathers. I could see from his eyes that his mind was on a journey.

"Surrounded as he was by servants, a bowl of chocolate before him, he neither knew nor understood the decaying state of his land. But he remembered me and treated me cordially. It was I who had designed and supervised the construction of his great house. I asked him courteously where I might go with my family.

"'You have no reason to go from here,' he said.

"'The building is done for a time,' I replied.

"'Harvest your crops.'

"'The crops are poor.'

"'They will be better next year. Pray to your gods,' he said, fanning himself with a feather fan.

"I remained silent. It is not prudent to argue with a prince, even a prince who has ceased to rule but knows it not. He looked at me for a time, then ordered a scribe and said, 'Write that I, Xieuktal, lord of all the earth, admonish all lesser rulers to deal courteously and hospitably with

Abraham Binyan, master builder, and let him pass to the lands which by this document I give him, to wit all the land beyond the peopled lands that he chooses for himself, his progeny, and his servants.'

"I heard him speak, watched the scribe write and when the document had been sealed with the prince's own seal and given to me by his own hand, together with a gold ring bearing his seal, I thanked him and asked, 'What land would that be?'

"Without hesitation he answered, 'Why, that land to the north which is unpeopled. I cannot describe it, for I have never seen it.'

"'Does it exist?'

"'If it exists, it will await your coming. If it does not exist, then you lose nothing by not finding it.'

"Impressed by the prince's reason, and having no alternative, I returned to our estate to begin preparations. (There follows a list of possessions carried by sixty of the peasants who agreed to accompany the family, including a scribe who had traveled to the north with the prince's emissaries and who knew several of the tongues.)

"'Don't look back a second time, or you may be turned to salt as was Lot's wife,' I told Miriam, my wife, as our procession left the low gardens around our house and entered a grove of Pxtepl trees.

"She replied, 'That which is already salt cannot become salt.' Our seven children were not so sad, for the path in front of them was the way of their life, as yet undisclosed, and did not God admonish Abraham, 'Leave your father's house and

go to another land.' It is fitting that he said it to the son and
not the father.

"About the first portion of our journey much or little can
be said. Much can be said because the days were filled with
new sights, dangers, injuries, sickness, even death. Little
can be said because the days merged into one another with a
sameness: the landscape was the same, flat and covered with
dense low trees, pierced only occasionally by the platform
of a temple. We passed these temples quickly, dedicated as
they now were to the dead, inhabited only by carrion birds
and rodents. No more than two years had passed since the
great rebellion, but already weeds were growing in the cracks
of the great stones that covered the ceremonial plazas, small
shrubs had taken root on the sloping sides of the pyramids,
the bright colors of the reliefs were already fading and the
sites had been picked clean of anything that could be used or
carried away. The villages and the surrounding fields were
not abandoned, but neither did they have the appearance of
well-husbanded and tended farms. Some fields were returning to their ancient forest masters, and had already lost their
symmetry, while those which were still tended had as many
weeds as domestic plants, and the maize, like the people
and the dogs, looked puny and vulnerable to disease. They
watched us pass with sullen indifference, and whether we
camped near or far from the villages or temples, we posted
strong well-armed guards around our encampments, and the
men slept with their weapons at their sides. It was with relief that, as we approached the frontier of the Land of the
Maya, these melancholy settlements with their crumbling

mud walls grew farther apart, until finally we put the last of them behind us and had only the road winding beneath the thick canopy of the forest to remind us that we were both leaving and approaching great civilizations. Sooner or later we would leave the forest and enter the country of either the Mixtec or the Zapotec. Which one we knew not, since they were engaged in perpetual warfare and the boundaries were continually changing.

"Our days were hot and the humidity drained our strength by mid-morning. The nights weren't much better, but in spite of the heat we lit a fire, carrying the embers with us, carefully protected through the day, so as to have some hot food, but even more to scare the jaguars, whose dreadful screams frightened all of us. The forest was morbid like the grave: sunless, smelling of mould, crawling with stinging insects, poisonous centipedes, scorpions, and snakes. The air was as heavy as a dead man's wrappings. Only occasionally would the sun thrust an arm down through the foliage and touch a spot on the ground, and God would remind us that with perseverance we would again see the sky.

"Only when it seemed to the stoutest among us that we were turning in circles into the very bowels of the forest, the scout who moved ahead of our column came on a *Stella,* more a carved stone. On the side which we approached was a Mayan glyph and on the other side a strange sign, the sign of the Mixtec Kingdom, according to our guides. It was the boundary marker. We gathered around it with solemnity, apprehensive, not knowing the reception which we would receive when at last we encountered these strange warlike people, certain only that as we left the marker behind us we would be burying our old life.

As we stood there, each with our own thoughts, Miriam took my hand and said to me, 'We could still turn back.'

"I answered, 'With God's favor, we'll find a dry place to camp this night.' Among us there was silence, except for one of the bearers, who sang alone of the girls of his village.

"Late that afternoon we broke out of the forest into full sunlight, and ahead we could see a hamlet, the houses thatched like those of the Mayans but long on two sides. Off the trail an old man, thin and knotted, was bent over a row of corn, pulling weeds. His skin was darker than the Mayans of our party, and seeing the alien the whole column grew as quiet as the hunter who gets the first sight of his prey. The old man, for his part, took no notice of us, or so we thought, but not for long...."

A sound pulled me out of the story, and I looked up to see Arin backing through the door, at the same time talking to someone who I could not see as yet.

"What you have been telling me is crazy," said the other person, in a cigar smoke voice. Arin turned, looking surprised to see me sitting at the table hunched over the book, my head turned up, no doubt with a curious if not stupid expression on my face. The other man came into the room and, seeing me, stopped. He was stout, of middle height, with a heavy folded face. His large brown eyes imbedded in two sacks of flesh, together with his golf course tan, gave him the look of a Saudi Arabian prince, except that instead of a robe and headdress he was wearing a well-tailored pearl grey leisure suit and a silk shirt open at the neck to expose a tuft of chest hair. Over his wrinkled prominent forehead was a well-tonsured bush of graying hair which he was smoothing with his hand.

"This is Mr. Traig," said Arin. "He's helping me with a library project. We can speak in his presence." Why did he say that, I wondered?

To me he said, "This is Marvin Windel; we have a business relationship. Just go on with your reading if you like. You won't bother us."

"No, I really should leave," I protested, feeling ill-at-ease but at the same time not wanting to go, responding to the tug of my devilish curiosity. I got half-way out of my chair, but Arin, pressing gently on my shoulder, pushed me down, saying "Stay, stay." And then to Windel, "You've never seen the library before, have you?"

"Yes, once before," he replied, pacing about, looking but not seeing. "Very interesting." Then a moment later he snapped his head around and continued, his tone sharper, "I still don't see how I let you get me into this mess, Arin."

"You got yourself into it," he replied softly and without a pause he said to me, "What do you think of that manuscript?"

"Fascinating! I can hardly wait to finish it, but it raises so many questions for me."

"Perhaps there will be time to answer some of them. How long will you be here?"

"A whole month."

He shook his head in disapproval, "Not long enough." Then he turned back to Windel, who was standing in the center of the room looking annoyed. "Do you celebrate the Sabbath, Windel?" Arin asked.

"Arin, you've known me long enough to know that every day is business. I inhale and exhale business, at least that's what my wife tells me."

"How are your children?"

"When I see them, I'll let you know. What do they call it, they are into their own thing." He continued with an edge on his voice, "You know, Arin, I'm completely out of patience. I gave you over half a million dollars four years ago, and I've still got nothing to show for it but heartache."

"Patience, Marvin, it's the Sabbath, you know."

"Not for me. I've had four years of Sabbath, while that lawsuit dragged through the courts..."

"Everything comes to an end, even a lawsuit."

"And now, after all this time, I get this letter from the Defense Department..." He took the folded letter out of his pocket and shook it in front of him.

"Would you like some refreshment, before you leave?" said Arin. "You're welcome to stay the night, and we can talk about it tomorrow."

"I haven't time. I've got a meeting with my lawyers tomorrow in L.A."

"Not another lawsuit, I hope?"

"What can I do when the Navy says they definitely won't permit a restaurant on the tower platform because of the security risk." His jowls began to tremble.

"Windel, your high blood pressure. Nothing is worth getting sick over. Besides, as you know, they've opposed the restaurant since they got into the project two years ago."

"If I sue, I'll have to sue you, too. You're the one that caused the problem with your three independent contracts. It's like selling the same building three times over."

"I didn't seek out the Defense Department. They came to me. We've been through all of this before," and in the same breath he said to me, "What's the reading today? Do you have time for a little discussion after..."

"I know. We've been through it many times. I only hoped it would work out in the end."

Arin looked at him with weary patience and said, "If they hadn't joined the project when they did, you might have lost your entire investment, Marvin. Now at least they've got to buy you out."

Windel nodded with a painful grin. Then, extending his hand to Arin, he said, "I'm sorry I bothered you today. I should have known better. But I was in town and wanted you to see this letter before the next meeting."

"No matter. You're leaving, then? You're welcome to stay. I can have Miriam get one of the spare bedrooms ready for you. Dinner won't be so special tonight, but salad will do you good. You're gaining some weight again. Too much of that rich French cooking in Beverly Hills.

"You don't have to say it." He moved toward the door, turned and nodded with a gaseous smile on his face. "I'll be down again next week for that meeting with the bureaucrat, the stiff bastard."

"Don't forget the Reverend."

"Who could forget him."

"Safe journey, Marvin." He turned to me, his face serene, and said, "Would you like to discuss today's Torah reading? I get such little opportunity to do it with anyone."

"Why not."

"And you'll stay for supper? A sniff of the spice box?"

"You don't have to ask twice, that is, if I'm not intruding."

"The Sabbath is meant for guests, at least that's what my father used to say."

"And his father before him?"

"And his before him," he answered.

After Windel left he suddenly opened up to me. It was as though I had undergone some initiation rite. And I must say I responded to him. Later, I saw it as only an encounter of two very lonely men, with a common love of old books and slightly outdated religious practices. That afternoon I didn't give it any thought. It just felt like infatuation. And as we browsed in the library and he discovered and admired books that he had forgotten about, he told me some things that people only tell strangers encountered on a train that they will never see again, or the closest of friends.

When at last we went down the wide stairs to dinner, it was with the chuckling whimsy of old friends. The dining room and table was set with white linen and ornate baroque silver service. There were flowers, fresh cut and fragrant, and tall silver candleholders. He must have seen me wonder at it, for he said offhandedly, "A family can accumulate a lot of things living in one place." Miriam, his wife, looked different than the night before. Her cinnamon complexion was polished and glowing in the light, and it contrasted with her black hair and her simple black gown.

"I see the table's set for Zev," he said.

"He should be back soon," said Miriam.

"We'll have to begin without him."

Then Arin officiated at a little ceremony that, like the night before, was both familiar and exotic. He sang, or rather chanted, over a smoking candle, lit it and in time extinguished it, then passed around a silver dish of aromatic herbs that he inhaled like snuff. I did the same, and felt an almost immediate exhilaration that left me wondering whether it was due to the spirit of the ceremony in this tranquil evening light, or some stimulant in the spices.

Within a few minutes after we sat down Zev appeared at the door, wearing a faded blue plaid shirt and muddy worn jeans, and for the first time I got a really close look at him. Zev was of middle height, with broad shoulders tapering to a narrow waist and short legs. With his mother's narrow onyx eyes and complexion I would have taken him for an American Indian. By the look of his face, he was in his early twenties.

"Miriam looked glad to see him as she said, "Have you cleaned your boots, dear?"

"They're tolerably clean, mother," he responded, looking at me with what might have been apprehension or curiosity. When Arin introduced me, his acknowledgement was shy, if whimsical. "My substitute," he said. He sat down and forthrightly turned to his soup, eating quickly like a very hungry man, his head bent low over the plate, a shock of his black hair falling over his forehead. Arin watched him with what I took to be a mixture of censure and parental indulgence.

"Sorry to be late," Zev said. "The repair of that pump took a lot longer than I anticipated."

"That's the third time this month," said Arin.

"Time it was replaced."

"There are a lot of things that need replacing, Zev, but there are times when we must make do." Arin looked down at the table for a moment.

Unexpectedly, Zev looked at me with a shy smile and said, "I hope that our little service last night didn't confuse you too much?"

Before I could answer, Arin looked my way and said with confidential irony, "Zev is a man of science. The Sabbath is a day of recreation to him."

"And a day of work as well when it suits you," interjected Miriam quietly.

"I suppose a farmer sometimes must have his sabbath in the heart," said Arin, passing me a heavy silver bread tray.

"You've noticed that Father has a way with words," said Zev, looking at me, and I began to feel uncomfortably like a juryman who has been given the task of adjudicating the merits and faults of each of them.

"Your father is a man of rare sensitivity," I said. This seemed to please all three of them. At least it closed the question, for Arin and Zev turned back to a discussion of the farm, something about whether all the tomatoes had been set in the southwest 100 acres. Zev told him that they had only planted 70 acres so far, since apparently Miguel the regular foreman had under-ordered. Arin looked gloomy when he heard this and began moving his fingers through his red hair, making it stand up like flames.

"I've called all around, but can't get any except for a new variety just developed by the University at Davis..."

"Spare me that," said Arin. "We still haven't recovered from the last variety they developed."

"I'm only trying to be helpful," Zev said.

Arin didn't look like he even heard that. "You could put lettuce in on the other forty. But it's probably too late for that. So when we need the money we are likely to be out $40,000 in profits." His hair looked like it was about to consume his head. Remembering me, he said, "Now you're getting a notion of what it takes to put food in the supermarkets."

"Every business has its problems," I said thinking of poor Sidney Cantor, may he rest in peace. At the same time I was wondering why he wasn't more involved in the day-to-day management of the farm himself.

Telling Arin that he would continue his search for tomato sets, Zev then asked for twenty acres to experiment with wild grains. At the time I wasn't aware that this was the subject of his dissertation. Arin said, "We need all of our acreage in production, Zev. You know that. The University ought to provide land for your research. That's what we pay our taxes for."

"All I've been promised at Berkeley so far is some glass house space. But the seed is available now, and I could change some of the valves on the drip irrigation system to provide precise controls for equating protein content with soil aridity and nutrition." He went on to talk about needing 40 test plots and explaining that he could even come down once a week to supervise. His voice took on enthusiasm as he talked about species of wild grains gathered from Africa, Mexico and the Middle East, the promise of increasing the world's food supply and so on. Arin listened, at least he seemed to be listening, but his look was that of a person who didn't want to be convinced.

He even interrupted Zev to ask me, "Are you interested in biology, Mendel?", as though he had already heard enough. Before I could say that I was interested in everything, he turned to Zev and said, "I can't make a decision today, Zev. You're asking for an $80,000 subsidy to your research from the family at a time when we just can't afford it. Maybe you could get a grant from one of those foundations..."

I could see Zev's enthusiasm leaking out of him. Miriam was watching it as well and she said, "You know your father doesn't make a decision like that quickly. Give him some time to think it over." Then to Arin, she said, "You will consider it, won't you? It's important to him."

"It's important to the world food supply," said Zev as he stood. "If you'll excuse me, I've got to check out the irrigation crew before they go home." He looked at his mother and in response to an unspoken question added, "I'm going on to Francesca's. I'll probably stay the night." He bent over his mother and kissed her, looked at his father and I could see him deciding whether to approach him or simply leave. Arin looked up at him with an expression not lacking in feeling, but definitely reserved. It was enough to put Zev off. He nodded and left the room.

Arin looked after him. When he was gone he said to Miriam, "I'm trying to save our land and he wants to save the world."

"He's young, Arin. He doesn't understand." Arin didn't reply. She watched him for a moment, her flat face impassive, showing only attentiveness and nothing of her thoughts. Then she turned to me and said, "Isabel has baked a lovely almond cake. I'm sure you will have some, won't you, Mendel?"

"Of course," I said.

When I tried to leave after dinner, he again asked me to stay in a way that told me he wasn't simply being polite. That was all I needed, for I was becoming more and more curious about him and his family. As for Arin, I seemed to be having an emetic effect on him.

We returned to the library, now draped in deep shadows that disappeared into the dark wood of the high ceiling. The lights, when he turned them on, were glowing pools and cones flowing out of luminous green glass shades, reminding me of an aquarium. No doubt about it, the room had its own atmosphere, as though the books were all of them alive in the quiet way that a plant is alive. And I, breathing this dry, leaf mould-tinged air, felt as though I were somehow absorbing something of them. I felt as though I were in touch with something indefinable yet reassuring, calming. Who knows, it may only have been the spices I sniffed, but I don't think so. The feeling returned to me again and again in that library.

Arin had pulled a book off a shelf and as we sat down at the table side by side, he opened it to the cover page. Without even speaking about it - I don't even remember what *it* was - he began to talk about his son. He spoke with pride tainted by bitterness, and it wasn't until later that I understood the source and complexity of his feeling. This night, Arin was more interested in relating events, not in any given sequence, not like a historian.

Some tea and a plate of dates had been left for us on the library table. He looked at the dates, picked one up, admired it, and began to speak about the grove as though the date had, through its glazed, sticky surface, transmitted its own history.

"You asked about the size of our farm. We have 640 irrigated acres near Indio."

"A lot of land." A square mile, I thought. He was like the landed aristocracy of Poland.

"We had much more; maybe 10,000 acres. But little by little it was lost or sold to pay off debts. That's a long story. Sometime..." He left off and gestured at the shelves as if to say it's all here, in these books. He took another date. "Please eat one. It's from here."

"You mean your garden?"

"No. From our date grove. We had a date grove. It was the first in the entire United States. I sold it a few years ago. It was a luxury we couldn't afford. It cost more to operate than it yielded in income, something my son doesn't understand. We still lease back part of it, at least until they build the rest of the condominiums. They are stalled, too, you see, like the tower." He picked up another date, thought about eating it, dropped it on the plate. "Zev has never forgiven me for selling the date grove. I did make a mistake in not discussing it with him. But he was just a kid. He learned about it from one of our workers, rather than from me. He confronted me, we had words and he hasn't forgiven me. It would be nice if we could take back some of the things that we have said."

"Still you should be glad that he's studying agriculture."

"I am proud of him. But I doubt that he'll apply what he learns to our land. I suspect that he'll go off to some university and do something theoretical. That's the way he does it. He even backed into biology. He discovered some species of wild grape out in a canyon on Francesca's father's land. Francesca is his girl friend. He discovered Francesca the same way. He had classified all of the plants in a small area of the canyon. There's a year-round stream and it's very lush. He did it for a high school science project. Some professor at college found out about it and encouraged him to become a botany major. Otherwise who knows what he would have studied."

"That's quite an achievement for a high school kid."

"He's smart, all right, but impractical, as you might have gathered from our discussion at dinner. This tower has put us in a tight money bind. We need all the earnings we can get out of our farm. And believe me, even that is speculative. One bad decision can wipe out a whole crop, turn it into a $100,000 debt overnight. It happened two years ago with the tomato crop."

Then he told me about a new hybrid tomato that Zev had convinced him to plant on 100 acres that had developed some kind of leaf curl and had to be plowed under. Although they never found out just exactly what had caused the loss, it was clear that Arin blamed Zev for not paying more careful attention. He even blamed Francesca for diverting Zev's attention with swimming, long rides in the desert and late nights and early mornings.

"What I would do with $100,000 now, although much of it would have gone for taxes. So you can see why I'm skeptical when again he tells me to plant some new kind of tomato. Or, even worse, take land out of production to save the world from hunger--not that it isn't a good goal. I respect him for it. But it all shouldn't fall on us. We're not the Rockefeller Foundation." He got up suddenly and began scanning a shelf, finally returning to the table with a bound pamphlet. It had some long name dealing with grain classifications. The author was a Stanford professor named Helvig. On an inside page was a special acknowledgement to Zev Binyan "for his invaluable assistance."

"Well, that's what Zev has been doing at college," Arin said with a kind of skeptical pride. "This is probably boring you, but as you can see I go to sleep with it and wake up with it." He looked at me with anguish and fatigue and said, "Here you come down on a vacation and fall into my troubles. If I don't stop you'll never come back here."

"We all have strength to bear the misfortunes of others," I said.

"Shakespeare," he replied, an intimate look in his eyes. "God must have sent you to divert me, Mendel. Do you believe that?"

"Well, I..."

"You don't have to answer."

We went on like that for hours. Only to get him off the painful subject of his son and his finances, I asked him he was doing on the roof just before *Shabbat*. Looking like he wanted to tell me but was afraid that I would think him crazy, he began with, "Have you ever heard of the *Matronit*, the Sabbath bride?"

I told him that I had in fact read a book about the subject. Reassured, he initiated me into one of the rituals of the Binyan tribe, the belief that what might be called the female side of God brings the Sabbath across the sky. While the *Matronit* never lands, because of the low moral state of mankind, people who look carefully for her can see her manifestation.

"You have seen it?" I asked, hardly concealing my skepticism.

"I think so."

"What do you see?"

"Sometimes it's like a faint violet shadow rolling west, like a veil. No more than that." His eyes grew calm as he said this, as though he were seeing it then. When I finally left and followed the beam of my flashlight through the silent fragrance of the garden, I found myself fascinated not only with the library, but with Arin's almost irreconcilable emulsion of materialism and spirituality. I was somewhat overwhelmed by his needs, but also flattered by his unexpected trust in me, a stranger. And finally I was saddened by the realization that this man with everything anyone could want was so desperately alone. I was no stranger to loneliness

4

REVELATIONS

Smog in the desert. No one had told me about that when the travel agent sent me here. Probably he didn't know about it either, but there it was, taking a holiday from its home in Los Angeles, looking like airborne mould, and smelling like an indoor swimming pool. And I thought that my bronchitis was on the mend. What could I do: shut it out, turn on the air conditioner, close the drapes and go back to bed? None of those. I did what you do when you're face to face with something all-pervasive, something inescapable like inflation, an incurable disease, or even worse things, things I've seen. I put on my sunglasses, oiled myself with suntan lotion, and went out into it, hoping that it wouldn't be so bad, and that in any event it would soon go back to where it had come from.

I walked along the balcony looking down into the patio, at the surface of the pool vibrating in the sun, and I learned something else about smog: when you're in it, you can't really see it. Why, you even begin to deny it by thinking that it is hovering over someplace else. It must be what the mind does with something that is simply too big to handle. Which is not to say that I didn't resent it. We want our vacations to be perfect, to contrast with our everyday life. Rationalizing that the smog wasn't so bad now that I had gotten used to it, I went down the stairs directly to a reclining chair next to a well-oiled Sarah Cavanaugh, seated under the same floppy hat but wearing only a yellow one-piece bathing suit and a layer of lotion.

She didn't see me. At least she didn't allow that she had. I couldn't tell what was going on under the hat, although I suspected that she was again reading a book. The bottom of her bathing suit was hiked up about an inch, and I could see that under her Polynesian bronze was a Nordic complexion. I spread my towel over the chair and sat down, unsure whether it would be right to bother her, wanting to say something, wanting to see those eyes again and at the same time wondering whether she had actually gotten thinner in the last week or whether the pattern on the bathing suit was creating an optical illusion. Perhaps it was the suntan lotion, I mused, a kind that conceals the configurations of the body. I was both surprised and glad to see her. It had been nearly a week since she had gone off to Los Angeles and having looked for her around the pool, I assumed with some disappointment that she wasn't coming back. Fortunately my two visits with Arin Binyan had partially met my need for companionship. Under her floppy hat were those grey eyes. There was only one way to see them again.

"Smog," I said, or rather expelled, with more contempt in my voice than I actually felt, and feeling surprise that I had said anything at all. It had the desired result in any event, for she lifted the brim of the floppy hat and turned a half-annoyed expression on me and said, "Pardon?"

I repeated in a more subdued, self-conscious tone, "Smog. It's the first time I've ever experienced it."

Her eyes warmed a little as she recognized me. "I suppose you're surprised that they have it all the way out here in the desert?"

"Nothing surprises me, really. I didn't know what to expect. I'm like Marco Polo in China."

I hesitated, not sure whether to pursue the subject into deeper waters, or to drop it. Would she think me a bore if I did so? Probably. She was looking at me, showing no emotion, and seemed about to get back under the hat when I said hastily, "It looks like the diet course is having its effect, not that you needed it, but you seem like you have lost some weight in the last few days even."

"That's very gallant of you to say, but I don't think it's true," she said, turning her eyes toward the double roll in her bathing suit that was cushioning her waistline. "I've still got a long way to go, but since you mentioned it, I have lost four pounds; probably just fluid." She looked proud of herself.

"No, I don't think so..." I said, but the thought trailed off as I had this sudden memory of the steady loss of weight which comes with starvation. I saw skeletal shapes and shuddered.

"Is something wrong?"

"No, nothing, why?"

"You got sad all of a sudden."

"No, I was only thinking that you should go easy with your diet. A sudden loss of weight can be bad for your health."

"I was under a doctor's supervision at the clinic."

Her expression, one of patience but detachment, told me that she wanted to go back to her reading. I hesitated, wondering if I should withdraw honorably from the conversation. Impulsively, I said, "Would you like to have dinner with me tonight? I've never had Mexican food. Who knows, it might go well with the smog..." My voice trailed off, and I watched her.

She snickered at my joke, almost a horse's whinny, looked down then up again and nodded slowly, as if she hadn't quite made up her mind. "Why not? It's not the best place for my diet, but I'm sure that I can find something to eat; maybe a plate of cilantro."

"I'm not imposing on you?"

"No. Not at all. But if you don't mind, I'll go back to this book. I've got to finish it before noon."

"Say 6:00? I'll knock at your door," I said.

"Or I'll knock on yours."

Relieved to have gotten through that conversation, glad of her decision, I went for a swim, dressed, and went down to my habitual place for breakfast, realizing that now I have two people to get to know. And to think how anxious I was about being lonely.

This pleasant thought, combined with the relaxing combination of the swim and a hot shower, added a bounce to my step as I left the compound of the motel only to see what was either a demonstration or a parade, at first I wasn't sure which. Just abreast of the motel and moving, not really marching, in the direction of the center of the town was a band, more an assortment of musicians than a band, dressed in outlandish costumes no two of them the same, walking together but not in step in a non-formation, without files, and led by a caricature of a strutting Harpo Marx with a six-foot baton. They were playing what sounded like a Viennese waltz adapted to a minor key, with all the usual band instruments except that some of them were painted bright colors, with the horn of the tuba the most bizarre, a ring of teeth to make it resemble an open mouth. Behind the musicians came two people supporting a banner which proclaimed, "Halibut League Marching Band and Chataquah Society."

Behind the band came several diverse contingents, including six, possibly seven men in electric wheelchairs supporting signs, "Disabled Veterans Against the DoD"; the vanguard of the Halibut League which according to its placards wanted to save the environment from microwaves; a group of dancing Indians wearing feather headdresses, foot-stamping to the rhythm of a skin drum, who wanted their sacred Taquitz Rock back; about twenty middle-aged men and women dressed in polyester, identified as the Constitution Party, who wanted to keep church and state separate. They were followed by three or four very excited barking dogs bearing no resemblance to one another, except that they were all dogs, participating more for the sheer excitement of the spectacle than to make a political statement.

I identified most of all with the dogs. A parade has always sent a little thrill through me, and I walked along briskly beside them wondering what it was all about. This wasn't George Washington's birthday or anything like that and, except for people who happened to be on the street at the time and who turned from their window-shopping to give the demonstration a moment's half-conscious notice, there were no lines of parents with children on their shoulders waiting for the floats, clowns, and fire trucks. The only spectators were the police and they were busy shunting traffic to one side of the wide street.

I had just reached my restaurant and was walking up the four concrete steps to the entrance when a young man with frizzy black hair rushed up behind me. He leaned his sign against the wall next to the door and rushed into the restaurant, leaving me to stare up at the legend printed in Chinese red poster paint, "Tower of Babble".

As I was about to go inside I noticed yet another group, also carrying placards, walking in the opposite direction on a seeming collision course with the parade. I squinted at the signs, trying from the distance to make out what they said and wondering what would happen when the two groups met.

As I watched, the man with the frizzy hair came out, grabbed his sign, turned to me on the way down the steps and said, "Thanks for watching my sign." Then he trotted up the street after the parade. He caught up with the three dogs and one, a black and white spotted mutt, jumped up at him in welcome.

With ragged, undulating shoving the groups converged, and it looked as if there would be more; but they simply wove together like one of those intricate formations that marching bands perform at half time. Whatever the ones in white supported, it was obvious that the marching demonstrators disagreed for, as the band wove among them, it switched to a kind of orchestrated braying.

I went inside the restaurant before the passage had been completed and found myself wondering what would happen if warring armies had to pass through each other's ranks close enough to see the color of the eyes. Well, it was an idea.

Enough speculation on an empty stomach. I bought a newspaper and entered the restaurant. Rowena, the waitress, a matronly type with lips like candied apples, smiled when she saw me. She didn't even ask for my order. She signaled with a little circle formed by her thumb and forefinger.

While I waited for the poached egg, I surveyed the other patrons, mostly tourists by their looks. With my growing ties to the town, Arin Binyan and Rowena, I was already becoming disdainful of strangers, like the new dog on the block who barks at everyone.

The eggs came with Rowena's self-satisfied declaration, "Just like you like them." How much loneliness had Rowena the waitress vanquished, if only for a quick twenty-minute meal, I wondered as I watched her pillow-like shape squeeze between two chairs on the way back to the kitchen.

I rummaged through the newspaper, thinking that I might as well have brought along the one from the day before. Maybe in small towns they just recycle the same articles at intervals of a few months. The only thing changed on the front page was the prime rate of interest and the unemployment rate; one was up and the other was down, I can't remember which was which. Even the tower was there again, this time on the front page. Work was resuming on the second stage this week; in fact, tomorrow, after a lapse of five years. I suppose I knew that already.

The article prodded my curiosity and made me want to return to Arin Binyan's library for the afternoon. More than that it set me thinking about the dinner that I had so rashly set up, wondering how I could possibly get through an entire evening of small talk. Beyond the tower, what would we talk about? Life in Los Angeles, the adventurous life of a synagogue administrator, the people of Bolton, her aspirations?

How long would it take before she found me boring? It takes so long before two people are comfortable enough to bear long silences. So it has always seemed to me at least, but then I don't go out of my way to meet people, not that I avoid them. My long term friends, Estelle and Nudelman, are as comfortable as old house slippers, but then I've known them since I was 14. I finished the last of my tea, already lukewarm, and wondered if I should bring along a pocket chess board (maybe she plays) or, even better, make out a list of topics and write them with a ballpoint pen on the palm of my hand.

Rowena saw me get up and she came across the room to the cash register especially to say good-bye and take my money with a "You hurry back now," and thirty-six cents change.

The thought that I might not be welcome came to me as I walked the now familiar twisting gravel path through the garden, inhaling the fragrance of cinnamon, lemon and honey from the blossom of some reclusive plant, but I dismissed it, so strong was my desire to immerse myself in the library. Arin had meant it when he told me to return, it was obvious. He had even suggested that if I had the time, I might help him with some cataloguing. "And if I'm not here, just come in and go on up. No one will be surprised to see you, and the front door is never locked, at least not during the day," he said, pressing my hand in his. The patio was empty, and quiet except for the trickle of the fountain and the distant chatter of birds.

I knocked and studied the paneling of the door, blackened with age to the finish of Chinese tea, as I listened for footsteps on the tile. Miriam answered the door. Gladly, I saw her expression change from curiosity to welcome as her smile nearly closed her narrow eyes. She said, "Arin is busy right now, but why don't you just go up to the library and he'll probably join you when he's free."

I hesitated at the door. "If it's not convenient, I can come back another time."

"Oh, no," she protested, her voice nasal. "He's very happy to have anyone use the library who wants to. He says books deteriorate when no one uses them."

"Certainly the ideas in them do," I said. "I'll just go upstairs then, I know the way."

"Yes, I'll bring up some fruit juice. I've just squeezed some grapefruit, nice and sweet, from our garden."

"Don't go to any trouble," I said, already climbing the dark wood stairs, watching her walk with small but energetic steps toward the kitchen, thinking that her brown skirt and tunic might have been hand-woven and -dyed.

The library was cool, and dark, redolent with the smell of old leather, dry paper and soap, the latter from the recently washed tile floor. My eyes were drawn to the table, and I was reassured to see the grey-covered folio resting just where I had left it. I wanted to sit down at once and begin reading, but instead I savored the expectation by walking around the room, letting my attention be drawn to details at random. To the right of the French window was a chest of drawers which, like the rest of the furniture, was of rough oak. On top of the chest in a rough wood frame was a picture of three children, a boy of about twelve, a girl possibly two years younger, and between them a boy of four or five. All three wore the features of Arin and Miriam, in congenial combination; the oldest boy resembled Arin, the youngest looked like Miriam with his Oriental eyes, dark skin and black hair. As for the girl, she had delicate Eurasian features, her hair dark and straight, while her intense eyes were both large and turned-up. The older son looked upright and bold in his glance, while the younger appeared shy and contemplative. The picture raised still more questions. The sound of the door opening startled me. It was Miriam, a small tray in her hands, with a ceramic cup of juice and a piece of nut cake still warm from the oven. She set the tray down and left before I could say anything, and I made no attempt to stop her. Feeling like a voyeur, I glanced hurriedly at a group of older photographs. By their appearance and clothes, these pictures were of 19th century relatives. I sat down at the table and, nibbling on the cake, quickly picked up where I had left off in Abraham's narrative.

"We were uncertain whether to enter the village or continue around it. All told we numbered 65 persons, although no more than twenty of us carried weapons. At best, we would command the respect of a few lazy watchmen, but would be no match for a group of warriors looking for adversaries, loot or both. Concealed in false bottoms of cornmeal sacks was a quantity of gold nuggets, as well as a smaller amount on my person for trade or bribery and a collection of small jade relics intended as presents to the many community leaders who might extend hospitality on the face of the Prince's letter.

"With apprehension we decided to proceed into the village, if only to find out whether we were in the territory of the Zapotec or the Mixtec, and to ascertain the state of relations between the perennial belligerents. A square-jawed handsome officer whose level wide-set eyes and broad nose identified him as a Zapotec official came out to meet us. Unarmed, accompanied only by the guide and interpreter, I approached him slowly, my hands extended forward in a gesture of peace. He watched us, showing no emotion. Behind him stood six warriors carrying spears, with stone maces in their belts. All were bare-chested and wearing little more than loincloths and sandals. Doing my best to show no fear, I handed him a small jade bead as a present and the scroll from Prince Zieuktal, which the guide ceremoniously translated into Zapotec. He listened impassively, then gestured us over to the front of a modest house adjacent to the road and bade us sit down on a woven mat. A woman came and offered us a gourd of water and some fruit. Only then did I relax, at least until I learned from him that the Zapotec and Mixtec conflict was again active, with the Zapotec victorious in recent battles resulting in the capture of five Mixtec cities and the flight of the Mixtec king from his capital.

"Fortunately we had chanced upon a village of the victor, for the vanquished might have given us an altogether different welcome. He was most interested in the purpose of our journey, as there had been very little traffic between the Maya and the Zapotec in recent years, due to the wars to the north and the chaos in the Mayan lands. I thought it unwise to tell him the real purpose of our mission, and had deliberately admonished Zepiq the guide to say nothing about the grant of land. Instead, I told him that we were on a trade and diplomatic mission to the ruler of the Zapotec and the Aztec to form an alliance against their common enemies, whoever they might be; I was certain such existed. This explanation satisfied him and, giving us peppers and tomatoes, he instructed us in the proper route to take to the Zapotec capital four days hence. With regret, he warned us that on two of those days the road would traverse a corner of the Mixtec lands which were not yet secure. In better times he would have sent a guide with us, but now he needed every man. He could do no more than mark his seal on a piece of bark and hope that it would suffice for any Zapotec warriors who we might meet along the way. As for the Mixtecs, owing to the breakdown of authority following their defeat, we were apt to encounter armed residuaries who would be glad to take our lives to gain our possessions.

"Now it was I who thought, but would not say out loud, that it was not too late to turn back to the relative security of the land of the Mayas. But I knew that our destiny lay in a different direction, the place before which the north wind made its home. God had always protected Jews in the wilderness. Like Moses, we too would reach the promised land. My hand on the shaft of the iron short sword given to my ancestor Jehushuah Binyan by King Solomon and wearing, on a chain around my neck, a small copper medallion engraved with the shield of David, I walked at the head of our line with my oldest son Noah at my side. And as I walked, I recited softly to myself a psalm taught to me by my father, finding in its words solace and even courage in the knowledge that it had been sung before by my forebears in the face of danger, that God had always heard it and would surely hear it again, and answer.

"We walked for two days, taking every precaution we could at night, before encountering the first but not the last of the defeated Mixtecs, three warriors who we met at the crossing of trails beside a stream. They were drinking and eating a handful of cornmeal when we surprised them at the turning of the trail. They were thin and little more than boys. The only weapons they carried were hardwood spears sharpened in the fire, and stone-tipped maces. We could have killed them; they were too startled to flee, but it was not in us to do so. Would that we had. We should have assumed that they were foragers for a larger party and that by passing them peacefully we were only revealing all that we had with us. This thought came to me, but I also assumed that, seeing our numbers and the arms which we were conspicuously displaying, they would stay away from us. As a precaution we marched longer and faster than usual into the night, hoping to put more distance between us and the warriors. In fact, we were moving closer to them.

"We made camp in what we thought to be a secure place, with a deep portion of a stream at our backs so that we had only one side of the camp to secure. In the vicinity was a large quantity of dead trees and brush left behind from a flood. These we piled as much as we could directly in front of the camp to create a defensive shelter, and twelve men were posted as guards in groups of four armed with clubs, spears and bows. Exhausted by the long march, the rest lay down, huddled close together, while I, sword belted to my side, faced the long slow night. The other guards took alternate watches. I had no intention of sleeping, but my fatigue and the quiet roll of the water over round stones made me doze after a long time, and the night, which seemed to be unmoving and itself asleep, passed into faint light.

"As we should have surmised, it was then that they came out of the trees, too many to count. We saw their weapons, knew their intentions and waited. The defenders crouched tense behind the barricades until they were completely in the small clearing, no more than a tree length away. At my signal we let loose a flurry of arrows, fully seven arrows of our total of twenty-one, and all of them, directed by the hand of God, found their mark. Seeing their comrades fall, the Mixtec warriors turned and ran back to the safety of the trees. Several of our men followed, brandishing spears and clubs, but I called them back, fearing a volley of arrows from the trees and not knowing how many of the attackers were hidden. Three of the arrows freed the soul of the Mixtecs, and they lay still, while the other four, though wounded, ran or dragged themselves back into the trees.

"We watched for their return, but there was no movement. Only the sound of the stream and bird songs broke the silence as the morning light grew in strength. We were certain that they were still there, and we could not move. Our security was in remaining in this place until we were certain they had given up and left. Time was in our favor. We had ample food and water. We assumed that they would not attack us by night as the people of this area believed the night to be inhabited with evil spirits. We were right, but it gave us little consolation.

"For three days we waited, our patience flagging, the tension growing. Some of the younger men wanted to attack, but reason told me that we would suffer the same fate as they. On the second day we sent out at dusk one of our quickest, a boy who could run between rushes and not disturb them. His task was to find out if they were still there, and if possible, estimate their numbers. We waited in suspense for his return as the night deepened, and when the horns of the great cow finally appeared in the sky, he returned to report that there were no more than thirty camped in the trees. Guards were posted, but the band appeared unruly and dispirited. While he watched, a fight had broken out among three of them.

"Could we take advantage of their fear of the night spirits and their lack of discipline and surprise them in the night? There were still too many, and we were poorly armed. Besides, our men had their own fears. Their gods were far away and wouldn't protect them, they believed. My assurance that our God was everywhere and the most powerful of all made no impression on them.

"'He is your God,' they said, 'not ours. We know him not, and he knows us not. We don't even have the words to summon him, and there is no time for you to teach them to us.' The discussion boiled, then became tepid.

"With my oldest son, I left the circle of men seated on their haunches. We must do something to put fear in the enemy and provoke them to rash acts, I thought. Joshua, my ancestor, faced with a similar situation, valued courage and guile over numbers. Leaving the rest of them, I, my son, and the scout who had returned from the camp and knew the position of the sentries, crossed the clearing, merged into the blind darkness of the trees and slowly crept to the edge of the camp. In the feeble light of the crescent moon that penetrated the clearing, we could barely see some of the men asleep on the ground, while a few who were still awake huddled together, talking inaudibly. Barely two body lengths ahead of us, partially concealed by a shrub, stood the sentry.

"Unmoving, we waited until the few that remained awake lay down, hoping that the sentry too would sleep, but he did not. He would not sleep, but neither did he see or hear us as we moved ever closer, finger length by finger length, until I was so close that I could hear him breathe and smell his rank sweat. All was still in the camp when I struck, plunging out and up with my sword into his torso, quickly drawing it out again as he slumped to the ground with a gasp. In the same motion I brought the sword down, cutting off his head. I seized it by the hair with my free hand and, motioning to the other two, returned to our camp, dropping the head in the clearing, midway between the line of trees and our barricade.

"Entering our own camp, we saw that nearly everyone was asleep except for the sentries and my wife, who looked from me to our son with relief, then recoiled at the sight of the bloody sword still clutched in my right hand. I went right to the river, to wash both the sword and my soul, now stained with the sin of murder. At least I had not seen his face, or it would have dwelt in the halls of my mind as long as memory remained. Not content just to wash the sword, lulled by the calm rush of the stream, I took some coarse sand, and sitting on a rock, I burnished my sword. My sword was finally clean, but I knew that the water rushing endlessly through my soul could not cleanse it. So must Joshua have felt.

"It was perhaps the lowest moment of the journey, yet at the same time that act renewed my confidence. I knew that tomorrow they would again attack, provoked by the death of the sentry. I returned to my wife's side. She rubbed my shoulders, and I fell instantly into a deep sleep, starting awake at the first light. We had little time to prepare, just enough to give my son the ram's horn, rouse our strongest men and move to the barricade.

"There was no time for fear before they advanced out of the trees, brandishing their spears, screaming some raging shibboleth. They attacked just at the moment that the sun rose above the top of the trees behind them, running toward us. As they closed half the distance, I raised my sword toward the heavens, rose and faced them, half expecting to draw their arrows. Their leader, the tallest among them, slowed, then stopped, confusion or fear on his face. What had he seen to affect him so? No more than the sun reflecting off the face of my polished iron sword, and the medallion on my chest. I raised my other hand and my son blew the ram's horn, three short blasts and a long blast. By then, all of them had stopped. I shouted a long incantation in Hebrew, again my son blew the ram's horn, and before he had finished they had turned and were running back toward the trees. We saw no more of them and continued our journey."

After a time, I looked up at the closed cabinet housing the relic of the voyage of Solomon's sailors. Was it possible that he actually had the sword, the medallion, or even fragments of any of them? The very thought sent a shiver through me and almost without willing it I got up and went to the cabinet. I was standing in front of it, undecided whether to try the brass handle when again the door opened. This time it was Arin, looking distracted, but clearly happy to see me. He came up to me and said quickly, "Glad you returned to us." Then without a pause he continued, an uncertain look on his face, "I wonder if you could do me a favor."

"If I can, I will gladly."

"Would you mind coming with me out to the tower? My son isn't around, and I would like a witness, somebody who is uninvolved with what he sees."

"I'll be glad to. When do you want to go?"

He paused and looked at me before he said, "Now, if you are willing."

"Of course," I said, reluctant to leave the narrative but pleased to spend the time with him.

He looked relieved for a moment, then worry returned to his features and he asked, "There's just one more thing. Have you ever ridden a horse? Our car isn't working, and besides I don't like to use it even when it is running. I thought since you were from Europe, possibly..."

"Yes," I interrupted, anxious to please him. In fact I had ridden my uncle's cart horse as a child, ridden bare back with improvised reigns tied to the halter. I had always liked horses and wasn't afraid of them in the least.

"Good. Come down in a few minutes then. I'll have a horse saddled and ready. Don't worry. It will be a good one."

"I'm not worried," I told him, "I'm looking forward to it..." ...a little, I said to myself, as he was already out the door, and I could hear his urgent steps in the hall.

There I was, riding a tall chestnut gelding at a brisk, spine-jarring trot, doing my best not to bounce around in the broad western saddle, the reins held in one hand, and resisting the temptation to steady myself with an occasional hand on the saddle-horn. Not bad, I said to myself. I'll regret it tomorrow. I could already feel the chafing of the inner surfaces of my thighs. It would even be enjoyable, if only we could go a little slower.

Even though I was gulping smog-saturated air into my poor lungs and the blurred visibility was like being nearsighted and forgetting your glasses, I was enjoying the adventure. I felt like John Wayne's lieutenant.

We were in the open desert, the last walled condominium development was behind us, the vegetation was sparse on the packed dry earth, but there were plenty of low bushes which didn't seem to bother the horse much although they worried me. The horse after all might stumble, or worse yet step into a hole, break his leg and catapult me head first onto the ground. Tshat is if the stirrups didn't cling to one of my legs.

I looked sideways at Arin and caught his appreciative smile. Erect, glued to the saddle of a white horse, wearing leather chaps, a white shirt and black cowboy hat, he looked like a Semitic Rudolf Valentino. A song from a Romberg operetta, something about the Riff rebellion but translated into Polish, began turning around in my head... "You ride well," he said. "How long has it been since you have ridden a horse?"

"Maybe forty years." Then, thinking of the chafing on my thighs, I added, "But it seems like only yesterday."

"There's something to that."

What he said must have thrown open some window in his mind, for his expression abruptly excluded me so that even looking at him I felt myself to be an intruder. He urged his horse into a gallop and mine followed. I leaned forward, attempting to let my pelvis flow with the forward roll, and found to my surprise that the horse's gait was so smooth that I could actually keep my seat, although my thighs were clamped to its sides like pliers around a bolt.

Ahead, through the plastic-cleaning -bag air, too far ahead for my tender thighs, standing like a spider on its splayed legs, was the tower. Five miles it must have been And as always when you want something to happen, it takes all the more time, and I was sure that the tower and its hill were rolling away from us faster than we were now trotting toward it. As my Uncle Heshe, the haberdasher, used to say, "When you really need the money, it seems like for every sale there are two returns and a theft." I can't remember what Don Quixote used to say when he was riding to some destination; I read it in Polish so long ago I can't think of a word of it. Some people always have a quote on their tongues, but I've never met one,. They must all be in books or the Reader's Digest.

I looked at Arin's back, hoping he would slow down a little, and wondered what kind of *mishugena* he was to build a restaurant on stilts out in the desert where everything that there was to see could be seen from the ground. Was it to make money? He lived like he had enough of that, at least he lived as though he had everything that he wanted, an eight-cylinder horse, a garden big enough to get lost in, a square-mile farm, precious books, a congenial wife, children.

I thought back on the folio, wondering whether I would ever get to finish it, what with the interruptions. Was this ancestor fact or fancy? I wasn't sure where myth ended and history began. Was the tower something each generation had to do? Was it like returning upstream for the spawning season, to build and build and build again something that would outlast you, something more than a granite stone with a name and two dates on it to mark your arrival and departure, the work of a stonecutter who didn't even know you, and between the dates, nothing but polished stone, as if your birth and your death were all there was.

Aha. The hill must have had a flat tire, for we were gaining on it and someone had removed the plastic bag, for the detail was coming into sharp focus; the aluminum grey of the tubular legs, the myriad of cross members, the yellow long-necked construction crane, resembling a grazing dinosaur, even the chain-link fence which now surrounded the base.

We ascended the first gentle hill that marked the end of the valley floor; Arin reined in on the crest. His horse danced in its place and dug at the ground with its hoofs while he sat immobile, gazing ahead of him. I reached the crest and saw what held his attention: at the base of the hill, leading up to the tower, a large semi-trailer carrying a long grey section of tube was stopped, and in front of it I could make out a line of men in motorized wheelchairs blocking the road. Now I knew the destination of the parade. And the men in wheelchairs weren't alone, for many of the other marchers, including the band, were arrayed behind them and on both sides of the truck. In fact, the band was even playing, a Kurt Weil-sounding "Hold That Tiger." Far to the right, a blue and white police car was racing toward the demonstration, its red light flashing hysterically.

"It's about time," said Arin, without looking at me. "I hope that I wasn't riding too fast for you," he added.

"Oh, I'm sure there are still a few layers of skin left on my thighs."

"You'll feel it tomorrow. Ready to go down there?"

"Don't you want to wait for the drum and bugle corps?"

"They've already arrived. Don't you hear them?" With that, he spurred his horse over the crest, just like they do in the movies. My horse followed and for a moment I thought that he had dropped out from under me, but I caught up to him and it wasn't so bad. At least we reached bottom together.

We crossed a dry stream bed and the road was no longer visible. Arin pressed on despite the rolling, rocky terrain and my horse must have had eyes in his four hoofs for he followed right along, going too fast to stumble on the loose rock surface. We got there just in time. Not in time to do anything about the confrontation, but in time to stop the needles that were probing the muscles around my kidneys.

The police car got there ahead of us and an officer with a belly that hung over his wide leather belt was already talking to an imposing man in a wheelchair, a man with the shoulders of a water buffalo and a head to match, but with no more than stumps for legs. The rest of the demonstrators were arrayed in an arc across the road. The band was on the right, playing a discordant, sour Horst Wessel that made my flesh crawl. On the left, the Indians were gathered in a tight group, moving rhythmically in place to the thump of a drum. The rest were sprawled across the road either sitting or lying down, but with signs held up so that they could be seen by two television cameramen that appeared to be making a record of the demonstration for the evening news. There were also a woman breastfeeding an infant, and two or three dogs that had apparently followed their masters.

I moved up to the edge of the crowd, but couldn't hear what was being said because of the band and the drums. The signs got the message across to me and certainly to the televiewers. They said, "Save Taquitz Rock," "Don't Make a Target Out of Canyon Springs," "Don't Trash Up the Desert," and "Tower of Babble."

Removed from the crowd, the second officer was standing at the patrol car door talking on his radio and the truck driver was sitting on the shady side of his cab, smoking a cigarette and leafing through a girlie magazine, looking as though he was the only one around for miles.

I had expected to feel tension, a *deja vu* of the televised clash of police and students during the days of the Viet Nam peace demonstrations, but I felt none. Perhaps it was the mood of the desert, austere - even vacuous - for the strongest emotion that I could see was irritability of the kind noticeable at a bus stop. Was it the bug-house band or the Indians which gave the scene a ritual color, lacking only floats to make me think that the participants were acting out Founder's Day. The Indians, for example, were looking impassive, stubborn, but grave. The unfinished tower of tubular grey aluminum, with its rusted steel interior, added to the ritual, standing as it was on the hill like some unfinished Easter Island deity waiting with petulant passivity to be served.

Absorbed by the scene, I had almost forgotten about Arin, at least until I heard him say, "Let's dismount."   I got down and stood there looking for a place to tether the horse and still feeling it under me.   Arin handed me the reins of his horse and began to walk toward the policeman.

As he stepped in front of the arc of demonstrators, I saw two people sit up.   The first was Arin's son, Zev, the other a thin woman with long streaming honey-blonde hair—presumably his girlfriend, Francesca.   They followed Arin with their eyes, looking both apprehensive and detached, like bystanders at an impending car accident.   Arin was about fifteen yards from the roadblock when he saw them.   It must have been their movement which caught his attention, for he stopped. The policeman turned towards him and walked slowly in his direction, a smile on his face.

Zev stood up and the blonde woman got up as well.   Zev began to stride toward his father and the policeman and the girl followed.   He turned and said something to her, but she shook her head and caught up with him.   I was having trouble hearing and took both horses closer, all the time watching the son approach his father, who by this time had stopped talking to the officer and was watching Zev and Francesca, as were all of the demonstrators except, I noticed, for a few Indians who kept their eyes fixed on some distant point in the sky.

Zev walked up within an arm's length of his father and stopped.   The policeman stepped back and watched like a referee.   Arin was the first to speak.

"I want these demonstrators to leave my property, Sergeant. They've made their point.   If they go now, there will be no prosecution for trespass."

"They're not trespassing, father," Zev said, his voice steady but tense.

Arin rubbed his hand through his red hair and stared at his son with cold fury. "They have no right to be here. I want them off, now," he said to the policeman, his voice snapping like a whip.

The policeman nodded and was about to turn to the crowd, when Zev said, "They are invitees, not trespassers. I invited them here."

Arin seemed to grow red and puff up. "What right do you have to bring a lot of hostile troublemakers out here?"

"Every right. It's my land too, isn't it?"

"I'm not going to make a scene out here, although maybe that's what you both want. Isn't there some reasonable limit to your childish opposition?"

"There's nothing..." but before Zev could finish Arin had dismissed him with a contemptuous wave of his hand and turned away, livid.

The policeman trotted after him and said, "If Zev invited them there's nothing I can do, Mr. Binyan."

"Just be sure they don't destroy anything," he said. He approached me and took the reins of his horse. Then he mounted in a surprisingly lithe movement and rode off at a fast trot without looking back.

I managed to mount shakily, clinging to the saddle with one foot in the stirrup as my horse on his own initiative began to follow his friend home, whatever my intentions. I wanted to ride next to Arin, even to rudely ask him questions, and my horse was of like mind, for without urging and before I had settled into the saddle, he shifted into a gallop. I felt the torque and the wind on my body as he quickly caught and pulled abreast of his friend, who acknowledged him by turning his head somewhat and nodding. Having caught up, my horse slowed to the pace of the other while I began to appreciate a form of transportation which, though slower and harder on the body than a car, nevertheless could be depended upon to take you home on its own initiative, no matter who was in control of the Iranian oil fields.

"Remember me?" I said, and he, turning a gloomy face my way, cracked a bit of a smile more in the eyes than the mouth and replied, "I never forget an old friend." So much for that exchange. At least he slowed down, perhaps recalling that I might by now be a little saddle-sore.

We rode together silently for a time, until I began to cough, the smog was apparently irritating my bronchitis. He looked at me as though he'd been sucking on a lemon and said, "The air used to be as pure as the runoff from the snow fields. Now we have this when the wind changes."

"It's the price we pay for the car," I said, glad to see him opening up a little. Apparently I said the wrong thing, for he closed up again. But despite his mood, he wanted to talk, for eventually he said, weariness in his tone, "Do you have children? I don't suppose you do; I think you said that you are not married."

"I have no children."

"They can be a great joy." And in a softer, more melancholy tone, he added, "And a great sorrow."

"Pardon my saying so, but I can understand your son's feelings about the tower."

"I imagine you do." He gave me a dour look.

"Lots of people feel that things like your tower, understand I'm not personally judging it, to put it their way, crap up the environment, and in this case, bring the nuclear holocaust a step closer. They didn't go through World War II and they don't look at a strong military as a deterrent. They see it as a threat."

We were silent for a while before he said, "My son's a scientist, a dreamer, like my father. He doesn't understand that there are practical considerations to the tower."

"I'm sure."

"If he and I could talk, if we could communicate instead of talk over each other's heads..." he said, seeming to agonize over these words. "He might accept that I didn't intend it to be as it is." He looked thoughtful and pained as he turned to me. "Besides, it's his girlfriend who goads him into it. She doesn't care if she ruins him in the process. It's in her blood."

He was talking in ciphers at this point. "I'm not sure I understand," I said. Then he told me that Francesca, Zev's fiancé, was the great-great-granddaughter of Cyrus Messer, and told me something about the man.

He sounded like a scoundrel, but it was a long time to hold a family grudge and I said as much. He frowned and said, "As you can see, the family hasn't changed. They're still making trouble for us. But don't misunderstand me; I don't hold her to account for old Messer's manipulations; not at all."

"Obviously, she is just as independent as your son," I said. My horse stumbled on a rock and I lurched forward.

"Horses have to be sure-footed out here. They can step in a ground squirrel hole and break a leg. Once it happened to me as I was galloping. I came out of the stirrups, but I had to shoot the horse. Be sure you just rest your toe in the stirrups," he said. We rode quietly for a while.

"I saw pictures of three children in the library. I guess Zev is the youngest," and my voice disappeared into a cough.

"Yes." He was becoming withdrawn. I could feel it, and I let my horse fall a little behind him. He must have sensed my discomfort, for he said, "You're not too sore, I hope."

"No, no more than could be expected."

"I'll give you something for that cough. Remind me."

"Thanks."

"You must have a lot of questions."

"Yes, I do; but I really don't want to intrude on your privacy. I'm after all just a transition."

"Sometimes it's easier to talk to a stranger than it is to talk to people you love." His voice choked off on this.

Yes, that's true. It must be why people in a small town compete for the attention of tourists; although you must be bored with tourists here."

"Oh, I hardly notice them. I don't go into the town much anymore. But you're right."

"Where are your other children?"

"Dead," he answered, letting the word drop like a heavy stone. It landed on my heart and for a moment I couldn't even look at him. We rode quietly again, walking our horses. Mine was sweating; he had been for hours, his flanks were dark and the sweat looked like shaving cream where it met the saddle. My nostrils were full of it. "Let's let them walk a bit," he said, "they must be a little tired by now."

"Suits me," I answered, trying to sound light-spirited.

He looked at me. "Don't feel sorry about the question. It's been some years now. The sorrow has scarred over mostly."

"I am sorry."

"Please don't be."

"How long do you expect this smog will last?"

"You don't really want to know that." He looked at me, amused skepticism in his large eyes. "You want to know what happened to my children: childhood disease, accident or what? I suppose it's all the same to a parent. Whatever the cause of death it's unacceptable, unbearable for a while, and you say again and again to God, Why, why?. You get no answer to that one. His voice trailed off. Again silence and I turned to watch a flight of birds wheel and plunge.

Abruptly, he began to speak. "We're programmed to grieve, you know. It's healthy; it lets us put the matter of death behind us. Every animal grieves: elephants, I suppose, even mice, although I've never seen it. It's that seminal commitment to the life process. Untimely death defeats it. The young are supposed to grow and have children. It's the old who are supposed to die, after they've produced another generation. It's against nature for the children to die." He wasn't saying anything to me particularly. He was saying it to the whole of the desert, looking straight ahead of him. Then he stopped and turned his head toward me, and I saw for a moment an older, weary man. For a while the only sound was the irregular scraping of the horses' hoofs on the dry surface of the desert.

"My children died needlessly, my son in Viet Nam. He was a lieutenant, blown up by a land mine. There wasn't enough left of him to bury, the Army said. My daughter died two years later in an automobile accident. The gas tank exploded on impact. She was a passenger. They had stopped at a crosswalk and somebody behind them didn't. We couldn't identify her. The dentist had to do it, by her teeth. I've not been able to ride in a car since that time."

Again the stone fell on my chest, leaving me without breath. "As you might expect, Miriam and I took solace in the fact that we had a third child, the youngest, the baby. Maybe we concentrated too much on him."

"That's understandable, under the circumstances."

"I suppose so. Maybe it was too much responsibility, for a young child. It had the opposite effect of what we had hoped. Oh, he was always a quiet sort, reflecting more his Indian stolidity than the Semitic volatility. But he has become a kind of stranger to us, still a son, capable of love, of feeling for us, we know that. But we feel that we don't really know him. Maybe it's just a lack of communication between the generations. Although we, Miriam and I, thought that we understood the first two..." He sighed, and his shoulders slumped a little. "I suppose we're just getting older..."

"I'm sorry."

"Don't be. As for having said it, it's kind of cathartic. I feel actually relieved. You know, I hated to see my son there, demonstrating against the construction of the tower. Never mind what the tower means to me -- so much is at stake. It does me good to talk about it before I get home and fall into a black silence. Miriam will thank you. She hates the silences. You'll stay to dinner, I hope?"

"I would love to, but I have other plans."

"Too bad. Are you done with the journal?"

"No,"

Eventually he left me to swallow his dust. And it was just as well, for I was feeling much like a grated potato and was relieved to make my own pace. This was not easy, due to the competitiveness of my mount. I finally got the best of him, or possibly he just got tired. Whichever, he and I returned slowly, he knew the way, and I was free to let my mind or eyes wander.

It is an unceasing source of wonderment how much there is to see, and hear, even in the most unlikely of places. Here, in the desert, I saw what I hadn't noticed on the way out to the tower. We were riding on what looked like an ancient Roman road, or if not Roman at least a road no more than six feet wide, surfaced by flat stones and graded so that the water from heavy winter rains would run off the sides. After a while I realized that my powers of observation were not that bad, since my horse, apparently having in his mind a more precise sense of direction than the person who laid out the road, didn't stay on it for long, although the path which he took repeatedly converged with the road. Without knowing something about the Binyan family, the road would have posed one more thing to speculate about, but already knowing as I did their propensity to build, I assumed that it was an all-weather road from their estate to the ceremonial platform. I later found that my speculations were reasonable, but wrong. History, like a con man, deceives. Well, sometimes it does.

Eventually I moved the horse into a cantor, since the sun was already settling toward the ragged, hilly horizon like an orange balloon, and my thoughts were turning toward dinner with Sarah Cavanaugh. When I arrived I found that Arin had already unsaddled his horse and gone into the house. I dismounted outside the door. The horse found his stall and began immediately to munch some hay without so much as a "Nice to meet you."

I returned directly to the hotel, walking as if my legs had been wired together, smelling the horse's sweat and thinking how good a hot bath or even a shower would feel. And as I walked through the familiar corridor of the garden, I found myself wondering what it would be like to have two of your children die and to feel your self a stranger to the third. My curiosity turned to Zev and I wondered what it must feel like to be him.

5

ZEV AND FRANCESCA

It wasn't until much later, after Zev had opened up to me, that I began to understand him. Arin's bitter words explained a little. Before Francesca, Zev had lived in his older brother's shadow. Everything he did or didn't do had been seen by Arin in relationship to what Arye would have done. Arye, the first born, was so different: social where Zev was shy, charming where Zev was awkward, practical when Zev seemed abstract. At least this was Zev's perception as he grew up.

In spite of his self-doubt, Zev shone with a natural brilliance in biology. The study he made of the plants of an obscure canyon, done before he had completed high school, was its first real manifestation. For him, it was nothing out of the ordinary since it came naturally, without conscious effort, like putting together a model airplane.

But no garden has ever grown in the seed envelope, my uncle used to say. Zev's genius needed a catalyst, and Francesca's strong personality provided it. Without Francesca's influence, who can say what Zev might have become? And if the two of them hadn't happened to be in the same place at the same time, Zev's ability might have shriveled. Life is full of ifs.

How did they meet? Zev used to ride his horse, Cabal, up Lost Miner's Canyon, past the 'No Trespassing' sign posted at Francesca's papa's direction. The land belonged to Beneveste, although he had probably never been on it. Zev and his brother would go there to bathe in a pool fed by a hidden spring at the canyon's head; water that ran fresh and cool even in the driest, hottest time of the year. Later it was the micro-climate, cool and moist when the desert was a furnace, and the variety of plants and trees that attracted him.

It was in the last stages of his plant classification project, about the time that he had identified, with certainty, the wild grape, that he first saw Francesca bathing nude in the pool and later saw her stretched out on the flat rock beside the sluice in a circle of sunlight.

I used to bathe in just such a pool sheltered by a bank, an ancient elm overhanging the dark water of a slow river. Not far downstream, cattle would be drinking while a farm boy fished beside them. When we came out of the water, Clara might have been nude, for the white cotton of her shift clung to her in places like a second skin. Remembering my feelings then, as we lay side by side on the grass looking up into the crown of the tree, gives me a sense of what Zev must have felt as he first watched Francesca lying on the rock.

But for another coincidence, Francesca might have remained no more than a remote sexual fantasy to him. He was enrolled in the local high school, while Francesca was attending a girls' school in Switzerland. He lived in his enclave surrounded by Canyon Springs while she, when she was home, lived in a sandstone Italianate palace on the edge of Lost Miner's Canyon. But they both liked to ride horses and that was, some six months later, the source of their second encounter.

What he saw one morning, before the sun had baked the night's chill out of the air, was two horses, one white and the other black. He rode up to them and saw what seemed to be an Arab in a long white robe and black kefir. So incongruous was the image that at first he didn't see just who or what the man was bending over. He dismounted and saw that it was the bather.

His breath caught in his throat when he recognized her. She lay there on her back, her long honey-colored hair fanning out around the delicate features of her face. Their eyes met and he had the notion that, despite her pain, she recognized him. She seemed even longer and thinner than she was. One leg was straight but showed where her faded jeans had been cut, a bulge that was already red and blue from the fracture.

"She has fallen and broken a bone," the man said, his voice soft and a bit hoarse. "I cannot leave her, but we would be grateful if you would go for a doctor." Zev took his eyes off of Francesca and looked at the man. He had a thin, tapered face the color of oiled walnut, a nose like the blade of a knife and deep-set black eyes.

"The nearest phone is four miles from here. I'll ride over and call the sheriff. Then I can wait for them and bring them back." He turned back to her and asked, "Are you in much pain?"

Summoning a wisp of a smile that turned up the corners of her blue eyes she said, her voice breathless and catching, "I'll be all right." He was already mounting and he urged Cabal to a gallop as soon as his right foot touched the stirrup. Zev normally was slow to move but there was no holding back this time as he let Cabal have his head. More than that, he was feeling the euphoria of the rolling flight of the gallop enhanced by the thought that not only had he met her, he was coming to her aid. The phone at the Meador Ranch was working. Luckily a deputy sheriff was actually cruising no more than three miles from the Ranch, and it took Zev no more than half an hour to return to the site of the fall with a tan sheriff's station wagon jouncing along behind him.

The officer put a temporary splint on the leg, and they got her into the flat bed of the wagon. With the gratitude in her eyes fixed in his memory he watched as the wagon slowly drove off. He barely heard her companion's thanks. Zev rode home resolving to bring Francesca flowers at the hospital.

When, several hours later, he arrived at the hospital receptionist's desk carrying a bunch of yellow roses he was disappointed to find that she had already been released. He went home, not sure whether to drive directly to the Palacio or telephone firs, but. the decision had already been made for him. Yas'r, the man who had been with her had already telephoned, inviting him to visit two days hence so that he could be suitably thanked.

How fickle time was when I was Zev's age. Sometimes it vanished like an after-image, while at other times it completely abandoned me to a single, endless, boring event. How long it seemed when I waited for Clara outside the cinema, and how long it seemed when she went with her parents to the North Sea. How long the two days before his meeting with Francesca must have seemed to him.

The Palacio Beneveste, as the place was called, was even more impressive from the flagstone courtyard than from the valley floor. It presented a flat facade, three stories, its French windows recessed into the thick sandstone walls. Geraniums and vines spilled over the balconies, but with the exception of the ornately carved stone lintels the facade was tightly dressed flat stone, giving off the warm golden color of sand when the sun strikes it at an angle. Immediately across from the entrance was a stable or a garage with living quarters above it. Yas'r must have heard the clatter of Cabal's shoes on the flagstones, for he approached Zev almost as soon as he had dismounted. He took the horse to a stall in the cool, dim stable, and escorted Zev, by inside stairs, to his apartment, a small area appointed with Oriental rugs, pillows, blankets, a low couch and a brass table.

After an hour of conversation, including two strong cups of sweet, muddy coffee that left his nerves twanging, Zev was beginning to feel that he wouldn't even see Francesca. Several times he asked how she was. Having answered with an abbreviated medical report of her condition like "recovering nicely," Yas'r would return to his somewhat rambling discursive manner of speech, punctuated by questions about

Zev's family. It developed that he had a mild curiosity, never before satisfied, about the "aboriginal" population of the valley. He spoke English with a slight British accent acquired when he had served in the British Army. Yas'r had come to the "American desert" when Francesca's grandfather, or "Papa" as she called him, enamored of the Italian Renaissance, had taken up falconry.

"Now that Mr. Beneveste is sick and cannot move about except in a rolling chair with a motor, he is no longer interested in the sport," he said.

"Where are the birds now?" Zev asked.

Yas'r made a flourish with his hand toward the window and the sky. "We let them go. Francesca insisted. She became quite good at it. I taught her. But she insisted. They are free to hunt. Sometimes one comes back and perches just there, outside my window, or on her balcony, just to see if we are still here. They are quite fierce, but surprisingly affectionate."

After Zev refused a third cup of coffee, Yas'r offered to show him the house. Almost as an afterthought, he suggested that they might go up to see Francesca as well. Accustomed to the quiet elegance of his own home, Zev was stunned by the scale and the opulence of the house. The central hall housed a curving stone stairway illuminated by a massive church window. Within the rooms on each side of it, he saw a museum-like array of antique furniture, tapestries and paintings. His eye took it in as one might see a landscape from the window of a fast train. His mind was on Francesca.

Francesca's bedroom was blue and white. In contrast to the elaborate taste of the rooms below, the room was feminine yet simple with pine country furniture. Bathed in streaming light form the French window, Francesca was reclining on a chaise lounge wearing a long gown of a pale blue fabric that floated, more than hung, over the side of the couch. Her hair was loose and fanned about her shoulders, radiant where the sun caught the gold. The cast was just peaking out of the hem of the gown and alongside of the couch were two light wood crutches. Seeing him, she put her book down and offered him a seat. Yas'r remained in the background for a few minutes like a harem guard. Observing that they were getting along, he quietly turned and left the room.

Feeling tongue-tied at first and unable to turn away from her eyes, Zev remained for what must have been two hours. It was, for him, the other side of time. Francesca spoke in a light, melodious voice. She told him about her life at the Swiss school and hinted at the loneliness of her life in the house with her grandfather, who was increasingly withdrawn and hard to reach. In fact, she had spent more time with Yas'r than with her grandfather, riding, building small fires in the desert to brew coffee, and falconing, a sport that she had grown to love through him. She was curious about Zev and made him tell her almost as much about his own family, but true to his nature, Zev said less.

At length, a housekeeper interrupted them and reluctantly he left, but with a request from Francesca that he return to "relieve the boredom of my convalescence."

"Is after dinner soon enough?" he asked her.

"Stay to dinner if you like. Nianne is a tolerable cook."

Zev had half a mind to stay, but his shyness curbed the urge out of fear that he would have nothing to say and would make her see what a clod he really was. He rode home surrounded by a fevered late-afternoon light that, for him at least, was the product of his happiness. He was, in his own words, "just wild about her." And what made it all the better was the fact that they were both enrolled at Stanford and they would have the whole summer to get acquainted. And so they did.

What a summer Zev and Francesca had, that first summer of their love, for they loved from the start in that effervescent bright way of beginnings. Theirs was all the sustained anticipation of a bus trip to summer camp. For them, drinking fresh orange juice under an umbrella in a cylinder of shade next to the turquoise mosaic of an Olympic-size swimming pool, there was a prolonged expectation of what they could do together, once Francesca's cast was off. Until then, she would watch him, lean, tapered, and naturally bronze. She would watch as he ran across the searing stone, and with a leap, slice the glazed surface of the pool, glide quietly to its center and break suddenly to the agitated surface doing, as he said, "Alternate laps, one for you and one for me." He would return to her, lean over and drip water over her thin body, trying to fill the seams of her belly. Or he would give her a wet playful kiss, playful but one that held, in its gentle sustained touch, a longing and a promise.

Mostly they talked; rather she talked, for she was more verbal. They learned all about each other, holding back very little; there is always something held back, after all. And they talked a lot about what they would do at college; how they came to choose Stanford. Zev could have gone anywhere, with his grades, but something held him back from the customary choices. Raised in an isolated semi-rural setting, he was afraid of the East, afraid of the pace, the climate, and the scale of the cities.

"At least at Stanford, you can walk out of class and go into some trees," he said.

For Francesca, going to college in California was coming home. She had spent so much of her time in Switzerland; she loved it, but she wanted to experience California for a while. "It isn't New York," she said, "but nothing is. And San Francisco is one of my favorite cities."

"I wouldn't know. I've never been to New York. And I've only been to San Francisco once. Our family doesn't travel."

"The one thing Papa and I did, after my parents died, was travel--every summer to a new place. It was too hot for him here, he said. Now, of course, it's harder for him, and he's lost interest in it."

She told him about the places she had been: Europe, Japan, Cambodia to see *Ankor Wat* (her Papa liked old things and especially ruined cultures). "He must have been a bat in an earlier life," she said. She had even been to *Machu Pichu* and Yucatan. "I must have seen every ruin extant in the world."

She didn't believe him, although she wanted to; the mythology of his family went beyond history. It was more like a fairy tale. To look at him, of course, was to believe him, but the side of her that wanted to be a lawyer denied it.

"One day I'll prove it to you." But he didn't. It was like Arin always telling me that he would show me some relic of

King Solomon, but never getting around to it. Maybe it was some kind of family joke, or ritual.

It didn't make any difference to her. She loved his essence but mostly she loved what she saw, the narrow eyes, oriental in shape, dark as night; the long thin hands that always seemed to be in motion; the gentle, sometimes melancholy look. And she loved what she heard: his ironic humor, the brilliance that he took for granted and didn't believe in; this more than anything. She had so much confidence, enough for both of them. She resolved to give him some, and that summer, even before her leg was out of its cast and soon after seeing his Lost Miner's Canyon plant survey, she began. She began with the obvious, insisting that he show his plant classification to her grandfather.

So far that summer he had only seen the elder Beneveste twice, both times in his study where he spent most of his time. The drapes were drawn, keeping the room in constant dusk with light from several floor lamps that gave highlights to the dark wood paneling of the walls. To look at him sitting stooped in a grey velour wingback chair behind a desk with his long, tapering face, the white skin beginning to fall under the eyes and cheekbones, it was not readily apparent that he had just enough movement in his arms to feed himself. He kept his knotted hands hidden below the desk

He had managed a little warmth and wit when Zev had been introduced to him, with proper emphasis on his intelligence. Having lost the physical side of his life -- he had at one time been a competitor in amateur tennis competitions -- he now identified more with the intellect.

"You are like a myth come alive, Zev," he said when, at Francesca's prodding, Zev told him something of the family history. "It seems that Francesca has finally found a unicorn in her garden. And it's the one thing I always wanted to give her."

"When I was a child I loved unicorns," she said, looking fondly from her Papa to Zev. "I had pictures of them all over my room. One time Papa gave me a lamb for Christmas. It had a single *papier mache* horn about this long," she said, extending her hands four inches.

Beneveste smiled and looked nostalgic. "You know, Francesca, I had completely forgotten that. You were so sad, though, when the horn came off in your hand."

"It was my rite of passage from childhood fantasy to reality," said Francesca, looking from her grandfather to Zev.

"You cried, and I had to console you with the thought that unicorns were all the better because they were unobtainable, and lambs were all the better because they were here, or some such humbug."

"It wasn't humbug, Papa, it was beautiful." She reached out and touched his arm and he looked at her appreciatively.

"Humbug or not, it consoled you. I understand you've been putting the pool to good use, Zev. Francesca tells me you were on the swim team. Do you play tennis as well? We have very good courts, although they don't get much use these days."

Francesca had a hard time convincing Zev that he should show the plant classification to anyone, least of all to her grandfather. She argued that it was his duty, since the canyon belonged to her Papa, and this rationalization finally convinced him. Her grandfather was pleased with it, gave Zev no end of praise, and even wanted a copy.

As the six week period of Francesca's immobility progressed, Zev found himself spending longer and longer days with her. For the most part, he would arrive at mid-morning and stay until after nightfall. Then he would ride home on Cabal, enjoying the silence and the moonlight on the shrubs and the quick nocturnal chill.

Sometimes, after Zev's acceptance, her grandfather dined with them in a more intimate dining room than the one that would have accommodated at least one of the tribes of Israel. Zev saw both the extent of her grandfather's disability, and other dimensions of his personality. Primed by a bottle of 1961 Cheval Blanc, his pale grey eyes took on the warm light of the candles that were the only illumination, and he talked about the past, about current politics, about art and the great collections of the world. But between such bursts of conversation, his head would lower and he would pick silently at his food. Francesca could always cheer him up, bring the light back to his eyes with teasing or a recollection of something ridiculous that had happened to them on one of their trips together. Sometimes she would even get out slides and the three of them would look at Peshawar, or Goa.

Once they got into a long discussion of religion that began with Zev talking about the archaic Judaism practiced by his family.

"Believe it or not," Beneveste began, looking from Francesca to Zev, "there has always been a vein of paganism concealed in the Beneveste family. A certain disdain for the formalities of the church. For example, I once researched back seven generations, have I told you this, Francesca? And there was not one member of the family that had taken up a vocation in the church. Strange, isn't it, for a family that can trace itself back to the Roman nobility."

"The Italian side of our family has an estate in Umbria that is supposed to have been in the family continuously for 1,800 years," she said.

"We've got you beat," Zev said.

"Ah, but we can prove it," said Beneveste. "Given the tempestuous history of Italy that is no mean achievement."

After dinner Zev and Francesca often went back to her room, where they played chess with an ivory chess set that was reputed to have been designed by Cellini. Chess was something else she had learned from Yas'r. Sometimes they would lie on her bed together and touch, silently looking into each other's eyes, caressing every part of the body, but always holding back from the final intimacy until they could choose the place, or rather let the place choose them. Francesca had told him that she was still a virgin and wanted it to be perfect, "not with a cast on her leg like a popsicle." They waited.

After exposing him to her Papa's praise, Francesca dropped the question of his future. One day, as they were seated on the patio, she began again. It was hot, nearly 100 degrees in the sun, but the shade of the umbrella, combined with the barest breeze, made it tolerable, especially for Zev since he kept dousing himself in the pool. The patio was like the foredeck of a ship, running to the edge of the cliff on which the house had been built. Beyond the ornate balustrade could be seen the whole valley. Francesca was wearing a spare two-piece bathing suit of blue, the same color as the sky, and her eyes. Except for the white that could just be seen at the edge of her bathing suit, and the cast now a little grey and adorned with designs, her nubile body was nearly the burnished gold color of her hair.

"You know, Zev, you must give more thought to what you will do with yourself when you finish college," she said, as though they had been discussing it for the last fifteen minutes. She probably had, but with herself, according to Zev, who claimed that her mind was so quick she was always assuming that everyone else was right in step with her.

"I don't even know if I'll finish. I'm not sure what I even want to study. I suppose I'll farm our land."

"You've got a gift that shouldn't be wasted on early-to-market tomatoes."

"Somebody's got to grow them. I suppose I could become a landscape gardener. There's plenty of demand for that down here, what with all the planned communities."

"Seriously, Zev."

"You be serious for both of us. If you want to be a lawyer, spend your life in an office, or in a windowless courtroom, that's fine for you. As for me, I like this valley, I like our land, I like to make things grow out in the sun."

"You've got something to give. You should at least declare a botany major and work toward a Ph.D."

"And end up in a classroom."

She looked up into the pulsating blue of the sky at the silhouette of a hawk soaring on an air current. "Look at that bird. He has a very different view of the world than a snake. This cast itches like crazy. Will you pour some water down it for me?"

The cast came off on schedule, although one glance at the shrunken, scaling, pale limb made her want it back. But they lost no time in breaking up and making a fire of her crutches and drinking a bottle of Dom Perignon in the firelight. Francesca had made a duplicate of the key to her grandfather's wine cellar and at least twice a week she was instructing Zev's palate against the time when they might spend a week-end in San Francisco. Up to then, his wine drinking had been limited to Passover and **Shabbat,** except for a few jugs passed around at high school parties. In the next few days she swam a lot to limber up her leg, and before a week had elapsed she was back on her horse, a spirited white Arabian stallion called Shaka.

As the weeks had passed, their closeness had become an exquisite prolonged pain. They had come closer and closer to consummating their love, but always she resisted and he respected her. They must have shared an almost Victorian romantic experience: a painful deferral, the heart rising into the throat, pressures in the head, euphoria, longing, delirium, an eternally back-lit vision of beauty. These feelings come back to me as I remember those translucent days of courtship when Clara and I shared the ecstasy of first love, of emotions gladly out of control, of senses heightened, like sunlight seen through a daffodil.

Finally, when they were free to pick the place, circumstance frustrated them and they had to wait another two weeks. For it was then that Yas'r came back out of the shadows, insisting that he ride with her until he was sure that she was strong enough, and Zev saw for the first time the more than paternal feeling that Yas'r had for her. For a whole week, they were not able to ride alone. For another week Zev was unable to see her except for an hour at a time in the evening. Arin, resenting the fact that Zev had spent little or no time working on the farm, insisted that he help supervise the crews during the lemon harvest. This engaged him from 5:00 in the morning until 6:00 at night.

The peak of the lemon harvest passed, and with just two weeks to go before they went away to school, they finally found themselves alone on horseback. Without speaking about it they rode to the canyon, tethered the horses near its mouth and walked together up the shaded path listening to the small flute-like voice of the stream and feeling its moist breath. Francesca had brought a small basket of food: a Boursin, rolls baked that morning, a bottle of Mondavi Fume Blanc and some apples.

The pool beneath the sluice was still four feet deep, chill and striated with gold and topaz down to its burnished stone bottom. The flow down the sluice was languid. Stripping off their clothes down to the pale negative of their bathing suits, hand in hand they slid down off the edge of the flat rock and into the pool, churning up just four small eddies where their feet touched the varied bottom. Chilled for no more than a few seconds, they found the water simply cooling to the skin and they stretched out their backs against the sluice, letting their legs float out in front of them.

They must have kissed then beneath the sluice, as Clara and I once did, and the stream brought us together as water flowing into it from another source merges and loses itself. Caressed by the flow of the stream, by the dappled moving light falling on us from the overhanging tree, we lay together on the grass as they must have on the flat rock, fused yet fluid, succumbing to the ebb and flow of the stream sucking, drawing and touching every part of them.

We lay together for a time, Clara and I. Later we drank the German wine, with the white farmer's cheese that we had bought at a nearby farm, and only at dusk, when the insects began to swarm, we rode our bicycles back to town as they must have quietly walked their horses.

For Clara and me, our summer was the best of it. The rest of our time together now seems like still shots of a play, meetings and partings until the last. For Zev and Francesca, that summer was the beginning. Their future had a stronger spring.

6

FIG LEAVES

I managed a long soak in the tub and a ten-minute nap before a knock on the door reminded me of my dinner engagement. Staggering a little as I got off the bed, I went to the door and opened it to face her gentle ambiguous smile and in her eyes, an expectant curiosity as before. And, as before, the eyes had the same effect on me, only more so. Perhaps the ride had emulsified my reserve, the bath had brought me to a simmer, but as I looked at her, dressed in a silk blouse of a sherry hue and a darker skirt the shade of twilight, full and fluted, I felt a visceral pulse which startled, even embarrassed, me with its suddenness. She must have seen my dumb discomposure, for her smile widened, showing her even teeth, and she asked, "You didn't forget about tonight, did you?"

"No, I dozed off. But I was just getting up when you knocked. I'm not late, am I?"

"No more than a few minutes. I was sitting there watching the early news and thought, why stand on formalities, we're neighbors." She stopped speaking and simply looked at me. "Mexican food still O.K. with you?"

Recovering my composure, I nodded. "Yes, I've been looking forward to it all day, in fact."

As we rode in the cool evening air under the sky with the reflection of the day still on it, she said, "Did you feel the quake?"

"Yes, it lasted for hours," I retorted, thinking about my ride.

"Seriously, there was an earthquake today; 3.4 on the Richter scale. I thought that I had felt it, like one quick jolt, and I heard about it on the news."

"The way I was bouncing around, it could have been strong enough to flatten the city and I wouldn't have known the difference." A traffic light changed abruptly and the sudden stop threw me forward against the seat belts. "You know you would have made a pretty good bus driver."

"You do say the nicest things."

As we were stopped, I looked around me and saw that we were no longer in what I took to be Canyon Springs. The stores on both sides of the street had a thrift shop, day-old-bread outlet look about them, with poorly painted signs, cheap furniture stores, a finance company, a used car lot with $600 transportation specials, and not a single Cadillac with enough room for a Honda in the trunk.

"Did you make a wrong turn or something?"

"The cashiers at the Safeway have as much right to retire down here as the automobile dealer. Besides, the waitress at the place where you have breakfast can't afford a condominium with a view of a golf course and clubhouse privileges." The light changed and the acceleration threw me back in my seat.

"Are we late?"

"Alright, I'll slow down. I'm sorry. I'm a little wound up. It's the pills I'm taking for my diet," she explained.

"You mean you don't always drive this way?"

"Only some of the time. I spend a lot of time in the car. I live thirty miles away from where I work, that's why I have a car I enjoy." She had shifted down or up, I'm not sure which, and the car was running more quietly now.

"Why do you live so far away from where you work?"

"Circumstances, I had the place before I got the job. A small condo, but with a view of the ocean, and I wouldn't want to give that up. Do you like the ocean?"

"I don't know. I've never lived near one. We went to the Baltic once when I was a child. It was nice, playing in the sand and the waves." I saw myself in the sand with a bucket and pail sitting between my father and mother, both of whom were planted on canvas chairs wearing an embarrassing amount of clothing, at least it seemed so to me at the time. A friend was there, too, kicking over my sand castle, running away out of sight down the beach to my mother's consternation. The grey sea stretched to the horizon, with only a small coastal steamer trailing a plume of dark smoke adding perspective. Where was it going? I remember thinking I had recently discovered geography and the names of cities were associated with unfamiliar buildings and people who looked and dressed differently. Had I ever heard of Pennsylvania, or for that matter California?

Probably the latter. Even school-age children knew about Hollywood. Not even in my dreams, as rich as they were, not even in my fantasies would I have imagined myself to be here at some time in my life, let alone the circumstances which brought me to America. This thought projected me forward, and I began to wonder what, if any, cataclysm would face future generations of Americans, even this generation perhaps. If so, let me no longer be here, once is enough for anyone. I had met a man once who three times in his life had been a refugee, and who was finally running a small food market in upstate New York. As near as I could perceive, he enjoyed life, his work, his family. This man, something like the peasant in War and Peace, was still in my mind when our car stopped in front of a parking attendant.

The restaurant was a replica of what I imagined a Spanish colonial mansion to be like: a Romanesque stone colonnade with a vaulted plaster ceiling and tile floor, enclosing a roofed court in which a stone fountain played. The place was crowded with people who by their appearances were spending a lot of time on the golf course. As we had to wait for a table, we were shunted to the crowded bar. At the far end of it, a man in tight pants and an ornamented bolero jacket was playing a guitar and singing Spanish songs. Sarah ordered a Perrier and urged me to try a Margarita, a drink made from salt and cactus liqueur, with a little lime juice and ice thrown in. I'll try almost anything once, and I do like a drink now and then, especially when I'm feeling a little self-conscious, as I did then. My eyes wandered over the crowd. Was it something they were saying or not saying that was affecting me? Was it something that they were exuding? Was it the make-up on the faces of the women, the carefully styled hair of the men, the concern for personal appearance, who knows? I turned my back on it and just listened to those schmaltzy songs sung by the guitarist, who looked so happy although no one seemed to be paying him the slightest bit of attention.

The *maitre de* called us, and we were given a quiet table across the court and far away from the bar. Alone with her at the table, insulated by the sound of other conversations all around us, I was feeling at ease, and her eyes were making me go soft inside. I watched her pick the crabmeat off the top of her salad (no dressing) and asked her about her diet.

"I was about forty pounds heavier when I started," she confided, looking like she'd dripped salad dressing on her blouse.

"I can't believe it. At the rate you're going, you'll be Audrey Hepburn's size."

"That's my ambition. How did you guess? At least something like that, given the limitation of my body type."

"Have you been at it long?"

She shook her head. "You don't really want to know that."

"Oh, but I do," I insisted.

The waitress came, we ordered coffee, and haltingly she told me about herself. "Seven years ago, I was overweight, addicted to sugar, a highly paid executive secretary in a firm of engineering consultants, married to an accountant who drank a little too much and had lost most of his interest in me. We had a life, not a good life, but a life. We came down here, we went to Vegas, he liked to gamble, we had a condo, stereo equipment, a Buick Riviera and a couple of signed Dali prints."

"Sounds like all anybody could wish for," I said, choking on the words, and I saw that she understood my irony.

"Right. At least I never questioned it seriously. We drifted along from steak house to stockbroker. We both enjoyed playing the stock market, that was our common interest, you see. We had about $75,000 when we split up, I forget now just how much. Enough at least for me to start again."

"What made you split up?"

I saw the hurt flow into her eyes as she said, "One day after dinner - a good dinner mind you, that I had prepared, it was pot roast, I'll never forget it. If he had done it before dinner, I'd have dumped it on his head. After dinner he told me he was leaving me. No warning, no discussions, no arguments, just like that; as if he'd decided to give up taking the Times."

"Was it another woman?"

"That's what he said. But whoever it was didn't last longer than the divorce. I think she must have been a catalyst."

"And so what..."

"What did I do? I got angry, I felt hurt, rejected, I cried, I felt betrayed, I felt empty, worthless, all of those things." Her voice got a little fluid, and I could see the recollection of the pain, then she looked at me, a look of tempered metal, and said, "In the end I concluded that it was the nicest thing that he had ever done for me. But that realization didn't come easy. If you really want to know, it took about two years going to a psychotherapist three times a week before I understood it." She breathed audibly as if she were expelling the memories and looked at me refreshed, self-satisfied. "The rest you know. I went back to school, worked part-time. I figured that I could be as good an engineer as any of the men I worked for. I worked on my weight problem, really on what I thought about myself, and I decided that I could do just about anything I set my mind to do, given some breaks of course. So here I am, working on the second five-year plan." She gave a little bow. "Did you like the food?" The waitress had brought the check and, opening her wallet, she dropped a Visa card on top of it.

"Wait a minute. Didn't I invite you to dinner?"

"What difference does it make? I chose the cuisine. Besides, I'm on a per diem."

"But..."

"No buts! If I didn't want to, I wouldn't. You buy the next time." She said this in a gentler tone. She must have seen me recoil, at least she thought she did, but all she really saw was whatever registered on my face as I thought of Major Barbara. Funny, the things that pop into the head.

"Do you mind if we drive out to the tower?" she asked me as we waited for her car.

"Not if you put the top up."

"Don't you like the wind blowing in your hair and the stars above you?"

"Remember me. I'm supposed to be out here recovering from bronchitis; acute but with some caution, hopefully not chronic."

"I've got a jacket in the trunk for myself and a blanket if you want to wrap up, if you don't mind. It's too nice a night to put the top up." She gave me the blanket, and I put it down on the seat, preparing to wrap it around me if necessary. Off we went.

"Did I ask you why you go out to the tower every night?"

"Yes," she replied. When she showed no inclination to say more, I told her about my earlier trip to the tower and briefly described the demonstration.

"You've gotten to be friends with Binyan, haven't you?"

"I guess I have." That was the end of that line of discussion.

After we checked the instruments, she asked me if I wanted to see a real Mexican restaurant. It was still early, so I agreed, and we sped over dark desert roads across the valley, scaling and descending hills, moving toward a cluster of faint lights, no more than twenty or thirty small houses straddling the road. On the far side of the town was a building not unlike the rest of them, except for the pink neon Coors beer sign in the window and a few cars parked in front. Near the door was a bar topped by linoleum, and a few chrome and plastic bar stools, glazed with fluorescent light. About ten tables, a quantity of chairs, none of which matched, a juke box and a pool table filled up the rest of the place. Eight or ten men wearing jeans or tan work pants, a few of them with straw wide-brimmed hats, were seated at the tables drinking beer and conversing in Spanish. Several of them looked at us in passing, their expressions unchanging as they turned back to their friends, but the man behind the bar nodded with a familiar smile to Sarah. We sat down at a table along the wall, and the bartender, probably the owner as well, a lean man with a heavily lined dark brown face, almost the color of maple syrup, came over to the table and took our order, beer for me, soda water for her.

My eyes ranged around the place, taking in the details, the sign advertising Montezuma beer in Spanish, the Mexican flag hanging on one of the glossy wood slatted walls. My gaze returned to her, to see that while I was scanning the place, she was watching my reaction to it with the attentiveness of an experimental psychologist. "I suppose you've never seen a place like this before?" she said, nodding to the owner as he placed the drinks on the table and waited for someone to pay him. "Let me," I said, fishing two dollars out of my pocket. "I didn't know the border was so close."

She shook her head. "Down at this end of the state there is no real border."

"These people work on the farms, I suppose?"

"Yes. I suppose so. I don't know much about it. Another engineer brought me over here one time. He said they had the best *menudo* in the country. I don't suppose you know what that is."

"No. I wouldn't even guess."

"Don't feel bad. Neither did I. It's tripe. I thought since we were already out of town why not show you a real Mexican place." Someone baited the music machine and a trio of men performed a castrato harmony to the moon, or so I assumed. We drank in silence, looking around the place and at each other like spectators at a show. I was searching my mind for something to say, something to talk about, but by the look of her she didn't mind if we said nothing, and of course I didn't mind either, as I have no love of chatter."

"Do you know the difference between chitter and chatter?"

"No," she said, a questioning smile on her face.

"Nor do I," I responded.

"Is that some kind of joke?"

"Maybe it is, but it isn't intended to be. It just came to mind, that's all. American slang."

"You don't have to make conversation, you know," she said quietly. "I'm not much for talk myself."

"Then I won't say another superficial word."

"I bet you will," she said.

Not to be trapped, I simply compressed my lips, thinking as I did so that I hadn't played games like that since... and the thought brought her back again; Sarah's eyes – no, Clara's eyes. The light had been different then, as was the table, polished walnut and octagonal, and the room in the light from the overhanging fringed shade was like the inside of a rose. It was some silly card game, something to do with matching your opponent's card. Her long brown hair tied with a brown velvet ribbon was cresting over her shoulders and fanning over the front of her white dimity blouse. An open smile on her wide mouth, her eyes filled with amusement, she turned from the cards to me as though she were savoring a perpetual joke on her tongue like a sugar lozenge. My sputtering laugh colliding in the air with the tumbling water of her laughter, the slap of the cards, the exaggerated seizures as one or the other of us took points, the scent of lilac overlaying the smell of chicken soup from the kitchen, her hand touching mine as she reached for a card and a sudden drifting tenderness in her eyes as I tentatively turned my hand and took hers...

"You've gone all dreamy on me, Mendel."

"Yes, I'm sorry. Just a transient memory, a drop in."

"I have a question. And I expect an honest answer. Promise?"

"It depends on the question. I may be a voyeur, but I'm not an exhibitionist."

"You don't have to give me a truthful answer, if you don't feel like it," she said.

"Tell you what; I reserve the right to receive the fifth amendment."

"You mean take the fifth," she corrected me.

"I'll never master the eccentricities of English," I said, shaking my head.

"Anyhow, the question is, do you find yourself looking backwards more often or looking forward more often?"

The amusement fell from my face for a moment as I recorded the question. "Neither, I guess. I try to stay right in the here and the now. I suppose I'm a little frightened of the future, and as for the past it's better put behind me."

She said nothing, she just nodded a few times too may and looked at me, a teasing interest in her wide eyes. So I looked back, trying to be casual and oblique, letting myself be drawn into her eyes. Then, to break the deadlock, I took a sip of beer. "I forgot to ask, did the earthquake, you weren't joking were you, there was an earthquake? Did it do anything to the tower?"

"Yes and no. There was an earthquake. Have you ever experienced one before?"

"No, and I don't think I'd care to, either," I said, thinking of a film I'd seen about an earthquake and fire in San Francisco, a vision of tumbling walls, and inferno. "That's one of the things that people in the East associate with California, those earthquakes."

"Do you know anything about earthquakes?" she asked me.

"Only that it has something to do with parts of the earth rubbing together."

"In school I did a paper on the effect of earthquake on structural metals, buildings made of steel to be exact. You know there's a measurable earthquake almost every few days out here? And a big one every fifty years. The odds are that we'll have another blockbuster like the one that destroyed San Francisco within another twenty years."

"Why would people build anything with this prospect hanging over their heads? It's like living under an active volcano."

She became more animated as she engaged the subject, tilting her head and gesturing with her hands. "People do live under volcanoes. There's an island off of Italy that is just that, a volcano; nothing more. And people live on its slopes between the cone and the sea." She stopped and observed my reaction. "We can't do much about most of the really awful things that happen to us, and we can't just stop living, either," she said, looking pensive and revealing a side that I hadn't seen before. "You should know that," she added, looking right at me, and the thought stung. The music shifted to a more melancholy solo song, something about *corazon*. A few of the men got up and left with lugubrious good-byes. We heard their muffled voices, then rhythmic engine noises receding to a hum.

"I had a friend in high school," she began. "She had everything. She was lovely, smart, a great personality, even rich, although she didn't need money, what with everything else. She was going to be a biochemist, which is a pretty sophisticated ambition for a senior in high school. The night of the senior dance she and her boyfriend -- he was driving -- skidded off a wet road, over an embankment. He was killed. She suffered brain damage. The accident wiped out two-thirds of everything that she had stored up in her brain for the first eighteen years, and a lot of her personality."

I looked at her, thinking again of Clara, wondering whether that would have been better for her than the camp and the naked- choking death which was her fate.

Watching my reaction, she continued, "Piece by piece she tried to put her life back together again. Biochemistry was out, so was even a liberal arts education. So she went to art school and became a potter, starting all over again. I saw her a few years ago. She seemed happy. She was doing some beautiful work, really skilled and creative. She had put a whole new life together for herself, as if she had died and been born a second time, almost a different person. I did not let on to her, but I went into the ladies' room and cried for her. Not just because of what had been lost. No. I think I cried for what people are capable of."

"Perhaps you were even thinking of yourself."

I thought of survivors. People who like me had spent the time waiting, for months in the same camps while the English and the Americans and the Russians and the Polish tried to decide what was to be done with us. Some had never lost the capacity to laugh although the humor was dark, while others could not even cry; their humanity had left them, not all at once but piece by piece, until they were literally dis-spirited, absolutely.

She was watching me again. I felt the need to say something, but not what was in my mind. "Some people are capable of regeneration, I suppose. Have you seen her since?"

"No. But six months ago I read about her. I cried a second time when I saw it. She had been killed," she said, as grief crossed her face and was gone.

"What happened?"

"A drunk wiped her out in a crosswalk. He went through a red light."

"When I hear things like that, I want to apply Old Testament justice," I said.

"Oh, he didn't just get off. He was tried for manslaughter. I read about that in the paper, too. It seems his wife had just died of cancer, leaving him with four young children. His wife's funeral had been just three days before the accident. The jury came back with a not guilty verdict. Sorry to get so gloomy. I don't usually talk this way. I don't know what made me..." She looked at me self-consciously, her eyes seeking absolution.

"It's not your fault. I think I bring that side out of people. I'd make a great friend for a comedian, wouldn't I?"

"You'd probably make a great friend, period."

I smiled, moved by what she had said. Then she reached across the table and gave my hand a squeeze, and I responded again, this time to her touch. "We'd better go if we're gonna hit the discos in Canyon Springs."

"Hit them with what, a bomb?"

"I thought that's just what you'd like to do at the end of an evening. You Eastern folks," she said, shaking her head as she got up and mechanically straightening her skirt.

There was a CB radio in her car, and she turned it on as we drove back across a landscape as empty as the night sky itself. "Why do you have that thing?" I asked her.

"Communication. It gets lonely driving, sometimes."

I looked at her and said nothing, but I thought how poor a form of communication was even the telephone, even when it was used to talk with friends. "Do you have one of those pseudonyms that they all use?"

"Yes. I'm Slide Rule."

"Have you ever met face to face with anyone that you talk with?"

"No."

"Have you ever talked with the same person twice?"

"No." Then there was silence between us.

We were on the balcony of the hotel facing each other between her room and mine, not sure what else to do. I took her hand and said, "Thanks for dinner," not sure what else to say.

"Remember, it's your treat next," she said, her head bending toward me.

"I, uh, don't think that there are any Polish restaurants around."

"How about the closest we can get, then."

"What would you say to tomorrow night?"

"I would say yes." She leaned toward me and touched my cheek with her lips, then she quickly turned toward her door, and I did the same, suddenly feeling buoyant.

I went to bed thinking about the evening: how it had progressed from superficiality, to tentative understanding, a sharing of feeling. I understood something of her now. She was more than a stranger, more than a professional, more than a person who was staying next to me, rustling and thudding through the wall. She was more than a powerful evocation of dead but not forgotten associations, and I knew that if I never saw her again, I would think fondly of her, and others might one day remind me of her just as she had called up Clara from my past.

As it was, I saw her even sooner than I expected, about 3:30 that morning to be exact, when the ringing of the telephone jarred me out of a narcotic sleep.

"Mendel?" she said, in a voice that called for help. "I'm so sick. I feel like I've been poisoned."

"Is the door open, I'll be right over," I said, the urgency in her voice jarring me awake.

"I'll open the door, oh God."

"Take it easy. I'll just be a minute." I put the phone down and quickly got into my clothes.

I found Sarah in a semi-transparent white nylon night-gown, doubled up on her bed. She was groaning, holding her stomach, and rocking a little.

I went to her side feeling quite helpless. She looked up at me and appreciation broke through the agony on her face, like sunlight through rain clouds. Touching her shoulder, I asked, "Can you describe what's wrong?"

"Stabbing pains in my stomach, like I've eaten glass."

"Have you had your appendix out?" I asked, the only medical question that came to mind.

"No."

"Maybe it's that. Or it could be food poisoning. Can you get dressed? I'll drive you to the hospital."

"I'll just put my coat on and some socks and shoes. The socks are in the top drawer." I went to the drawer and found some white socks amid her underwear, feeling like an intruder and at the same time feeling intimate as I did so. I got the socks and shoes on her, then the coat, and with Sarah leaning on my arm we moved toward the door.

"The car keys are on the bureau," she said, and leaning her against the wall, afraid she would collapse, I returned and found them.

"Do you know where it is, the hospital?" I asked her as I helped her into the passenger seat. She nodded, her breathing coming in sighs. She gave me directions both for the hospital and the operation of her car, and I managed to bring us to the emergency entrance in no more than five minutes.

We were a sorry, incongruous-looking pair: she with her blue nylon bathrobe, socks and tennis shoes, her face contorted and puffy, her hair disheveled. With my greying stubble and my shirttail hanging out in the back of my pants, I was looking no better, but there was no one in the waiting room when the automatic doors admitted us. A nurse's aide looked out at us through the glass window, like a clerk in a cheap hotel and with about as much interest. If she's been here long enough, she's seen just about everything, I imagined, and it was clear that, sick though Sarah was, it was no life or death matter. Between gasps Sarah explained the symptoms, and the woman nodded without writing anything down, then asked for her hospital insurance card. Then she realized that in our haste we had left her wallet behind in the room.

"I'm sorry, but we can't admit you without it, this is a private hospital," the aide said impassively.

"What do people do who don't have insurance?" I asked, my tone showing impatience.

She looked at me with mild condescension and replied, "There's a public emergency facility at Indio. But nearly everyone has something, a Medi-care card or a credit card."

Sarah sat down and I asked her, "Will you be all right here until I get back and get your purse?"

"I don't know. I feel... I'm so sorry..."

"Don't worry about that. I'll just..." then a thought came to me that we didn't even have the key to her room, so that getting her purse would entail waking the couple on night duty and another fifteen minutes. I turned to the aide and said through the baffle, very politely, "Just admit her for treatment now, and I'll be right back with her insurance card."

She looked at me. "I'm sorry, but the rules."

"Forget the rules, this woman is suffering, she's very sick."

"We can only do that in cases of imminent loss of life."

"Is there somebody in charge that I can talk to who can go around the rules?" I was doing my best to be polite, but I could feel my blood rising like mercury in a thermometer.

She looked at me silently with reproof and said, "Just a moment."

Sarah was bent over and gasping when the door opened and an imposing woman in her early sixties with pale, wrinkled skin and rimless glasses, who apparently never left the hospital by day, came over to us and said, "Now I understand that there's a problem here." She listened to my explanation and at the same time fixed a clinical eye on the bent-over Sarah. "Is she your wife?" she asked.

"No, just a friend, she is staying in the motel room next to me, in fact. But what difference does that make, she's sick and this is an emergency room."

"You're right, and I assure you that if she needs to be admitted, there will be plenty of time for you to go get her card. Now, if you'll just sit down over there, I'll see what I can do in the meantime." She sat down next to Sarah and in a comforting tone asked her a few questions such as what she had eaten, where it hurt and whether she was taking any medication. She disappeared behind the door, leaving me chewing on my lip, wondering where Indio was and how long it would take to get there. She returned on her soundless shoes with a small bottle of something.

Holding me with her eyes, she said, "It's probably just food poisoning, combined with those diet pills. Have her take a tablespoon of this right away and that should bring it up within a few minutes." Observing my skepticism she added, "Don't worry, it can't hurt her. If she's still as sick in a half an hour, bring her back with her card, and we'll admit her. And one thing more," she said, a vein of conspiratorial irony on her face, "You were never here, you understand? What I've done is strictly on my own. If the administrator heard about it, I would be looking for a job. If our insurance company heard about it, we would be looking for a new liability insurance carrier." She waited for my visual assent then she patted Sarah on the back and said, "You'll be just fine, dear. Just stay away from the crab salad. This isn't Cape Cod, after all." She turned and went back through the door.

As soon as we got into the car, I let her have a swig of the medicine and started back toward the motel, jerking through the gears. I had no idea just how quickly that stuff would react, but just as we drove into the parking lot she erupted like Krakatoa, all over herself and the floor of the car. The choking spasms came until she leaned back sweating and panting, the remains of dinner filling the car with a sour acidic smell. I leaned over her and pushed her hair out of her eyes and got in return a weak but sincere smile of appreciation,

"Feeling better?"

"Yes," she said softly, "much."

"I'll just go and get the key. Will you be all right by yourself?"

"Fine now."

I rang the night bell a few times, finally rousing a dour puffy-eyed night clerk who looked from me to the car with the world-weary eye of his profession and gave me the duplicate key without a word.

Sarah was recovering, it was clear, for she was well enough on the way up to the room to be embarrassed at the mess.

"Don't even think about it," I said, "I'll just help you get into the shower, robe, nightgown, and all, and in a few minutes there'll be nothing left of it. Feeling better?"

"Weak."

Once inside, she went right to the bathroom and gargled with toothpaste and water. I helped her get into the shower, robe and all, left the bathroom and sat down on the lounge chair listening to the rush of the water.

"Mendel," she called through the door, her voice stronger, "will you get me a clean nightgown, better yet, pajamas. You'll find them in the second drawer." Once again I found myself on sensual and forbidding ground, my hand slipping in among the lace and nylon, looking for what turned out to be nylon pajamas with a light floral pattern, and feeling as I did so both stimulated and embarrassed. I handed the pajamas through the door, turning my head aside, and in a few minutes she stepped out, her hair wet and plastered down, her skin shining, smelling of something at once delicate and provocative, probably concocted by some French wizard from ram's sperm, mare's urine, and jasmine, for all I knew. Whatever, its effect on me was aphrodisiac, although I'll never know whether she intended it that way. The pajamas hung loose, a fluting film around her breasts and waist, clinging like a stocking to the azimuth of her thighs as she sat down on her bed and leaned back on the triple pillows.

"Come sit down here on the bed, Mendel," she said, her voice blurred and drowsy. I hesitated, but drawn by the invitation which lingered in her eyes, I went to her and sat down on the edge of the bed, not knowing what to expect but feeling as if my heart were caught in my throat like a fish bone. "I can't thank you enough for what you've done tonight. A really close friend couldn't have handled it better."

The words made me feel like the night I had gone to Estelle Cantor's house to comfort her after Sydney died. I'm sure that I must have gone all pink, for I saw amusement flow into her expression. She reached out her hand weakly, took my arm, and pulling me down to her she kissed me on the lips, kissed me softly and lingeringly. My pulse levitated, and the kiss went straight to my middle. Lightheaded, I drew back and she too fell back onto the pillows. Confused, I looked at her, not knowing what she expected. At my age, what I was feeling doesn't happen as with a teenager, three times a day. On the other hand, I didn't want to mistake her sincere gratitude for something more, especially considering how sick she had been. Nor did I want to exploit her weakened condition. Wrong. I wanted very much to exploit her weakened condition, but only if she wanted to as well. I felt that there would never again be a moment such as this for the two of us, but Hamlet, Hamlet, Hamlet that I was, I hesitated and the surge of feeling ebbed like a receding wave, leaving only popping foam in the dark wet sand. "Well, I guess I should let you get some sleep. Tomorrow is after all another day."

A plea crossed her face, and she said, "Mendel, please don't go just yet. There's just one thing more."

"Yes?" I said, the word catching in my dry throat.

"Could you, would you, just rub my shoulders a little bit?"

"Sssure," I stammered. She turned on her side, and I rubbed her soft thick-skinned back through the nylon of her pajama tunic, feeling barely able to contain my excitement as I did so. In a few minutes the regularity of her breathing told me that she was asleep. I turned off the lights, quietly closed the door and returned to my room, where I fell across my bed, wrung out like a washcloth and exhausted.

7

MOVING FORWARD IN REVERSE

Morning! Was it really morning? The sun had burned a piece out of the floor and was advancing toward the bed. I turned onto my elbow and squinted out the window through sandpaper eyes. The body isn't what it once was, I thought, feeling the dead weight of my limbs. There was a time when being up half the night wouldn't have moved me even one degree off course, but that was too many years into the past even to count.

I shaved, facing the wrinkled skin of my face in the bright fluorescence of the oversized bathroom mirror, a light that was as revealing as an FBI wanted poster. Time, the insensitive sculptor that it was, had been too industrious. The crevices on my forehead were too deep. So were the arrowheads pointing at the corner of my eyes. As for the rest of my face, it was literally coming apart, though not quite yet. For now it was content just to divide into sections, a section under each eye, a section bounded by my lower lip and chin, another section from my nostrils to the dropping line of my jaw. A Rodin it wasn't, but for all of time's wear there was character and a certain definition. Strange how being here in front of this showroom of a mirror made me look at myself this way, or was it only this whole earthshaking vacation. So far, it had been a little like hiring a dredge to clear the blocked channels of my memory. I thought back on my feelings of the night, or morning, before. My widow in McKeesport didn't make me feel that way, not that she didn't arouse me. As for Estelle Cantor, I never let myself. Sydney was still hanging in the air. This feeling for Sarah was something more Dionysian. Yes, that's a nice way of putting it, Dionysian.

Hunger was gnawing away at my stomach as I started on my way down to the restaurant for breakfast. I stopped at the office and found a letter from Estelle, in a scented violet envelope no less. As I walked to the restaurant, still the same one, I read Estelle's letter only tripping once on a crack in the pavement.

I had sent her a postcard of Mount Har telling nothing of my adventure; there would be time for that. Her letter was matter-of-fact: a little gossip, what she was doing, a play she'd seen in Pittsburgh, a visit with her son. And she missed me. I missed her, too, but not as much as I thought I would.

Thinking these thoughts, I looked up to see a recent model car pursued by a middle-aged and overweight man in a jogging suit. At first it appeared that the car was simply pacing the man, but that was not it at all. It was more that the driver of the car was taunting the jogger, for he would pull forward, then stop to give the man a chance to catch up. When he was almost abreast of the car door, the driver would lurch forward out of reach for twenty yards or so, only to repeat the cycle. By the look and sound of him, the man wasn't enjoying the game at all. He was florid, sweating and breathing hard. His gait was still quick but heavy, and as I looked at him, he was shouting hoarsely, "Stop, you son of a bitch, or I'll have you locked up!"

In contrast to the runner, the driver, a young man in his late teens was, by the look of him, enjoying the game as he watched the runner in his rearview mirror. I moved to the curbside to better see as the car stopped just abreast of me and the driver craned his neck out of the window and gave the runner an obscene gesture.

Seeing me, the man shouted between gasps of air, "Stop him, it's my car!" What got into me, I don't know. Without thinking, I jumped in front of the car just as the man was closing in on it. The driver accelerated and the car lurched forward, but seeing me he jammed on the brakes stalling the engine, but not before the bumper had given me a hard rap on the shin. He threw the car door open, slid out and ran down the sidewalk, just as the man caught up with the car. His chest convulsing, he slumped against the open door and watched the boy disappear between two buildings.

Then he turned to me, and watched as I hopped on my good leg and touched the throbbing bruise on the other.

"Here, sit down," he said. He opened the car door on the passenger's side and I limped around the hood and sat down. He got in, drove the car to the nearest red zone, and parked. "Lemme look at that," he said. I raised my pant leg to expose a red knob on my shin.

"Do you want me to take you to a hospital?"

"No," I said, thinking of the last trip. "It's feeling better already."

"Can I take you anywhere?"

"I was just going in there to have my breakfast."

"C'mon. I'll buy you breakfast. It's the least I can do."

I got out of the car and said, "You don't need to thank me. To tell the truth, I don't understand why I did it."

"You're just a good Samaritan, that's why. You don't like to see punks stealing other people's cars."

"Shouldn't you move the car?" I said. "After all, it's in a no-parking zone."

"Naw, it'll be fine," he said, as we entered the restaurant.

"Hello, Sergeant, out for a jog?" said the cashier.

"Yeah, tryin' to get in shape," he replied, patting his sagging stomach. "The doctor says I gotta get my blood pressure down."

I found a table and he sat down across from me. Rowena, my usual waitress, came and he said, "Whatever he wants, Rowena, it's on me." I ordered my usual, but added a large fresh orange juice. When I had that in front of me, I asked him just what had happened.

"The kid knows I leave the keys in the car when I go jogging, I've got no pocket, you see. Besides, who would steal a car with a sign on the back that says Police Officers Benevolent Association?"

"I thought you looked familiar," I said. "You were out at that demonstration at the tower."

"Yeah. Were you there? Which side were you on?"

"The builder, I guess. I was with Mr. Binyan."

"Oh," he said, looking at me as though he didn't quite understand what I had said.

"Have you ever seen that boy before? Would you recognize him if you saw him again?"

"Yeah."

"What is he, some kind of local troublemaker?"

"You could say that. He's my wife's son."

I finished the orange juice and watched as the poached eggs came. "He's a pretty wild kid, but lots of them are at his age. He was getting back at me for not letting him take the car last night. The kid'll kill himself the way he drives out there on those desert roads, and his friends with him. So he thought he'd play a little trick on me. He hasn't seen the end of it," he said, his eyes smoldering. He looked at me and added, "I really appreciate what you did. Not for me, but for him. Maybe it'll make him see that I'm not the only one he's got to contend with." He looked at his watch. "I'm on duty in about an hour, so I'll be going."

He stuck out a broad sweaty hand and mangled mine. "Just call me if I can help you with anything. Matt Redo, R E D O, not the French way. You know where to reach me." I watched him go, nodding to acquaintances on the way out the door, thinking that I would never see him again, but I was wrong.

"Do you want the newspaper?" Rowena asked, handing me a copy. "It's only been read once. Some guy left it. I know you like to read it in the morning."

"Thanks." I unfolded it, interested in reading about the demonstration of the day before. Not that there was any point in reading about something that I had seen with my own eyes, except possibly to compare my own observations with those of the press. This time the tower made the front page. A lawsuit was being filed today, by the Civil Rights Forum, the Halibut League, and the Anasazi tribe, seeking to stop construction of the tower, each for its own reason. Separation of church and state owing to the combination of religion with Defense Department uses was raised by the Civil Libertarians. The Indians challenged the violation of their sacred ceremonial site, while the Halibut League claimed that the rock, a unique geological formation already on a list to become a national monument, should be free from any development. Actually three suits had been filed, two yesterday and another expected today.

More attention was given to the demonstration than to the lawsuits, however and, as described by the reporter, it had come close to being a riot. As I read the account, I thought that maybe I had attended the wrong one or had left before the main happening.

There was nothing much else going on, according to the paper, other than the monthly price increase in crude oil, sub-zero temperatures and blizzards throughout the northeast, and the usual school district that was going broke. I was glad to be here in my shirt-sleeves rather than back in Bolton, shoveling snow or dealing with frozen pipes.

Like a salmon returning to the spawning ground, I finished my breakfast, and pointed my bleary eyes and fatigue-ridden body toward the serenity and quietude of Arin Binyan's library, thinking how much of this place I was probably missing. Every other tourist seemed to be walking around and looking through the stores when they weren't playing golf or cards. As my grandmother used to say, a mouse crawls into a hole and a squirrel climbs a tree. Mouse that I was, I made for my hole, hoping that nothing would intervene.

Limping a little, I made it. Miriam let me in with the usual show of welcome, and I went straight up to the library, relaxing only as I entered that quiet room, breathed the dusty old book smell, and watched the play of sunlight on motes of dust and the dark oak table.

Someone had closed the folio, and I turned the pages looking for the place where I had left off. They were on the trail passing through a zone of conflict between the Mixtec and the Zapotec, as I recalled.

"News of our supernatural powers must have passed from village to village, for we were treated respectfully throughout the land of the Mixtecs by the villagers, who almost always met us with offerings of food. Later we learned that it was more than our powers that they feared.

"It was with relief that we left the disorder of the Mixtec and entered the land of the Toltec. Here I would present my credentials and, in return for service, we might even be given quiet and fertile land in which to start our lives anew. In contrast to those now left behind, here was a land blessed with order and harmony: well-tended fields, well-fed animals, happy children, well-thatched roofs, and a salubrious climate in pleasant contrast to the humid, insect-infested land of the Maya. The women still walked straight and with the grace of the Heavenly Mother, and the old sat among the young in the doorways of tight houses, dreaming of their youth. The Toltecs were not strangers to our family, for long ago my ancestor Natan Ben Hayuda Binyan had journeyed to Tula to assist in the construction of a great pyramid, for which he was richly rewarded in gold and jade.

"It was with no little interest that, reaching the crest of a ridge, we looked into a wide valley and saw spread out before us a ceremonial center of high, many-colored pyramids, plazas, and palaces surrounded by the houses of merchants, artisans, and peasants. So secure in their peace and strength were the Toltecs that not once were we stopped or challenged. Even as we drew close enough to the city to smell it, we saw nothing of the military, not, at least, until, threading our way through the crowds, we came to the imposing seat of government. There we were treated as emissaries, given comfortable quarters, and food enough for all.

"Seven days passed, seven days of welcome quiet and rest before I was called before Kanikulu, a high prince of the Toltecs, an old man with both the proud bearing of the warrior and a kindness and interest in his eyes.

"He lost no time in telling me why we had been met with awe and respect on our journey. It seems that in the past season, strange white-faced people with round dog's eyes, he said, landed in a winged boat, having traveled across the sea from the distant place where the sun rises. This news excited me. For countless generations we had waited for another ship from our homeland, or at least one that would bring news of our people, but to our knowledge none had arrived until after many generations our family had ceased even to hope. We, or rather I, had been taken for yet another group of white foreigners since, like them, I carried a white metal burnished sword.

"In answer to my questions, he told me that the men at arms had been subdued and killed by his warriors, leaving only one gentle old man with strange eyes the color of the sky, who was dressed like night in a long colorless gown, and who wore as his only adornment a large wooden cross around his neck. When he heard that I spoke the ancient language of our fathers, he had the man brought to the palace, reasoning that since he had come from the same place as our ancestors, the tongues might at least resemble each other.

"The captive had spoken much but no one understood him. Toltec priests assumed that he spoke the language of the birds, since it resembled bird sounds. One of the chief priests even had the notion that the man was an emissary of the great god Kukulkan who, having been killed by the god of Evil, Tezcatlipoca, would one day return from the eye of the morning sun to redeem his place on the throne of good, banishing evil from the world. This, the old prince doubted.

"'Evil, like the night itself, is here to stay,' he said. 'And if there were no evil,' he continued, 'neither would there be good, but rather something that was neither good nor evil.'

I was not inclined to challenge this thought, for I had been taught that to engage a king in idle debate is to risk evoking his disfavor over a trifle, much like throwing away eggs because the shells are discolored.

"While we waited for the sky-eyed man to arrive, we were taken to a hall, my interpreter and I, and fed delicacies for which the Toltecs are famous, roast dog in chocolate sauce, and a stew of peppers and tomatoes. The taste has not faded from my memory, although forty summers have since passed.

"Having eaten, we returned to the great hall to find both the prince and the stranger looking exactly as described, with one exception: the prince had not spoken of the aura of gentleness which emanated from him. There was in his eyes and soft smile a humility and warmth which would have stopped a charging boar in its tracks. There was also a rope wrapped around his waist and a sack which hung behind his garment and might have served as a cover of his silver head.

"The old man stood slightly bent, watching us, showing a happy recognition at the sight of me for, despite my dress, not unlike the dress of the prince, he could see that I was of different stock. The prince asked me to speak to him in my ancient Hebrew tongue, and this I did. Even before he responded, it was clear that he understood.

"'Who are you and where are you from?' I asked him.

"'I am Brendan of the Order of St. Phaedric, come to this new land to bring the word of the true Lord to all heathens. And who might you be, that dressed as a heathen you speak the language of the Israelites?'

"'I am an Israelite,' I replied. This did not surprise him, for he had been told in a dream by the angel Gabriel himself that he would encounter, in some far-away place, the remnants of the Ten Lost Tribes of Israel.

"'What Ten Lost Tribes?' I asked. 'I know nothing of my people since my ancestor followed the sun to this land in the time of King Solomon.'

"'Much has happened to your people since that time. It is best that you know not of it. But then you know nothing of the birth of the Messiah, Jesus Christ?' he asked.

"'If the messiah has indeed come, I have seen no sign of his coming. You are good to bring the news. When did he come?'

"'More than 900 years ago.'"

"All this I related to the Prince, through my own interpreter, and through his as well, since I spoke in the Mayan tongue. When the old priest heard the story, of which I now relate just a little, he grew very excited, for what he heard convinced him that the old man was indeed an emissary of the deity Kukulkan and that this Jesus Christ was none other than Kukulkan himself, returned to rid the world of evil.

"What happened next only a prophet would have foreseen. The old man was removed from the empty cell where he had been kept and taken to the precincts of the temple of the high priest so that all he knew of Kukulkan might be imparted to the priesthood. This he was glad to do, for he saw it as his mission to bring the teachings of his Christ to all. This was not, in his eye, a matter of mistaken identity, but divine intervention, proof again that the coming of Christ had been prophesied the world over.

"For the Toltecs, the coming of Brother Brendan was a sign that they should in time embark on a conquest of all of the nations to bring the god's wisdom to all men, and to dispel evil thereby.

"My hopes too were fulfilled, for I was given not only the task of helping to teach the Toltec language to Brother Brendan, but to supervise the construction of a new facade for the ancient pyramid built by my forbear. This new facade was to depict, in its stone and terra cotta reliefs, the salvation of mankind by Kukulkan-Christ-Messiah, as taught by the old man and interpreted by the Toltec priests. As a reward, I was given a capacious residence and the promise of land of m own in only five years' time. Once settled in the house, I began this work willingly, eager to restore my skills as a master builder. These had fallen into disuse during the period of upheaval in the Mayan empire when there was little built and much destroyed.

"Those years were glad times for my family and me, what with the satisfaction of continuing work on the pyramid of my ancestor. Looking at the engineering and masonry of that edifice was like visiting with him and carrying on a timeless task which had begun with the Ziggurat and culminated in Solomon's temple for my family.

"It was also good to spend long hours of the night with old Brother Brendan, to learn of his faith in man's salvation through Christ, and Christ's death and resurrection; a history which matched the myth of the death of the Toltec God of good. To his sorrow, I could not bring myself to accept the notion that Christ was indeed the Messiah.

"'Accept it on faith,' the old man told me, but the faith would not come. In fact, when he told me that my people had been driven from their homes, enslaved and reviled by Christians, I concluded sadly that if Christ were our Messiah, he would not have permitted our people to be treated so. Even beyond this despairing thought was the possibility that our God, our strength and shield, had abandoned us, though not entirely, for according to the old man, our people continued to observe their faith even in the face of persecution.

"'If we are reviled, why did you learn our language?' I asked.

"'Because it is the language of the Bible preserved in the Christian world only in Ireland, so as better to study the ancient texts,' he explained.

"Over the years I grew fond of the old man. In his child-like innocence, he truly believed that the transliteration of his teaching would bring the 'true faith' to the rest of the world through the mouths of the Toltec priests, just as St. Phaedric had brought Christ to the Irish from across the water. Patiently he taught the meaning of the ceremony in which celebrants drank the blood of Christ and partook of the flesh of Christ, who as God's son had been sacrificed so that all men might be granted salvation and eternal life at least he explained it so. At the same time, the artisans translated Christ's sacrifice and resurrection into symbols which the Toltecs could accept. The cross, for example, at the hands of the Toltec priests and artists became a tree with tendril-like branches extending out from its three points. The design pleased the old man, who spoke of similar tree-like crosses in his own land.

"'New rituals must wear the trappings of the old order to win acceptance of converts. After all, was not the worship of the tree, which antedated the coming of Christ, proof that even the symbol of the cross had been preordained?' he explained.

"The poor brother had no idea to what extent the priests of the sect of Kukulkan would adapt his ritual, that is, until the dedication of the new facade of the pyramid. By this time the wars of conversion had begun with the conquest of the war-weary and debilitated Mixtecs. The banner of the deity, depicting his head, a combination of the sun and great thunderclouds, was carried at the head of the Toltec warrior lines, and it was said by those who returned with uncountable captives that the Mixtecs shrunk in fear from it. To my surprise, Brother Brendan accepted the campaign and the prisoners as part of the 'revelation.' To him, the victory was the beginning of the conversion of all the diverse people of the land, and he shone with a joy which I did not share.

"With the completion of the new facade of the pyramid, my obligation to the old prince was at an end. He alone, among all of the nobility of the Toltec, seemed to doubt the rectitude of the mission which consumed the Toltec nobles. My last meeting with him was somber. He thanked me for my work. With proper solemnity the old man handed me another formal grant of land, sealed by the King himself. It lay far to the north, across the great wasteland, and before reaching it we would traverse the lands of simpler peoples, among them the warlike Aztecs and the Yaquis, who lived in holes in the ground and ate small animals and seeds…."

Engrossed as I was in the text, I didn't hear the heavy door open, wasn't even aware of the presence of the others until Arin spoke my name. I turned my head to see him in the company of three other men, one of whom I recognized as the restaurant owner. I began to rise, but Arin pushed me back into my chair, saying quietly, "Just stay where you are."

To the others he said, "This is Mr. Traig, and.." He paused, then said quickly, "one of my lawyers." I was surprised, at least until he squeezed my arm. With that signal I sat back and listened, hoping that I wouldn't be called on to say something legal.

Windel, the restaurant man, shrugged. He knew I wasn't a lawyer. The other two said nothing. They all sat down around the table, and Arin introduced them to me. The first, a tall, angular man with a square face, tight lips, pinched nostrils and narrow dark eyes, was Reverend Collery-Matin. The second, Andrew McHadden, limped a little, his face drooped to one side, his hair was thin and what there was of it was battleship grey. He was an Assistant Deputy Undersecretary of the Navy, as befit his hair color.

"I suppose you called this meeting," Arin said to McHadden, "to deal with this new lawsuit that's been filed?"

"Yes and no," said McHadden, smiling in a disarming way.

What followed was fascinating to me. Maybe it was because of my new and transient career. McHadden tried to buy the restaurant man out, and he offered the minister some time on the Voice of America so that the Navy could have the tower to itself. I swallowed the impulse to mention a separation of church and state question. They went on, and on. Arin sat and listened like a bored spectator at a bad play.

I took a lesson from him, at least until, the meeting about over, McHadden began to gather up his papers. He looked at me and said, "Mr. Traig, is all of that agreeable to you and your client?" My heart stopped for an instant and I looked at Arin with a question in my widened eyes. He looked positively opaque. It came to me that Arin, having suffered through all the controversy, changes and lawsuits, ought to get something out of the meeting as well, so I stammered, "Arin, shouldn't there be some payment from the Government under the contract, now that things are getting closer?" Where this came from, I don't know.

Arin's eyes woke up at this and he said, "I was going to say the same thing myself. Give some thought, Mr. McHadden, to cutting loose two or three hundred thousand in the delayed progress payments."

McHadden responded with a toothy smile. "I'm glad you spoke up, Mr. Binyan. I'll see what I can do." Once again he assembled his papers, then stopped and looked at each of them in turn as he said, "I don't need to say that what we are talking about hinges on our lawyers booting those new lawsuits out the courthouse door. While I'm pretty optimistic, my father, who practiced at being an attorney, told me never to count on weather, women, and judges. I leave you with that."

They all stood up and shook hands warmly, like cousins leaving a family reunion, and left. I had no idea there was so much good feeling; I certainly couldn't tell from the meeting itself. Why, they even treated me like an old friend, and I began to wonder just what I had done to ingratiate myself.

Maybe it wasn't warmth. They were probably just relieved to get it over with.

Arin returned in a few minutes and asked me, "What did you think of all that, Mendel?"

"What did I think? It was kind of crazy of you to call me your lawyer. But I appreciate that you got them to put out the cigars."

"Why was it crazy?" he responded, with a benign smile. "You functioned as one. You raised the issue of payment. You deserve a fee. How about dinner?" He followed with a belly laugh.

"Never mind me. You must have been crazy to try to put the military together with a restaurant and a church. It's like putting a lion, a monkey, and a lamb in the same cage at the zoo."

He just leaned forward a little, and said in a weary if patient voice, "If you want the God's honest truth, I don't like what's happened any more than Zev does."

"So what got into you, then? At risk of alienating you, why did you spend your money on such a, a Rube Goldberg project?"

He just looked at me, benign, weary and a little all-knowing. "It's not as eccentric as it seems. There's more than one road to Jerusalem, my grandfather used to say. As I told you, when I first planned the communications tower, I approached Windel with the restaurant idea. I needed money and, after all, there's one on just about every major tower in the world, so he said at least. And there are still no restaurants with a view of

Canyon Springs. He thought that it would bring people out there."

"But I thought that the rock was a sacred place for your family."

"Even so, there are lots of examples of encapsulating a historic structure in a modern one. The Toltecs, and I think the Mayas, others as well, did it. They simply entombed a pyramid by using it as a base for a new one, at least a facade. There's a little Byzantine church in Athens that I read about that has an office building on stilts constructed over it. The church is protected and the modern structure is enhanced. It's better than tearing old buildings down like the worst of urban renewal."

He went on to explain the peculiar properties of the rock discovered by his father. Not only was it a good place for a conventional communications tower, but as the Navy found, the rock itself communicates low frequency radio waves in some complicated geophysical way through the molten core of the earth. I asked him if the tower was superfluous and he responded that, to the contrary, it will throw short-wave signals clear across the Pacific and is a second means of communicating with the Pacific fleet, "in case the Russians knock out our space satellites or their systems break down. It's two more back-up systems to get through in an emergency, according to the Department of Defense."

"You have an explanation for everything."

"Don't we all have an explanation for the things we do?" His eyes sought my assent. I suppose that I shrugged, and he continued with his apologia. "Understand, the rock is important to my family, but not just because of the stone platform.

It's because my grandfather started the first tower there. The tower is spiritual, you see. It's the act of building it, as well as what it is. A tower has always been special to our family, not a tower but a high place where man by his own efforts can get off the earth."

"There are the mountains for getting off the earth."

"Man didn't make the mountains. There's something special about man transcending his own limits by his own power, like in the legend of Prometheus."

"Or the legend of Satan's fall from grace."

He looked at me with both understanding and annoyance. "Don't tell me you're something of a Dukobor?"

"Not consciously. Who are they?" I asked.

"Some sect of Russians up in Canada that destroyed machinery. After all, you did fly out here, you didn't walk, and you have a car, I suspect."

"An old one. And what about you, you don't drive."

We looked at each other, each trapped in the other's paradox. He drummed on the tabletop and said with an expression of irony, "It's true that technology hasn't been around long enough for us to learn to live with it. It's like an obnoxious relative that comes to live with you."

"Be that as it may," I said, "I still don't understand why you got all of those conflicting interests involved in your tower."

"Pragmatism," he replied.

"What's that, a new religion?"

"Why, it's the American religion," he answered, looking surprised that I had even asked the question. "After getting Windel involved, I went to Alumaloy. I'd heard about this aluminum alloy that they had just developed as a substitute for structural steel, cheaper, lighter and easier to build with. They were interested. They thought that a tower would demonstrate its potential in a dramatic way, a structure that would not only show how good it was, but even be a symbol for the company - a logo, they call it now - like the Star of David is to us. They offered to sell us the materials below cost, if, but only if, I would let the church in."

"So that's how the church got into it?"

"Exactly. You'd never heard of Reverend Collery-Matin?"

"No, I can't say that I have, not before Canyon Springs."

"I'm surprised. He was on the cover of Time magazine."

"It must have been the time my subscription ran out," I said.

"Radio is his medium of reaching people. He has his own network, about thirty stations, all owned by a non-profit foundation called the American Church of the Air."

"So he wanted the tower for a symbol as well?"

"More than that. As it turned out, he wanted to broadcast worldwide his own religious ideas, an American Christian gospel; individualism, free enterprise and Christ."

"In that order?"

"I don't know. We've never talked about it."

"Are they compatible?"

"Ask him. To the point, the President of Alumaloy was on the Board of the Church, and a personal friend of the Reverend. It was his idea. I agreed, provided that the church paid a substantial part of the construction costs and time was provided for other religions, including Catholicism and Judaism."

"How did the Reverend feel about a division of the air, something like the loaves and the fishes?" I asked.

"No. He wanted a monopoly. But I held out and eventually he agreed."

"And the Defense Department?"

He must have seen the incredulity on my face, for his brow creased and he said, "I know, it sounds bizarre, but no more so than a lot of things that we take for granted. It happened gradually, you see. When we planned the tower, it was like any communications tower. How was I to know that the Defense Department would move in on it at the time? What was I to do, tell them to go find another rock? They would have turned around and appropriated it, as they've been threatening to do." He looked frustrated, even defeated as he said this.

I said to him, "If you had known what was going to happen, would you have begun the project?"

He looked at me, and for the first time I thought that I could really look right into him, right through his pupils into his very soul. What I saw was conflict, ambivalence, the conviction that he had to build the tower, eroded by the wish that he didn't have to, the anguish of the kleptomaniac. All of this I imagined from a weary shrug, a determined set of jaw, that and the fatigue in his eyes. At length, he smiled an ironic smile and said, "Somebody's always saying that to people who do things. Can't you just hear Columbus's mother, or one of the wives of the Pharoahs, or whoever got the idea for the Statue of Liberty, or the Golden Gate Bridge?"

"Or even Solomon's temple," I added, to be accommodating.

"They are all examples of man trying to transcend his limitations, like Prometheus," he repeated.

"Or the fallen angels?"

This was fascinating. For the first time, the riddle of the tower was coming into focus, not only as to the various interests, but the complex motivation of Arin. Now that I understood it, it didn't seem to be nearly as crazy.

A few minutes later, Miriam entered the library with a tray. For some reason she had decided to finish off my bronchitis. The tray had a large cup of bitter-smelling tea and a small piece of cake. "I've heard you coughing. This will cure it," she said.

"What is it?" I asked her with a pucker.

"An old remedy, made from local plants, *mechawal* and *atukaul.*"

"If that doesn't work, the sweat house will," said Arin.

I took a sip to be polite. She must have seen my reaciton, for she said, "Drink it with the cake and it won't taste so bitter."

"What's the cake made with?" I asked.

"Some local seeds. Do you like it?"

"Compared to the tea I do." I finished the tea with one penitential gulp, thanked her and impulsively kissed her hand. It seemed somehow appropriate, although I hadn't done it since Poland. In Poland, it was the polite way to greet a lady. In the United States, it seemed somehow stilted. But she was delighted by it. In this house, where time and custom stood in suspension like a specimen preserved in alcohol, even a bow might have seemed natural.

By then, the sun had shifted to the other side of the house, leaving the high-ceilinged room in dusk. I walked to the french windows and looked out at the dense green overlay of the garden, beyond it to the pastel shades, mauve and taupe, of the far hills and the perfect sky. Arin had gone to a shelf and pulled out an old book. He took it to the table, sat down and opened it.

"What was it McHadden said about the Wisconsin grid?" I asked, still not understanding the government's motivation.

"They wanted to bury thousands of miles of wire all over Wisconsin, and the farmers didn't want them to. It was all over the papers at the time. Then some geologist told them about our rock, and how it would be even better than turning half the state of Wisconsin into a radio antenna, and much cheaper. So they approached me. They were willing to pay for the rest of the project and help with the suit. At first I didn't like the idea. But then I thought, if it becomes the government's project, not only will they defend the lawsuit and have a good chance of winning, but they're the only ones around to pay for it no matter how much it costs in the end. I had gone into debt to start it and was in no position to go on." His lips tightened with this admission.

"Why did you want me to sit in on that meeting this morning?"

"It never hurts to have an impartial witness when there are lawsuits in the offing. Somebody who can testify to what was said, rather than what somebody says was said."

"You didn't say anything at all."

"Yes, that's true. The whole thing is beyond me now. It's in their hands. One way or another it will get built."

The man is so complex, I thought, a mixture of shrewd businessman and quixotic dreamer. "You were going to show me a memento of your family. Something from biblical times, wasn't it?"

"Oh, there's enough time for that. Why don't you finish reading the memoir first?"

8

BARING AND CLEAVING

So there we were again, Sarah and I in the violet dusk, whistling our way from one red light to the other, this time bound for a "rib place," or so she described it. The rib place turned out to lie in the purgatory between Palm Springs and Palm Desert, a simple storefront with an open kitchen smelling of charcoal and vinegar, with Formica-topped tables, noisy people and an overall country-and-western din. Here the people were just not as well-fashioned as at the Mexican restaurant: their bellies didn't quite fit, they were either too big, hanging over their western belts, or they looked malnourished. Their clothes were the same: either the colors weren't right, too bright or too sticky, or they were too tight for the job. But for all the mismatching, they and their children were enjoying life every bit as much as the tailored people. Sarah stood out, wearing champagne crepe de chine, looking even thinner than the day before, no doubt because of her illness.

"You do eat pork, don't you?" she asked me. "I never even thought to ask you if you did."

A fine time to ask me that, as I was halfway through with what I had assumed was beef. The sauce was so pungent that it might have been buffalo for all I knew.

I looked down at it. "I never even thought about what it was. I suppose it's too late to worry about it now."

"You don't eat pork. I'm sorry." But the amusement in her eyes told me she wasn't.

"I suppose the harm's done now. Will I get trichinosis, or something?"

"No, the meat is well-cooked and inspected. How do you like it?"

I didn't know what to say and fell back on, "Very tasty. So how was your day?" I asked.

"Breathless. I had to drive in to Los Angeles to a meeting to discuss the earthquake."

I watched her tear a piece of flesh off a bone with her teeth and said, "I wasn't going to mention this, but have you given up on your diet?"

"No, but you are supposed to stop it periodically. Not stuff yourself, of course. This is my sabbatical."

I said, "Oh," but wondered whether it had more to do with her job than the schedule of the diet. By the look of her, she seemed willing, even eager, to talk about her work. The more that I learned about the tower, the more curious I was to find out just exactly what she was measuring, and so I asked, "You know, I still don't really understand what it is you're doing out there with those instruments. Can you explain it in simple terms?"

Using some poor sow's rib as a baton, she proceeded to explain, as had Arin, that Alumaloy was using the tower as a test for a new building material. "This is the first time that it's been used in any form of construction anywhere in the world. And if it meets its specifications, it could very well replace structural steel."

"It has some advantages over steel, then?"

"Sure. The obvious one is weight. With that is an enormous reduction in cost and ease of construction, especially in high-rise buildings. The company has a patent on it. If it's successful, it will make them not just millions, but literally billions," she said, blotting her lips with the napkin.

"You missed some," I said, observing a patch of barbeque sauce near the corner of her mouth, not that the business about the metal wasn't absorbing my attention. Looking uncertain, she rubbed the wrong side. "Permit me," I said, and leaning over the table, I went right to the point with my napkin. I know it was forward of me to do it. It was the eyes again, so familiar to me.

She flushed a little, looked around her to see if someone might have noticed, and said, "You do take good care of me."

"Sorry if I embarrassed you."

"I'm flattered by your attention." Her eyes, lively and sincere, focused on me.

"You were talking about Aluma, Alumaloy. Is the tower so strange-looking because of the material, then?"

"Partially. The design is intended to compensate for the fact that the aluminum tungsten alloy has somewhat less tensile strength than steel."

"Tensile strength," I repeated, trying to recall just exactly what that was, but reluctant to ask. "So you were happy with the earthquake, then? The thing didn't fall over, at least." She didn't reply, and I went on. "It seems like you've got a pretty important job to do. If the results are good, you could find yourself going all over the place, working with plans for other buildings."

She smiled dubiously. "Yes, that's partly true. But it's sort of like dancing on hot coals, too."

"Why?"

"Well, in the first place, the data are susceptible to more than one interpretation. So whatever I say, I'm sticking my neck out a long way."

"What do you mean?"

She looked at me as though she were trying to decide whether I could be trusted. "Mendel, you don't work for U.S. Steel or anything like that, do you? You're not one of those industrial spies. Not that it matters. Even if you were, you could go out there yourself and find out the same thing."

"Do I look to you like a spy, Sarah?"

"Well, you're not James Bond. I guess you're not Smiley, either."

"If you'd rather not talk about it, there are lots of other things..."

"I don't have to say anything that isn't suggested in the scientific journals in theory. The laboratory tests have all been written about. Right now, we assume that we can build four-story buildings with complete confidence. That gets us up to the restaurant platform. After that, it's kind of up to me. If I say no, they've got to change the design and the construction material, which frustrates the whole concept."

"And if you say yes?"

"If I say yes, they go all the way to the top with Alumaloy, the tower becomes the company logo, and I get a twenty or thirty thousand dollar raise."

"So, what are you going to do?"

She looked pregnant with irresolution. "Before the earth-quake I was pretty sure. Now I don't know. That's why I went to LA today, to tell them that."

"You're under a lot of pressure then. What will they do if you tell them it's unsafe?"

She raised an eyebrow. "I really don't know. But it couldn't be any worse than if I said it's safe, and it turned into the Leaning Tower of Pisa. Can you imagine the egg on the face of the engineer who designed that suspension bridge up in Washington, without taking into account the high cross winds?"

"What happened?"

"The bridge blew apart."

The waitress, complete with hairy armpits smelling of sweat, brought the coffee in mugs, splashing it on the table as the mugs landed. I pulled a napkin out of the dispenser and mopped it up. "I never heard about that. When did it happen?"

"Just before the Second World War, I think."

"Could be it was an omen." Her expression clouded at this. "Why did we come here?" I asked her, looking around and flinching a little at the noise.

"Does the place put you off? I like it. The atmosphere's not much, but the food is good."

"I didn't say it wasn't. It's just not the kind of place that I would go to at home, let alone out here. But I'm just a hick."

"Anybody who goes through middle age without tasting pork..." For the first time, there was a slight mocking tone, and I recoiled.

"I suppose that I could list a lot of sophisticated people, scientists and philosophers, who never tasted pork. Then if you want to discuss beef, we can start with Gandhi and go on to Shaw."

"I'm just teasing you, Mendel," she said, and I felt foolish; in fact, I could feel the flush in my face. She noticed it and added, "I like a man who can blush."

"It's probably just high blood pressure brought on by diet."

We were in the car again. The top was up and the warm glow of the instruments was like a miniature fire log. She had grown restless back in the restaurant. It must have been the stress of her day. She seemed to be alternating between a forced cheerfulness and a morose reflective state. Now, in the car, she was again calm and self-possessed. "The car suits you," I said. "You should spend more time in it. It's a kind of incubator for you Californians."

"And where do you go to escape, the bathroom?" She was turning her head toward me slightly, but her attention remained on the road.

"Me? A good book. I crawl in between the covers and close it on myself."

"Not a good woman? Or is that something to escape from?"

"I wouldn't know. I'm not married."

"You don't have to be married to want to get away from someone." She had pulled into a parking lot. We left the car with the parking attendant and entered a softly-lit Victorian sort of bar, with lots of dark wood, odd chairs, many of which looked authentic, random prints on the walls and a pianist playing nice, innocuous music. Not the kind I like to listen to, but still pleasant.

"Does this suit you more?" she asked me.

"To tell you the truth, I never go to places like this either." We found a table in the corner and ordered a couple of Remy Martins.

"You didn't answer my question."

"What question?" I asked.

"The one about getting away from women into a book."

"You didn't answer mine, either." She looked quizzical and I continued, "The one about why we went to the rib place."

She shook her head, smiling to herself, listening to an inner voice. Then she lowered her head and looked at me out of the top of her eyes. "It's a place that we used to come to, my husband and I, when we were still happy with each other." Her eyes drifted up over my head and she continued quietly, "We used to come down here, stay in a cheap motel, we didn't have much money, go for walks, look in store windows, dream about having our own place. We'd fantasize about being invited to Frank Sinatra's or some other star's place for a party. Pretty silly."

"Everybody has to have dreams. Dreams are as important as food." I swirled the cognac in the snifter and watched the ridges and fingers recede, thinking how long it had been since I'd had such dreams. I no longer thought about having a wife. I had two half-wives; the widow in McKeesport below the waist, and Estelle Cantor from the waist up. Was there something wrong with me that I had shut off my dreams? What happens when you stop dreaming, I asked myself. Should I ask her? No, not yet. Instead, I said, "That song is nice, even if it is a little melancholy. What is it?"

"I don't know."

"I listen to classical music at home. But I can see why people like this. You're more relaxed now. Would you like another cognac?"

"Yes, thanks. I am more relaxed. It was a hard day. But you could probably figure that one out for yourself." The waitress brought her another cognac, and she sipped it appreciatively. "I don't know how this stuff mixes with spare ribs."

"In our society, it all goes together somehow,"

"I suppose you're right."

"You feel your meeting didn't go so well, then?"

"I don't know. They were pretty high-level management. And even though they didn't say as much, I got the feeling that what I said wasn't what they wanted to hear."

"How do you know?"

"They were kind of condescending. There were glances that seemed to say, to me at least, we should have given this to somebody with more experience."

"So why didn't they?"

"I think that they wanted to have a fall-person if things didn't go as well as they wanted them to."

"What do you mean, a fall-person?"

"Somebody to blame. If they don't like my conclusions, they can chalk it up to my inexperience, a woman and all, and send out one of the old hacks to fuzz up the data."

"Would they do something like that?"

"Maybe. After all, they've got a billion dollars in eventual orders riding on this report of mine. And when it comes down to it, I'm just dealing in probabilities, the one chance in two million that something will go wrong," she said into her glass.

"Isn't that what they say about the nuclear power plants?"

"Something like that. Do we want to accept the risks to get the benefit? That's the argument, at least."

"Seems to me we ought to have a vote of the people who might be affected."

"We've already voted, Mendel. We voted for convenience, bright lights, fast elevators, air conditioning."

"Not me. It gives me sinus trouble."

An indulgent, sympathetic smile, "That's part of your charm, you're above it all."

"Just out of it all. I think I heard some teenagers use that expression once or twice."

"That's what I mean. Even your slang is out of date. What kind of a car do you drive?"

"Nothing fancy; an old Chevie."

"I suppose it has a name."

"Tevya. I call it Tevya."

"You see?" she chided, wagging a finger, "Even you give human qualities to the machines around you."

"Nobody said I didn't."

After the tense beginning, we really started to enjoy ourselves, drinking the cognac slowly, just chattering - loose, familiar, easy talk that came out as smoothly as the cognac went down. She asked me about the women in my life. I told her about the widow and Estelle. Well, something of them. I wasn't going to go into detail about each of the women since Clara. After all, this wasn't one of those sensitivity sessions and she wasn't my analyst. I did tell her that she reminded me of someone, someone special. That confession made her glow a little. Saying so made it even more real. It was as though by saying it I had opened the gate of my feelings all the way.

"You don't remind me of anyone that I've ever cared about," she said when we were back in the car and on the way to the motel.

"I suppose for that I should be thankful."

"Why?"

"You don't have very fond recollections about your husband, for starters."

"Perhaps I simply haven't shared them with you."

"I could remind you of your father, or an uncle you had a pre-teen infatuation with."

"Come on, Mendel, you're not that much older than I am. And anyhow, after thirty-five years, it all levels out." She said this last sentence to herself by the tone of it. "To return to your comment, it is good. You see, I've grown quite fond of you these last few days."

"And I of you, Sarah. Even though you're a reckless driver," I added as she jammed on the brakes at a stop light.

"Nobody's perfect."

She stopped the car in the parking lot and we climbed the stairs to our rooms.

"You'll come in?" she asked. "What can I lure you with? A night cap?"

"It's past one I think."

"I'm not tired, are you?" She fumbled with the key, opened the door and turned with her back to it, facing me. I hesitated, wondering how far it might go, wondering about her intentions, wondering if she desired me, wondering whether to make advances, wondering if I would feel the same as the night before.

She looked at me with an expectant, ambivalent smile and said, "Come on."

Putting my doubt aside, I followed her into the room, sat down, and watched her pour the cognac. I was feeling alternating waves of fatigue and uncertainty, and a gentle awakening of desire brought on as much by the fragrance of perfume in the air as by the open warmth in her eyes as she picked up the glass and reached out to touch mine, saying, "To us."

"*Le Chaim.*"

"To life."

We sat there drinking quietly. She saw me finish the last of it and said, "Would you like another?"

"No, it's already past one and I guess I'd better let you get some sleep. You've had a long day, and you'll probably have another tomorrow." I said this with a question in my eyes and the hope that she would give me some sign that she wanted me to stay. She did.

"If you're tired. But I don't have to get up early tomorrow."

"No, I'm not particularly tired," I lied.

"Then stay. As long as you like."

Did she mean what I thought she meant? We hadn't known each other very long, but this was, after all, California. "Should I take that literally?"

"Sure."

Her words bounced around in my head, touching yes, no and yes again. Last night's desire wrestled with my shyness. I was exhausted. What if nothing happened? What then? If not tonight, there was always the morning. I looked into her waiting eyes and saw Clara instead. What memories would return to me if we did? I was afraid.

She saw the conflict on my face, she saw my hesitation, and her mood changed to reassurance. She said gently, "Don't worry, Mendel."

"Well, I'll, uh, just get my pajamas and robe." That was it, like jump-starting a dead battery. The blood was already pumping to my head and desire, or was it adrenalin, was heating my blood.

"Don't forget your toothbrush." She gave me a little pat and a shove.

Out of her sight in my semi-dark room, my feet got cold, as the saying goes. I looked into the bathroom mirror at myself, my steel grey hair, the fine wrinkles surrounding the deep-set blue-grey eyes. I suddenly wanted to cough. Toothbrush in hand, I still hesitated. I could call her and tell her that I wasn't coming. No, I couldn't. She needed me, and I wanted her. Yes, I did, wanted to lie beside those grey eyes and swim in them. I put on my pajamas and robe and returned to her room.

"Mendel?" she said, responding to my knock.

"It's me."

She came to the door wearing a pale blue silken gown and smelling faintly of lilac. She had combed her hair and she looked fresh for the hour, fresh and attractive. So much so that on the way in the door, following the flow of her body in that fluid gown, I was stirring. She turned to face me, the deep shadow between her breasts visible behind the lace of her nightgown.

I felt a flush in my face and said, "You really have lost weight."

She chuckled, her breasts bounced, and she said, "That's not very romantic, Mendel, but you couldn't have said any-thing nicer to me." She looked across the void that separated us, maybe four feet, her expression open and inviting. "Which side do you want?"

"It makes no difference." I watched her sit down and swing her legs onto the bed. She leaned back on two propped-up pillows, turning slightly towards me, and the outline of her legs under the thin nylon made me come alive, made my heart do a handspring. It would be good. Again I had passed the test.

I took off my bathrobe. I got into bed beside her, more aroused than I imagined I could be. It was more than her eyes now that stirred me; it was her confidence, her weakness, her strength, her need, her shape, her touch, her scent of lilacs, her soft kiss. We played touched, stroked, read with our hands and lips, arousing and arousing and arousing, stretching as long as we could. Later we slept for a while. It was different then, a longer gentler pull for both of us and again we slept, this time until morning.

I awoke before she did, at first surprised to see her. I lay there still, so as not to wake her, looking at the serene expression, the gentle undulation of her breast, her hair tousled and over one eye. I couldn't see Clara's eyes, and for the first time there was no Clara lurking just behind her, looking out at me through Sarah's eyes, I thought both sadly and with relief that Clara had gone to live in another part of me, and Sarah was just Sarah. As I thought that, her eyes opened like a child's, at first seeing nothing. Seeing me, a warm, sweet smile came into them, a smile meant for me.

Later, I went back to my room to dress. One of the maids saw me leave Sarah's room and stop in front of my own. I nodded to her as she passed me, pushing her cart filled with sheets, towels and cleaning supplies. "*Buenos dias*," she said. I went into the bathroom and looked at myself in the mirror again. It was the same old me, I thought, but there was a new light in my eyes, or at least so I imagined. I showered, dressed, waited for her to knock, as we were to have brunch together. Finally, I grew impatient and went to her door. She opened it, looking apologetic, and I saw that her packed suitcase was open on her bed.

I looked from the bags to her and said, "Was it something I did?"

She laughed at that. "I was in the middle of a shower when the phone rang. It was my boss, not my boss, but his boss. 'Pack your bags, you're going to Korea on the 8:30 flight to Seoul.' A major construction contract, a fourteen-story building planned for downtown Seoul, and he wants me to be there on the negotiating team." She raised her eyebrows. "So, off I go to L.A., with just enough time to get some clean clothes at my place, then a lengthy meeting with a couple of vice presidents, and dinner and drinks on the plane, first class, of course."

"No time for breakfast?" I asked, my libido plummeting.

She shook her head. "I made myself some coffee just now on the thing in the bathroom. I'll have lunch in the executive suite at the company. They have their own French cook."

"So when will you be back?"

"Who knows? They may even take me off the project altogether, although they didn't say as much."

There was affection and thanks in her look. I must have opened my mouth, but nothing came out. She turned away and inspected the room, opening a few drawers, even looking under the bed. Then she picked up the lighter of her suitcases and I took the other. She looked into the room for the last time, closed the door and handed me the key. "Drop that off at the lobby for me, will you, Mendel. Don't worry about paying. They'll send the bill to the company."

Clobbered, I helped get her suitcase into the car behind the seat and put the top down. One hour ago I had gotten out of her bed and now she was driving off down the road and very likely I would never see her again. It wasn't that I was planning to spend the rest of my life with her, far from it, but I had expected something more and she didn't even seem disturbed by it. I could see that she was already in the air, relieved not to have to commit any further to the tower, looking forward to meeting new people, seeing different things.

She turned to me, showed me an affection muted by the excitement of a new challenge, and, perhaps a little sadness at parting. She reached around my neck and kissed me full on the lips, a long kiss, one that brought back a shadow of the night before. She looked at me hard, as she got into her car and started the engine.

"Bye, Mendel," she said, her voice sweet and light, with a fluttering waive of her right hand, and she left me standing there inhaling the acrid vapor of her exhaust. A little wave of the hand and she was gone from my life. That was nothing new to me. I dropped her key at the desk, bought a newspaper and ambled down to my usual coffee shop for my usual breakfast, thinking all the while of her and of all the partings in our lives.

9

HEARING VOICES

After moping around in the wake of Sarah's abrupt departure, I found my way back to the library, and in my renewed loneliness got myself adopted into the Binyan clan. Well, not quite, but nearly so. As I look back on it, the greater the distance which Arin perceived separated him from his son, the closer he drew to me. But that's jumping ahead.

That morning I filled the emptiness left by Sarah with Abraham's Journal and other books. It was my way. What was missing in my own life, excitement--I had had enough of that in Poland--passion, the achievement of great things, I got from books. Through books, others, my own, I could be like God, everywhere, in every time, everyone, a man, a woman, a scoundrel, a saint. Through books I could make of life what it wasn't, straighten corners or make them crooked. A poor substitute for experience? Who can say?

I opened the folio of Abraham's Journal and joined his party as they once again left their home bound for the vague promised land.

"Most of our original group had remained intact, our two oldest sons had grown to manhood, and despite the silver in her hair, my wife had borne us another daughter who had already passed three seasons. We set out heavily provisioned and carrying even more gold and jade than before. At my request, the prince agreed to send a contingent of twenty soldiers to escort us through the lands of the Aztecs. Though subjects of the Toltecs, they were not to be trusted to willingly honor the King's wishes. The prince had assured me, however, that we need not fear the Aztecs because of the land given to us, 'it lay in the empty lands below the very gates of the north winds in a valley surrounded by mountains, dry yet with water, hot yet with snow, empty yet with trees, barren yet fertile.' This riddle was the extent of the prince's grant, and as with the original grant of the Mayan prince, I accepted it, not without some doubt.

"Once again my wife, Miriam, looked back with regret as our file ascended out of the valley, and we saw for the last time the spreading city dominated by the great pyramid now even higher than before. It was a good place to live she said, but we are leaving at a good time. Yes, a good time for leave-taking, I agreed, and with the child in her arms she strode forward.

"Accompanied by the Toltec warriors, we traveled without fear even among the Aztecs, who lived simply and looked to be a strong race. From their countenances, it could be seen that they had little affection for their masters, the Toltecs, who treated them with disdain. We were glad to leave them behind us, but sorry to lose the warriors, our escorts. Having seen us safely beyond the Aztec lands, they returned, all save one, Natalal. He was permanently attached to our party by the prince himself, with the duty to observe the lands beyond the Aztecs and report to the King on them, since the information that was borne by traders was more exaggeration than truth. The fifth son of the prince, he was a strong adolescent, and he made us feel in some way that the Toltec power still protected us. Most important, he carried in his head the Toltec trade route to the north. More than the Toltecs, we trusted the power of our God to bring us through the wastelands.

"The land which we crossed could hardly be dignified by that description. It was not land at all, just broken rock and cracked adobe with not a single tree to shade us from the unceasing, burning touch of the sun. From time to time we crossed what must at one time have been a stream, but was now just an erosion of the surface of this wasted land. Our water supply ever dwindling, we walked on thinking of our forefathers who, having escaped the wrath of the Pharaoh, wandered for years in the Wilderness of Sin. We walked on with thirst as our companion, following a path between the sun's rising and setting, resolute in the belief that we would finally be delivered from the turmoil which embroiled the world which we had left, into a mountain-fast land of our own where we might live in peace and isolation.

"Our road seemed endless, however, and in time we had only enough water for the children. We walked on, cherishing this small amount in a skin bag, drinking none at all except what we gave to them, and even that hardly enough for a mouse. Three of the oldest among us died during that hard time, and I saw when we made camp that there were others who would soon die. In spite of the hardship, there was no great complaining among us, owing in part to the stolidity and reserve of the Mayan people. Was it also the faith in our God?

"On the fourth day without water when, debilitated as we were, we could hardly return to the journey before the sun had climbed to the peak of the sky, we came to the dwelling place of a family of the Yaqui. They lived miserably, as might be expected, in a hollow dug out under a rock overhang. They were naked except for a cloth made of bark to cover their most private parts, that and a band worn around their lank uncut hair. The men among them, there were three, met us without welcome and without apparent fear at the sight of our numbers and weapons. The Yaqui women retired to their dwelling, taking the children with them. Observing their poverty, it was difficult for me to comprehend why, whether by choice or circumstance, they had elected so harsh a life. I faced them, my arms upraised in a gesture of peace, sure of one thing: here or someplace nearby was water.

"Unmoving, the Yaqui men stood before me making no reciprocal gesture, their opaque eyes shifting from one to the other of us. I made the signs of drinking with my hand. No reaction. Then I placed several jade objects before them. One of them bent down to examine the beads, showing no reaction to the beauty of the work. Next, I placed in a mound before them a pile of gleaming gold nuggets. The youngest picked up one the size of the first joint of his thumb. He brought it to his mouth, bit it and carelessly cast it away like a pebble. At this point my small daughter began to cry, either out of apprehension or thirst. My wife tried to comfort her, but could not do so. One of the Yaqui women heard, and she responded as a mother. Wearing nothing but her uncut hair, she approached us, holding in her hand a small basket. She walked past me to my wife and held out her hand with the basket in it, bringing my child a gift more precious than gold or jade, the dual gift of compassion and life-giving water. My daughter drank. The woman waited, then retreated under the watchful eye of the men.

"Seeing this, I felt sure that the men would make some gesture toward the rest of us, but they remained stolid and unmoving, as though they were not men but statues of men. Thinking what if anything might appeal to them, I opened a pack and laid out five shirts of soft Yucatan deerskin. They all bent down to feel and touch it, nodding among themselves. In the end they looked up, still making no reciprocal move, and regretfully I realized that the bargain was not yet complete.

"Then the tallest among them approached me and touched the hilt of my sword. At first I drew back, but he boldly touched it again. Reluctantly, I withdrew it and his eyes widened with awe as he saw the polished iron surface. He touched the edge and withdrew his finger, repelled by the sharpness of it. Then he held out his hand and nodded. I brought my cupped hand to my mouth. He nodded. He would give us water for the shirts and the sword. I lay before him five more swords, putting the sword back in its leather sheath, but he looked away.

"I knew that I had to give the sword up, even though it had been passed down from King Solomon himself. Then I clearly saw that it had been given for just this purpose, to save our people from certain death at this very hour, and with the realization that man's destiny is a continual unfolding and revealing of the hidden, I willingly handed the sword to him. The bargain struck, they took us to a cistern, deep in the rock but not far from their camp, and we took all the water that we needed. We took enough at least to restore our vitality, enabling us to cross the rest of the wasteland to the more hospitable mountains beyond. I have often wondered what has become of the sword of Solomon.

"With the provisions obtained from the Yaqui tribe, we crossed the remaining wasteland only to find ourselves at the base of a steep dry wall which to the naked eye looked insurmountable. It was a fearful sight with spines as sharp as swords running up to the very crest, their sides falling sharply into crevices filled with loose rock. We would have been heartened to see even a single tall tree or hear the murmur of running water, but there was neither.

"We camped at the base, speculating on what lay on the other side, perhaps the end of the world, thought some; a molten sea, thought others; but there was no remaining where we were, and we had neither enough food nor water to return. We had no choice. I remained awake the whole night, listening to a sad prowling wind, waiting for a sign. In the morning I saw it: the hopeful early light showed us what the feeble evening light would not. More than half-way up was a concentration of green, more than the scrawny shrubs

that clung to the mountain's sides. More than that, I saw
below the mass of green a faint reflection of the sun. It had
to be water giving back the sun's rays as only polished metal
and water will.

"For the second time on our journey God had pointed a
finger for us. With my eyes, I traced a path down from what
had to be a bench half-way up the wall, and I discerned a difficult but traversable route. We each ate a handful of meal,
each one of us took a little water, the last of it, and we set out,
buoyed with the expectation that before the sun reached the
top of its ascent that day we would at least have fresh water.
Even as we began the climb, breathing heavily because of our
weakened state, we realized that we had been directed by an
unseen hand to a place where other men had walked, for we
found ourselves on a crude barely perceptible path.

"As we climbed higher, I saw that in fact we were ascend-
ing to a bench from which spilled a small twisting course of
water. Perhaps there was even a lake where we might bathe
and rest, for we were all of us filthy and caked with dust, looking like men of clay. But I also saw that to reach it, we would
have to climb hand over hand up a steep rock face. A young
boy, lithe and strong, with nothing but himself to bear, would
have no difficulty in this climb, but for those who carried almost half of their weight on their backs, each movement was
dangerous. So it happened that our oldest bearer, loved for his
flute playing, lost his footing and tossed like a stone down the
steep slope as we watched horrified, hearing the sound of his
bones cracking on the rocks. I personally made the descent to
where his broken body lay twisted like a broken corn stalk. We

said the prayer for the dead, thanked God that more had not met the same end, and buried him under a stone cairn.

"When, tired and aching, we reached the top, we saw that the others had already made camp along the edge of a small shallow lake fringed by evergreen trees. Everyone had drunk their fill of the cold water and many were now bathing. The tense, tired look had given way to smiles, as if they had already reached their goal. I approached Miriam and found out why the abrupt change of mood.

Our young Toltec had been told by his kinsman of the string of caches of food along the trail north. Toltec merchants and soldiers sometimes traveled this way to trade gold for stones. He recognized this lake from the description and had already seen the pass that would take us over the mountains. Two parties were now circling the lake, seeking the food cache. Even as I stood there talking, a shout came from the other side, letting us know that it had been found lodged in a stone cairn, partially eaten by small animals but still intact. That night the sorrow over the loss of Taclat was muted by the hot corn gruel which we all shared, and nothing, not even a feast, could have tasted better than that handful of warm salted meal washed down with the clearest water any of us had ever tasted. We rested by that lake in the shadow of the mountain for three days, finding still another treasure, an abundance of small fish. On this island suspended above the earth, fragrant with the aroma of the evergreen trees, we felt as if we had already reached the land promised us. The trial of the wasteland was behind us. We recounted the wandering of our ancestors in the desert and the arrival in Canaan, and I prayed that, unlike Moses, I would live to see the land.

"The top of the pass revealed more mountains beyond, but our disappointment was tempered by the knowledge that we now had a marked trail to guide us, and we knew from Natalal, our Toltec guide, that beyond the mountains, across a river, beyond another desert and more mountains lay our valley.

"The way continued to test our endurance, our faith, our patience, but now there was water and game tucked in between the mountains and even wood for fire. We still could make a fire, for we carried embers like the flame of life itself, continuously renewed and watched over by Miriam since she last saw the hearth of our home in the land of the Maya.

"This last passage took thirty days. For most of us, it was more than a journey. There was in it the feeling which followed the first long climb to the summit when we paused and took in the sweep of the horizon before descending. We felt that we were passing finally to our home.

"At last we came over a rise of ground to see on our left a high, sharp-toothed mountain crested with bristly trees and a mantle of snow falling to a flat valley, beyond which rolled supine hills. In the very center of the valley stood a grove of palm trees. As we looked at it, a cloud erupted from the trees, a cloud resembling a swarm of insects, and, its shape constantly changing, it moved steadily towards us. We heard the wings, and, as most of the flock wheeled above us, then veered high as if borne up by the wind, a few, no, more than fifty -- one for each of us -- broke off from the pack and settled to earth nearby, and we saw that they were doves.

"If we had nurtured any doubts about this being the promised valley, the coming of the doves dispelled it. Here was a sign of welcome as if each of our souls, at least kindred souls, had been here before us. The sight of the valley alone was enough. After years of expectation, it was everything we could have hoped for. I turned and saw that my wife's face was wet with tears. I took her hand and with my daughter riding on my shoulders, we descended to the valley floor and approached the trees.

"When we arrived, we were again surprised, for these were not simply trees gathered around water. There were date palms among them. In the center of the grove was a small, fresh-water pool, no bigger than the length of a man, flowing into a rock-strewn stream barely a stride in width. Above us in the trees the mourning doves talked to one another and rattled the leaves.

"We lost no time in building shelters with the abundant dead wood and dry palm fronds. The nights were still cold and heavy rains had kept our clothing damp if not sodden. The permanent shelters would await the dry season, when we could make brick and cut trees for roof members.

"During those first weeks, we sent out parties to survey the resources of the valley and discovered that we were not the first to live here. Stretching from our spring across the valley to the low hills was a paved road, wide enough for two men abreast. Where could it lead, why had it been built, and by whom? Although it ended at our spring, we saw no foundation stones and assumed that if anyone now lived in this valley, they were not permanent dwellers. It was obvious from its condition that the road had been built carefully of stone, but long ago.

"We followed it and came to a great rock unbroken, rising like a tooth out of the valley floor and on the summit of the rock we found an altar. Near the altar was a single toppled column, nothing more. Seeing the column, I knew who had planted the date palms; people like us who had journeyed from another world long ago and who had remained long enough to worship their God before passing on. We stood in the sight of the altar, quietly, respectfully, sensing that here was a place abandoned, yet still consecrated to worship. What had been sacrificed, and to what God, we knew not.

"Awed and humbled by the experience, we returned to camp eager to describe what we had seen. Jews and Mayans alike saw themselves on a continuum of time born on the back of the generations, and here again in this remote place we saw proof of it, for this place in its solitude was not ours alone, but ours only to husband, entrusted to us by God to be passed on to the unborn, our unborn or the unborn of another, we knew not."

I had finished the Journal and was ruminating on it when Arin exploded into the library, more agitated than I had yet seen him. It turned out that he had just seen his banker, who had told him that a big loan would not be renewed. The due date was no more than two weeks away. He had been counting on the first progress payment on the tower construction to pay it off but, because of the new lawsuit, the Defense Department was being predictably evasive.

When I didn't follow through with questions, as I might have done in a better state of mind, he looked out of the cloud of his agitation and seeing my shade of melancholy, said, "What's happened to you? Bronchitis back again?"

Before I could say anything, Miriam came in and told him that his lawyer had called. "What did he want?" Arin asked.

"He said that the meeting with the judge is this afternoon at 3:00. And the lawyer from the Defense Department is coming from Washington. He'll be here on the noon plane."

"Should I call him back?"

"He said not to bother to come to the meeting with the judge. It's just for lawyers."

"The whole judicial process is just for lawyers," said Arin, looking like he had a migraine.

Thinking that I could play the court jester and distract him, I proceeded to tell them about my sundered friendship with Sarah. Since they knew her as the engineer, they were in fact interested. "It seems that my social life here in Canyon Springs has come and gone already."

"You still have us. Not that we're much company under the circumstances. Still, there are a lot worse places you could be, like jail or in a hospital," he said.

"Your companionship is a blessing. Without it I might have been driven to do something rash, like, like..." I let my hand circle as I searched for an example, "...joining the Odd Fellows." They both got a chuckle out of that.

"Don't go that far. But if you like, why don't you join us. We'll make you an honorary Binyan. We can do that, can't we Miriam?"

I went along with the joke. "Sounds good, depending upon the initiation rite. If it's circumcision, you're too late."

"I'm serious, Mendel. Move in with us for the rest of your stay."

"I've already used up all the hospitality I deserve," I protested, at the same time hoping that they would insist and searching their faces for sincerity.

Miriam touched my arm and looked at me tenderly. "Please. It would mean more to us than to you."

Arin drew closer and said, "We've got five empty bedrooms. You can have your choice. I'll even send someone over to carry your bags." Before I had a chance to respond, Arin said, "If you like, you can trade a little labor for the room and board. Catalogue a small section of the library. It might take you ten hours altogether." I couldn't refuse. I agreed, and he was very pleased until he remembered the hearing again.

Later he showed me several bedrooms, although each was about the same: tile floor, french windows opening to a small balcony, and dark oak furniture. I chose one adjacent to a bathroom that the family didn't use.

"I'm glad Miriam asked you to stay here. I'd never have thought that you would want to, it's so quiet."

"Do I seem to you like a discophile or a bar flea?"

"You never know about people, Mendel. You think that you know them, and you find that you don't."

Returning to the library, we found more tea and cake already on the table. He nodded with satisfaction. "What do you think of Miriam?"

"I should have been so lucky."

"We have an old-fashioned marriage, she and I, I suppose. It's just as well we live out here."

"Oh, you're not so unique. I know plenty of people back in Bolton who are paired for life."

"I'm sure," was his curt reply, as though he didn't want to discuss it. "This is the section that needs indexing," he said, walking over to the shelves.

I looked at the titles and saw that they were mainly Hassidic writers. He was watching my reaction. "You should enjoy these, coming as you do from Poland. I know next to nothing about Hassidism. I never got beyond the study of the Kabbalists. My father bought this Hassidic collection almost intact in 1937 or '38 at a book auction. It's been on these shelves virtually untouched since he died, and to tell the truth, I doubt that even he did much with it. The age of Miamonides was his particular field of interest."

"Sounds like he was quite a scholar."

"Yes, and in the old tradition, that is to say he did little else. Would you believe it, he could read classical Arabic. He had to, to understand some of the books from that era." We sat down and had our tea, and I thought about this family. The more I learned, the more unbelievable they were.

"You know, you still haven't shown me the memorabilia of your ancestors." He looked at me as though he didn't understand what I was talking about. "You said you had something from the time of Solomon." He didn't hear me. He was doing the best he could to ramble on about anything but he was as distracted as a husband barred from the delivery room. "You're worrying about that hearing."

"I'm used to it. The Binyans are born with lawsuits in their livers, you could say."

"The families have been in court a lot?"

"We could have added a courtroom to the house. You know the picture of the woman that hangs in the landing?"

"Yes, the one with the penetrating eyes."

"My grandmother, Tamar Binyan." With that introduction he told me something of Tamar's conflict with the railroad, mentioning nothing of the personal side of her story. Ultimately, he offered to let me read her journal as well. "You can write a history of the family if you're so inclined," he said with a flourish of his hand, taking in the shelves on which were kept family records.

"While I have your attention, are you aware that there are nude young people running around in your garden?"

"What else would you expect in the Garden of Eden?"

"I mean it. I saw them on the path."

"There's a school for disturbed adolescents next to our grounds. It used to be a public school, but the Board of Education closed it due to lack of enrollment or money. So they leased it to this private mental health facility. They seem to believe in letting the kids do what they please."

"Aren't they dangerous?"

He turned away from me, put his hands in his pockets and walked toward the door to the balcony before he said, "Not any more than Mr. McHadden." He let this settle, then turned and added, "They pick the fruit. There's so much of it out there, they're welcome to it. That goes for you, too. Eat anything you like except, of course, from the tree of knowledge."

"Which one is that?" I asked, playing to his whimsy.

"One of these days when I'm in the mood, I'll show you." He said this very seriously, as if he actually knew. Maybe he did.

He looked like he was about to say something else when the telephone buzzed. It was the first time that I was aware of a telephone in the library. He went to a corner table and mainly listened, his back to me. He hung up and turned to me, a wry smile twisting his lips.

"We've won a round. My lawyer says that the judge refused the T.R.O." I must have looked blank, for he explained, "He won't block the construction of the tower."

"Is that the end of the lawsuit?"

"No. There's a hearing on a preliminary injunction in 15 days. But the odds are in our favor on that one."

"So that means the Defense Department will cut some money loose for you, won't they?" I asked, thinking that except for my interest in Arin, why indeed would I care whether or not a tower gets built? There are already enough towers in the world, just as there are enough weapons and people. In spite of the essential vulgarity of the tower -- in my eyes, it was no cathedral and it didn't come close to the Washington Monument -- I found myself caring.

Arin went to the window. "We'll have some rain," he muttered. Then he turned and continued in the same tone. "Now there's a rumor of a strike by the construction workers."

"Over what?"

" They want the same number of workers as they have in conventional steel construction. Something like that. Even though Alumaloy is lighter and easier to work with, and should require fewer people to handle it."

"When will this happen?"

"In a few days."

"Are you anxious about it?"

Instead of responding, he threw his right hand out in front of him, a gesture that said to me, it's all out there, and how much can I do about it; and with that he walked toward the door.

I poured a little more tea, nibbled on the almond cake, comparing it to Sarah Nudelman's recipe. Here I was, essentially back in Bolton surrounded by books, occupied with light but stimulating duties, and enjoying it. I thought of Sarah Cavanaugh, my lady friend he had called her, and I found myself wondering what she was doing and I suddenly got the idea that I should go home.

Here I was: settled like a mouse in a hole as I like to be, with eight thousand rare books to peruse, including fifty or so incunabula, and suddenly wondering whether I should cut my trip short. I coughed tentatively, to confirm that my bronchitis was receding. I had no excuse to stay, and the work was probably piled up on my desk, a mound of bills, letters to write. I wanted to stay, and I would.

10

IN TOIL

The next days passed easily enough for me, doing what I often did at home. In between cataloguing, I searched for, but could not find, a continuation of Abraham's Journal. Later, Arin told me that it had been lost in a fire. Instead he gave me several other journals compiled by Gabriel Cardozo. Full of family stories, they had been compiled and typed by an anonymous Binyan on a 70-year-old typewriter. I decided to summarize them just to amuse myself. I alternated between total concentration on my work and cogitation over what I had read as I walked the shady green paths of the garden.

My mind often went back to Sarah Cavanaugh and that night when we had yielded each to the other. Every day I called the motel to find out if a postcard had come from her, but none came. I did get a letter from Estelle and I wrote to her, matte-of-fact narratives, saving the best for later. Postcards dutifully went to Nudelman, Rabbi Bing, and the widow in McKeesport, not to mention a reassuring medical report to Dr. Zucker.

All this time Arin was like a caged lion. There was the strike to worry about, the new lawsuit, as well as the ongoing negotiations between Windel and the Department of Defense.

For me the days were seamless. Except for my sympathy and support for my host, I hadn't felt so carefree since my days on my uncle's farm before the war.

It had grown darker in the library. I went to the window and saw a heavy blanket of steel-colored clouds. Below them a pendant luminous twilight blanched the dense foliage of the garden. The air was fragrant and heavy. Somewhere, not far away, a lone bird was rehearsing a baroque song.

I stood there dreamily for a time until I heard the door open. It was Miriam.

"Arin told me that before you leave this house he's determined to cure your cough once and for all."

"Really, the desert air is taking care of it just fine."

"Yes, but you need the _hashlish_ to balance the dryness and sweat out the poisons."

"I'm not familiar with the term, but if it's what I think it is, I don't even smoke tobacco, let alone narcotics. Not that I'm prejudiced against people who do."

She shook her head. "It's not what you think, it's the sweathouse, that's all. We've already got the fires going. You'll stay in there, breathe aromatic humid heat, sweat, then rest in your bedroom and you'll be cured in a day or so. No protests, Mendel. Just go into your bedroom. You'll find a terrycloth robe and a towel on the bed. When you've changed, Joachim will take you out to it." She stared at me with that flat obduracy of hers and what could I do but give in.

What could I say to her? Even if I couldn't stand steam I would have gone through with it after those preparations. I went to my room thinking of my Aunt Hannah. She, Uncle Meir and their four children lived in a village near Cracow. He was a grain dealer and, before the war, I sometimes spent a month in their large old house in the summer, cleaning the city soot out of my system, my mother used to say. I thought of her only because Uncle Meir had built a *shvitz* next to the stable. Like Miriam, there was no circumventing Aunt Hannah when she had decided what was best for your health and nutrition, not that she was authoritarian. I undressed in the room, still thinking of their house, of the dark room under the eaves that I shared with my cousin Motke. Once opened, the association blossomed, my senses inverted, and I heard the roosters call, breathed the cool dew-laden morning air as I stretched my child's limbs between the warm sheets and even smelled the sweet dusty hay piled in the stable.

As I thought about it, there was more than one similarity between those summers and the way of life of the Binyans, except that one was all gone. A quiet knock on the door and I opened it to find Joachim. "Please come with me, the *hashlish* is ready," he said. It proved to be a small mud house, more a bake oven than a house with a single opening barely three feet high. Wrapped in my towel, I crawled in, sat down cross-legged on a low wood platform, breathed the aromatic steam, and thought again of Uncle Meir's *shvitz*. When I had sweated about as much as I could, I crawled out, feeling both weak and relaxed, and returned to the house for a shower. No sooner was I in my seat in the library than Miriam entered with a tray with tea and cake.

"You look better already. There's a flush on your cheeks. Your circulation is perking up." As she set the tray down, I saw that there were two cups. "If you don't mind, I'll just sit down and have my tea with you. It's herbal tea--part of the cure."

Then, with a mischievous little smile that put dimples in her cheeks and closed her narrow eyes, she said, "You know you're half a Binyan now."

"How's that?"

"The sweat bath is part of an old initiation rite. It purges the spirit and renews it. We won't bother with the other half just now."

"What is it?" I asked, chuckling nervously. "Maybe I've already had it," I said, thinking about circumcision. "I'll tell you one thing, Miriam," I continued in a jocular way, "don't ask me to sign anything, I never sign for anybody."

"Mendel, does a child sign anything to be born into a family?" She poured me some tea. "Now you drink that down."

"I won't ask what it is," I said, puckering at the taste.

"I wouldn't tell you if you did. Family secret."

She became quite talkative as we sat there. I learned that she was Arin's second cousin and had been married just after high school. She asked about the places I'd visited, and she told me that she'd never been out of the Valley. She reminded me of some people back home, only more so. Most of my friends had their ritual vacations somewhere, but usually at the same place where they could feel comfortable among the familiar. Miriam had no desire to travel. Her sole interest was the house, raising the children, and gardening.

"Never even taken a trip?" I asked.

"Once we were going to Yucatan to see the ruins. It was Arin's idea. We were about to do it when we lost our daughter." Her voice fell for a moment as she said this, but her face remained placid. "We canceled the trip. Arin didn't want to go, after that. I'm content to remain where I am." She looked around her. "Who would want more?" She looked at me with a distant smile playing on the flat plane of her face and said, "Arin told me that you read Abraham's journal. Then you see that this house, at least a part of it, has been lived in for 1,300 years. It has a strong pull."

"I surmised that this was the oasis. But I wondered about the spring. Where is it?"

"It's in the garden. But it stopped flowing for some reason about 50 years ago. We get our water from a well now." She looked around her as though she were preparing to leave. "It has a strong pull," she repeated.

"I have to agree with you. Although I'm afraid most city people would think that you are," I paused, thinking for something diplomatic, "somewhat out of date."

"One of the virtues of staying put is not having to trouble yourself with what other people think." She got up, picked up the tray and said, "All of this talk isn't getting the weeds pulled out of the lettuce bed. It was so nice to talk to you, Mendel."

On her way out of the room, she turned and added, "I'll want a full report on your cough."

"I'll post a progress report on the library door, Miriam."

"You do that."

She left me to my reading and writing. My summary of Gabriel Cardozo's Notebooks follow, because it brings the story of the Binyans through the next millennium or so, right to the Nineteenth Century. Creating history is like imagining what a decorated ceramic pot was like from a few fragments, or giving someone who has never seen a beach a thimble full of sand. Even so, the stories left behind in time's tracks are important, not because they are accurate or even basic to what happened, but because they are what people remembered. As opposed to what they forgot, for it is their memory and not the vanished reality that defines them. Don't fall asleep; this isn't a treatise on history, just a few of my poor thoughts as a preface to my summary of Gabriel Cardozo's summary of 365,000 days and nights in Binyan Valley.

A generation after the death of Abraham Binyan, his party had already settled in a fine house, with walls of mud brick an arm's length thick. The house faced on a walled courtyard which enclosed the constant spring. Seeds carried over the mountains by the settlers had taken root, closed together, and become orchards and gardens. The Toltec guardian of the arduous road had by then married the daughters of Abraham and mixed their blood in the children.

The Binyan clan settled deeper and deeper into the valley until footprints in the dust had become a path worn like a signature on the land. Yet even then, they knew that it was not completely theirs, for the platform and the road leading to it reminded them that others had come before them. In time they made use of this high altar, making of it a sundial or solar observatory. Using a wooden pole, they charted the sun's movement and measured the passage of the seasons to regulate the planting of crops as the Mayan priests had done in Yucatan.

After a time they stopped wondering about who had built it, and accepted it as their own. Then, in the year 110 of the settlement, a lean, bronzed people with long black hair who called themselves the Anasazi returned and claimed it. Eli Binyan, the red-haired counsel leader, was the first to see smoke from their campfires on the dawn of the summer solstice. He and several of his relatives walked out to them with gifts of food and water.

Their leader was an old man named Taquitz. He was wrinkled as a buzzard, had long white hair, and was dressed in a white robe with a necklace of black beads that might have been made of the same substance as his serene eyes. In return for the water and food, Taquitz gave Eli amber beads and Jimson weed, which they used in their rituals.

The Anasazi spoke a strange language, but communicated with pictures drawn in the dust. They lived many days' trek away, on high plateaus cut with deep canyons. Like the Binyans, they were farmers and tilled corn and harvested pine nuts for their sustenance. Taquitz, their leader, was the living embodiment of their father deity who slept under the rock on which the mysterious altar had long ago been built. The rock, according to their legend, kept him in his place. He held the world together while he slept, grasping in each hand two ropes that stretched to the opposite ends of the earth. Sometimes he tried to escape from under the rock, and his struggles would make the earth shake. Once each century, the Anasazi returned to the rock to perform the ceremony of resignation to persuade the old God to rest in his place, for if he got away the world would fall apart.

They stayed for many months, enjoying the hospitality of the Binyans. Eli studied their language and learned something of their customs. He found the Anasazi story of creation to be surprisingly like their own. The Anasazi believed that a great flood had occurred, drowning all living things, and later a nameless Creator had fashioned all living things out of the mud left behind when the waters receded. This same creator later bound Taquitz, a giant created before man, and placed the rock on him after he had proved too destructive.

When the Anasazi left for home, two of their children remained behind to marry, and two children of the Binyan youth went with them so that the blood of the two peoples would flow as one and they would be as family through the generations. And to the silver of the Hebrews and the copper of the Toltec was added another element, the bronze of the Anasazi.

The Anasazi traded with the Binyans for generations until a great drought turned their canyon streams to stone and their mesa top fields to cracked adobe. In the end, the only water left was their tears. Many died of hunger and the remnants abandoned their proud canyon-shelf stone cities to the mice and owls. Of the survivors, most joined the Binyans in their high valley, since it was blessed even in times of drought with a constant water supply flowing from the feet of their great mountain. These few were welcomed as family and settled in what eventually became three villages.

Days, seasons, and years followed one another, borne on the back of time. Their life, tied to the cultivation of crops, changed very little from generation to generation, yet it changed like the face of a cliff eroding year by year. Ways of saying things altered; the Hebrew, Mayan and Toltec merged with the Anasazi language into a patois, as did the customs, rituals and beliefs. Of the four language roots, the Hebrew predominated only because it was the only one with a complete script.

Despite their isolation, travelers often passed through and were made welcome. The valley was a station on trails from the morning sun to the evening sun, and from the south to the north. They traded goods and told of happenings, stories of white men who came in winged boats like the Phoenician vessel that had brought their ancestor, Jacov Binyan. It was claimed these adventurers carried wands that spouted fire and brought death.

Once a white man with blue eyes like the Christian priest in Abraham's time was brought as a prisoner by Shoshone hunters. Yitschak Binyan, of the milky eye, the counsel leader, traded the man for his weight in red corn. Johan was his name, and he took his place among the Binyans and the Anasazi, learned their language and merged his blood in theirs.

Later the Spanish came, with dark beards, wearing polished steel, riding large nervous animals. They too were welcomed with hospitality, but they accepted it without gratitude for they had come to claim the valley for their Sovereign and mistook the hospitality for subservience. They planted a colored cloth on a pole and left without learning a word of the language. The Binyans watched the pole until the flag faded and disintegrated, and the story has it that it didn't grow. From this came the saying, "Conquerors should plant peppers and corn, not flags."

When the Spanish next returned, it was to stay. They made camp at the far end of the valley beside a spring and built a small church and a long adobe barracks, big enough to accommodate a garrison of twenty soldiers and five priests. The church was connected to the barracks with a square adobe wall. In the enclosure they planted grapes, olive and citrus trees, and settled down to an easy peaceful cohabitation. At first the Binyans and Anasazi were glad to have them as neighbors. Unlike the first Spanish visitors, Captain Areaga, Father Coparez and the others were polite and solicitous.

Areaga was a short, broad-shouldered man with a dark beard that partially concealed a heavily pocked face. He was a tanner's son and could barely read or write. His companion and spiritual guide was a man in his mid-twenties whose body was already going to fat. He seemed indolent in his manner, liked wine and eating more than prayer, and though quiet most of the time, had a good sense of humor that required priming with spirits.

After generations of isolation and peace, the Binyans had lost the capacity to suspect the motives of strangers, so at first the gift of a parchment presented to the current leader,

Micah Binyan, was regarded as a courtesy. It had a red wax seal and a long red ribbon, and it proclaimed that the Valle Agua Escondido belonged to the King of Spain, who magnanimously granted half of it to his loyal subject, Micah Binyan. All the captain wanted for this poorly-written parchment was a weight of gold. In the end he settled for an Aztec bracelet of gold, long ago obtained from a traveler in exchange for food.

Micah Binyan discussed the document with the counsel and they decided to accept it, given that the Spaniards were already established, and their king lived some six months distant and could do them little harm. Soon after the Spanish arrived, another group came and settled in the vicinity of their compound. These were Cahuillas, humble tillers of corn with digging sticks, who had been driven from their land by more aggressive Shoshones. At first it looked as though the Spanish and the Cahuillas would get on. In exchange for small lengths of cloth and cooking pots, they helped the Spanish farm and brought them wood for their fireplaces.

Later they were given little metal crosses and instructed in the Spanish alphabet to their amusement, for the words seemed as useless to them as a fifth leg on a dog. Over time, their relationship evolved into a pattern of menial servitude.

Work was related to function, the priests explained to Ha-Anosha, the elderly leader of the Cahuilla. "We must all serve the soldiers, for they protect us from our enemies."

"Death is our only enemy," he answered.

The priest replied, "We the priests protect you from death by giving your soul immortality."

And that was the beginning and the end of the conversion of the Cahuillas to Christianity, for until then they had believed that there is no life after death. Ha-Anosha accepted the father's offer of immortality and brought his tribe as one into the church for the rite of baptism.

Had the relationship between the Spanish and the Cahuillas been confined to work in return for salvation, the mission would no doubt still be standing. Had the Cahuillas suffered no more than long hours tilling the fields, repairing their walls, working their looms and serving their meals, they might have accepted their servile state as the natural order of life as they had been taught; a humble purification in preparation for heaven.

But it didn't turn out that way. Among the decent if indolent soldiers were more than a few given to venality and drunkenness. The Cahuilla women, often as not, bore the brunt of their churlishness in the form of harsh words, and beatings. When they withdrew from service the soldiers came to their simple wattle dwellings, dragged them out and forced them to work. Even this they might have tolerated until one day the most dissolute among them attacked and raped a young girl. When she resisted he savagely beat her. She was found by her brother on the edge of a field, unconscious and bleeding from her injuries.

Among the Cahuillas, the penalty for rape was death and the forfeiture of the wrongdoer's possessions to the family of the injured party. Ha-Anosha went to the Captain and demanded that the assailant be turned over to the tribe. The

Captain refused, explaining that he had already been punished by a whipping under the law of the Spanish King.

The old leader patiently replied, "Had he violated a Spanish woman, he should be punished under your law. But he violated a child of our people."

"But you are subjects of the Spanish Sovereign," said the Captain.

Ha-Anosha returned to his village and sat alone for two days, not speaking to anyone. When he finally came out of his hut, he knew what must be done. After a week, the girl's father came to him and urged him to act or the whole tribe would be shamed.

He answered, "The ground must be right for sowing corn."

No more was said until the eve of the next Spanish feast day, the Feast of San Carlos. Since San Carlos was the Captain's patron saint, it was an occasion for a feast. The native women had snared six rabbits and were preparing them when Ha-Anosha came to them with the sleeping potion to be put in the soldiers' cactus liquor. He had already spoken to the men and they were busy sharpening their digging sticks and tempering them over a fire.

The meal was raucous with jokes, bawdy songs and even an aborted fight before the drug put them all to sleep. Some managed to make it to their beds, while others collapsed on the floor of the kitchen or onto the table among the congealed grease and bones of the meal.

When all of the Spanish were asleep, the women returned to their village. It was yet two hours before midnight. The old leader nodded solemnly at the news and, muttering a prayer, he led the men, digging sticks in hand, to the barracks. They stole into the compound and each placed himself over a soldier or priest. The old man let out a cry and the men plunged the sharpened sticks into the chests of the Spanish. Screams tore the night's silence and blood gushed from the wounds, but the natives held fast to their sticks, pinning their victims to the ground like rabbits.

When all the Spanish were dead, they set fire to the roofs of the barracks and church. Then they returned to their huts, packed their belongings and left the valley.

The next morning the Binyans awoke to the sight of smoke. They sent a party to investigate and discovered the carnage. There was one survivor, Father Ignatius, who had made his way to the facilities to relieve himself just before the natives had entered the compound. The Cahuillas had discovered him cowering near the waste pit, pale as the moon and shaking, and had spared him. He was a gentle, kindly person and their desire for vengeance had already been sated. In fact Ha-Anosha had made him a witness.

A year later the Cahuillas again made contact with the Binyans. They had settled over the western hills near a spring. Asked why they had left, the messenger replied, "In another place it is easier to bear the memory of the shame of what we endured and the burden of what we did."

Father Ignatius stayed with the Binyans for the rest of his life, cultivating the abandoned Spanish gardens. The Binyans gladly shared in his work, for there were many species of tree and plant that they had not known. He planted the first date grove from seeds and gave each of the first trees the name of his fallen comrades.

Two years later, when Spanish soldiers again came through, Ignatius exonerated the Binyans and Anasazi from any blame. For whatever reason, they didn't come again until 1747, many years later.   Although the priest succeeded in propagating plants, he failed in the propagation of his religion. He died the only Christian in the valley, but his humility and gentleness were influential. He was buried in a corner of the Spanish garden not far from the ruins of the church, and his grave was marked with a rough stone on which was etched a cross. It is still there.

The next time the Spanish appeared from another direction, the west. There were only five and they had been sent east from the recently established Mission of San Diego on the coast of the Pacific Ocean to discover the land route to Sonora, which had been forgotten. They went no further than Binyan Valley, however, because three of them were too sick to go on. Two of the three died and the others established themselves at the old barracks.

Gabriel Cardozo was one of them. He had a long face, round, sad, intelligent eyes, and had lost his left arm at the elbow to a cannonball. He found his life's work in Binyan Valley. At first he simply spent all the time he could spare with the Binyans, observing their customs, learning their language. He particularly enjoyed the Sabbath celebrations and the feast of the New Year, when they blew the great spiral trumpet made from the horn of the local mountain sheep and the Spring Festival when they ate flat cakes and told the story of the flight of the Jews from Egypt.

After one complete season of observation he revealed to Adam Binyan, the counsel leader, that he was a secret Jew, what the Spanish call a Marrano. Persecuted generations ago, forced to convert or die, his family was outwardly Catholic but had practiced a few Jewish rites in the privacy of the home such as lighting candles on Friday night, although the dual observances had ultimately fused like a grafted tree limb.

After another year, Cardozo married the youngest daughter of Adam Binyan and took the family name. He left the Spanish Army and came to live at the Big House. Over his lifetime, he wrote down the history of the Binyans and, for that matter, the Anasazi. He also established commercial ties with an agent in San Diego and began to market dates and figs. He used the gold to buy books and began to build a library. The present Big House, with its wings, second story, and tile roof, is attributed to him.

There followed seamless decades in which people lived and died under the sun's burning wheel and the rain's renewal. For much of the rest of the world, the last half of the eighteenth century was a time of social upheaval and innovation. In faraway France, in what was to become the United States, in Mexico and the lands to the south, a new class, alien to the land-based aristocracy, was taking control. People were busy creating new facts, investigating natural phenomenon, inventing new social freedoms, and new forms of creating wealth. Man was even realizing the myth of Prometheus, harnessing fire to drive engines. A little of this reached them in books.

Gabriel Cardozo lived in the valley for forty years before his death. He was the last survivor of the second coming of the Spanish. About that time, the agent in San Diego stopped buying their produce, the steep trail down the western slope was closed in several places by landslides and never repaired, and the valley was again forgotten.

11

BONES

Despite the fact that I was now staying in the Binyan house, I still saw very little of Zev. He came to meals irregularly as his farm management duties were demanding, not to mention the time he spent with Francesca. These meals were moreover uncomfortable affairs, and I was always relieved when the place set for him remained empty throughout the meal. Although neither Arin nor Miriam mentioned it, I saw the pain of loss when he failed to appear. Miriam would steal a hurt glance at his empty plate and Arin simply avoided looking at it at all. Arin's way was to keep up a brisk conversation as though nothing was wrong.

When he did turn up, Miriam was all smiles and love. Zev responded, but when he looked at his father apprehension clouded his handsome face. These meals began politely enough, but usually deteriorated into a disagreement between father and son, words that were usually restrained if tense but sometimes shifted into acrimony followed by sullen silence. The first of these came with Zev's disclosure that he had substituted a new hybrid tomato for the ones he had been unable to get. He claimed to have left Arin a note. Arin claimed not to have seen it. To his credit, Zev was never the first to become angry. He explained with the patience of a professor the virtues of the new tomato: "They can be picked ripe, they stay firm for a week with longer market shelf life, and you don't need to treat them with sulfur dioxide."

Arin replied to Miriam, not Zev, "And they taste like cardboard and must be cut with a chainsaw." She winced at this and Zev's complexion darkened with anger.

His lips trembled a little and he spat out, "Manage the goddamned farm yourself."

"Zev," his mother said, looking embarrassed and apprehensive.

"I know, we have guests at the table," he said with a more gentle tone. "Well, if we hadn't I might have said more. And now if you will all excuse me," his angry eyes machine-gunned the three of us, "I'll get back to the cardboard tomatoes," and he rose and strode out of the room, dropping little chips of caked mud on the polished tile from his boots.

When we could no longer hear his boots, Arin ran a hand through his wavy carrot-red hair and said, "He was a different boy before he got involved with Francesca. She's turned him against us."

Miriam just gave him a look of suffering. There was silence for a moment, and then she said with firmness, "He's not a boy anymore, he's a man who probably knows more than you do about running a modern farm and with all your troubles you can't bring yourself to admit it." Arin looked at her as though she had thrown a glass of water in his face.

I was feeling more and more awkward and uncomfortable as an involuntary witness to this growing family conflict. I looked at both of them and said, "Maybe I should go back to the hotel. With all that's going on in your life it's embarrassing to have a stranger in your home. I'm sure Zev feels that way."

"Zev feels a lot of things," Arin said. "No, if you can put up with the tension, I'd like you to stay."

"Remember you're almost a family member now, Mendel," Miriam said.

I relaxed in my seat, took my napkin off of my lap and with trepidation said, "Then let me speak with the candor of a family member, at least a friend. I'm not taking sides..."

"Don't," interrupted Arin, glaring at me.

"But I'm not going to be a sycophant either, just because I'm in debt for your hospitality and love your library," I said, glaring back at him, feeling my own indignation rise. "I'm no psychologist, but I think you've got to learn to treat your son as an equal. Give him his due now before it's too late." The lines on his brow deepened and I saw that he was in fact weighing my words. "He may be the baby, he may be the only one left, but you'll lose him too, the way you're going." I could feel myself trembling a little. "There, I've said my piece, Arin."

His surprisingly gentle response was, "Thank you for your candor, Mendel."

Zev didn't return to the table for two days, and when he did it was to plant a mine under his father's plate with the casual disclosure that he had gone ahead and set up his experimental plot on two acres. He said this with studied carelessness.

With the disclosure, the flush crept onto Arin's cheeks, but he restrained himself with the comment, "I'm sorry that I hadn't gotten around to your request. I've been preoccupied, as you know." He looked at his son with seeming apprehension.

"Well, as I said before, I couldn't wait. I figured you wouldn't miss a couple of acres. It's very important to me, Father. I hope you understand."

"I suppose I do," said Arin with a sprinkle of understanding.

Miriam looked at both of them in a healing way and said, "How about some fresh apricot crisp?" We all nodded, and I thought to myself, my little outburst may have made an impression.

A day or so later the meticulous Zev performed another test of his father's tolerance when he appeared suddenly at lunch, not alone but with Francesca. This was the first time I had seen her at close hand, and she was striking. She stood beside Zev at the door of the dining room, looking expectant and self-assured like a guest at a good restaurant with a reservation. She was wearing tight worn jeans, tucked into well-worn western boots, and a white western shirt with blue piping. With her narrow upturned eyes and delicate nose, the nostrils flaring above sweet, bow-shaped lips, she might have inspired Botticelli. Her fine honey-toned hair was falling loose about her shoulders and in her dark blue eyes I saw both curiosity and the perception of a keen observer.

Miriam stood and with characteristic good feeling made her welcome and set another place at the table. Arin looked like changing weather, alternately gloomy and charmed by Francesca, who showed not the slightest discomposure and conversed with him and for that matter with all of us, with a light, fresh, totally unaffected charm, studiously avoiding any hint of a subject that might provoke disagreement. Zev was quiet for the most part, but it was the silence of a tape recorder, for I could see that he was registering every nuance of the conversation and measuring, as a scientist, the qualitative shifts of his father's mood. They ate their lunch of fresh tomato soup, fresh garden salad and bitter almond cake, even laughed a little over some family joke, and departed, leaving a residue of good feeling. We three were still at the table and I was surprised but pleased to hear Arin say, "Charming girl, totally beguiling. I can see why Zev fell for her." The warm nostalgic look in his eyes faded and he said in a harsher tone, "It's a damn shame that she's got the conniving disposition of those Messers."

And I said, "Maybe that's just the way you see her, Arin. She may not be conniving at all. She may be as principled as you are."

"You're a damned chaplain, Mendel. You try to find the good in everybody."

"And what's so bad about that?" Miriam declared, and before he could answer she said, "More Yerba Buena tea, anyone?"

I returned to the library thinking that father and son were on their way to a negotiated peace. If nothing more, the shooting had stopped. But my judgment was premature, for they both flunked Zev's next test of his father's tolerance.

Arin's reference to the "conniving Messers", Francesca's family, was an aphrodisiac to my curiosity. A day later I pinned him down about it and he restored another faded section of family history; what transpired in the late Nineteenth Century.

But for Francesca's background, she might have been welcomed from the start as a good companion for their only son. She was rich and lovely and intelligent, three characteristics that weren't exactly liabilities in our society. But she was the last of the Messers, and with her inheritance, a considerable fortune deferred until her grandfather's death under the terms of a trust, came a legacy of bitterness carried over from Messer's exploitation of the Anasazi and Binyani.

As the Indian Agent, Messer had profited by every change of fortune. More important, he had encouraged the Binyan's to give up the reservation status so that the land might be parceled out among separate families. To achieve this end, he maligned Arin's grandmother Tamar (whose painting hung in the hall) claiming that she had gotten rich by controlling the resources of the tribes, which was to some extent true. He worked tirelessly at this task, buying influence among village leaders, in other instances letting people build up debts at the store which he either never collected or threatened to collect unless they cooperated.

Despite his tireless, twenty-year effort, he might not have succeeded if Boaz Binyan hadn't built his radio tower on the site of the sacred Anasazi platform. Letting that happen was the greatest blunder of Tamar's life. She had succumbed to the pleas of her only son, reinforced by her husband Tyler's obsession with commercial progress. A bare majority of the Council went along and she closed her ears to the opposition. The tower would make Binyan Valley the radio communication center of the western United States, Tyler claimed, and Boaz would be next to Farnsworth in his contribution to the development of worldwide airwave communication. In time, they could even manufacture radio receivers and transmitters and sell them to the world.

Boaz Binyan got his tower, but it alienated the community. The festering animosity among those who considered it a desecration of the ancient Anasazi site led to the break-up of the land holdings into private ranches. Tamar Binyan was left with the big house and 640 acres split into two parcels.

Once the control of land was taken from the Tribal Council, Messer methodically bought up mineral rights and land whenever the opportunity arose. He tried to find oil but, as with gold, there was none. All he found was water, a great primordial lake, just two hundred feet below the valley surface.

He tried mining and had better luck. The hills produced several minerals, including titanium and molybdenum as well as phosphate. Between the minerals and his land dealings his wealth compounded. Ultimately he set up the Bank of A. Messer. Although the wastes from the initial processing of the minerals caused some water and soil pollution, at least the operations themselves were hidden between two canyon walls.

Messer lived into his mid-eighties, and actively controlled his finances to within a year of his death in 1925. By then he, rather than the Binyans, was the principal economic and political power, and it was Binyan Valley in name only. Tamar Binyan had died three years earlier and Boaz had already withdrawn from social and philanthropic activities to pursue his research.

Messer was more successful in business than in producing an heir, although what happened wasn't his fault. He and his wife Margaret had two children, a daughter, Olga, and a son, Carl. Carl died in the Argonne, the target of a bullet no doubt made in Stuttgart by another Carl and targeted by yet a third. Olga spent a year at the University of Southern California, married the only son of a Los Angeles flour mill owner and settled into a genteel Los Angeles life in an Italianate mansion in MacArthur Park, shuttling between the Wilshire Country Club and the First Presbyterian Church in her Packard phaeton, visiting her father at Christmas time and on his birthday.

Her marriage produced only one child, Veronica Messer Varden, Francesca's grandmother. Veronica went east to boarding school and remained through Radcliffe, where she studied painting and art history. In 1939 she got most of what she needed and wanted, a Doctorate in Art History, and on her twenty-fifth birthday a flat in Chelsea in London and the income from a trust to maintain it.

The following year, she married an art collection in the form of an Anglicized Italian art dealer. After the war they built the Palacio on the flanks of Binyan Valley to house their collection and spent more and more of their time there. They had one daughter, Carey, who followed her mother's path east to college. She married while still a sophomore at Sarah Lawrence and gave birth to Francesca the following year.

Francesca was only two when her parents both drowned after their kayak overturned in Frederick Sound during an Alaskan camping trip. That's how Francesca came to live with her grandparents, and eventually just with her grandfather, in the Palacio.

And it explains why the Binyan animosity was still so deep. Messer, rather than Boaz Binyan, was still blamed for the atomization of the Anasazi-Binyani community, and nothing that his descendants did in their cosmopolitan indifference broke down the distance between the two families. There was yet another reason, one that worked at a deeper, more emotional level -- Zev's attachment to Francesca turned him away from his father and deepened the silence and misunderstanding that separated them.

With that summary, wrung from a preoccupied Arin and supplemented by another journal, my overview of the Binyan history was almost complete. But there was still a large gap, the story of Tamar Binyan, of her war with the United States, her flight, and her return. The other secret was the promised relic of King Soloman. Tamar's journal I didn't see for years. But the relic was to come into my hands soon and under circumstances that I would not have imagined.

12

JACOB'S VOICE

The German soldier who was chasing me through the even rows of firs, firing his rifle intermittently, fled back into the neuron that housed him during the day. I had tried my best to evict him, but he refused to leave, although in the last ten years he had become reclusive, hardly ever coming out. He must be in his seventies now, and isn't up to the chase anymore. Still, I know he is there. He will be with me always.

I awoke to the sound of rain, low and determined, and the sound of a shutter banging on the other side of the house. My small digital clock was keeping its sleepless vigil, metering the night with equanimity. It informed me that I had just missed 4:13 a.m. I turned over, immobilized by the first decision of the new day, whether to get out of bed and investigate or let someone else do it. My body told me there would be no more sleep for me. I was rested, having gone to bed earlier than usual, and already drawn my customary six and a half hours, all that I needed. Putting on my slippers and robe, I set my crabbed muscles in motion. The sour inactivity of my mouth made me think that I should have brushed my teeth, just in case I met someone. As it turned out, I did. As I opened the heavy library door, surmising that the clashing was coming from there, the noise stopped, and I saw Arin in his pajamas returning from the balcony, shaking his head like a dog just out of water. Seeing me, he smiled and said, "So you're the only other one to meet the emergency, Mendel. The house of Binyan thanks you."

I hesitated at the door, not sure whether to go in or return to my room. He decided for me: "Come in, unless you feel like going back to bed." His eyes were puffy. He looked like he hadn't slept very well. Did he really want company or was he just being polite? "Come in and sit down. The early morning like this is the closest we can come to..." He didn't finish the thought as he left himself drop into one of the chairs at the library table. His eye caught on the place where the notebook had been.

We sat quietly. I was feeling that sluggish quiescence of the still-somnolent body and mind, although my appetite was beginning to stir, and I would have loved some coffee.

He looked up at me and said, "I'm going to make some coffee." Without waiting for my encouragement, he rose and moved, with surprising energy for the hour, out of the room.

It wasn't too early for my compulsive book browsing. I pulled something off a shelf at random and began to read it. What precisely it was I can't say, it might have been written in

Arabic except that I can't read Arabic. I always have a book with me, even in the car, in case of a serious traffic tie-up. It's a kind of meditation, I suppose. In no time at all Arin was back with a tray, bringing, not simply coffee, but cream, toast, jam and halved grapefruit.

"One of the best times of the day," he said, sitting down. "I used to get up like this all the time, before the children were up." His voice had dropped at this. "I would read quietly in here for an hour or so, with coffee, just like now. I did it for years, except on *shabbat*." He looked up from his coffee and swept the library walls with his glance. "Still, there's so much here that I'll never read. I seem to have less time for just reading. I know what you're thinking. I don't really work and should have plenty of time, but you would be surprised how much time is taken up with just managing things. There's the farm near Indio. Then of course the tower has taken so much of my time and energy over the last few years..." With mention of the tower, the pleasure drained out of him for a moment. He looked up at me, a mild question in his eyes, and said, "Tell me, what do you think of Francesca?"

"I think, frankly, that she's everything your son could possibly want in a mate. I know she offended you. I gather she's working against you on the tower project."

"I was angry when she flaunted that. She literally slapped me in the face with it. But there's a kind of justice in it. You see, I did the same thing to her father over fifteen years ago. You might have guessed that from the conversation. The farmers in the county were fighting industry, for all kinds of reasons. Some of us were fighting the developers, too. We knew what that would do to our taxes. Ultimately make it too expensive to hold on to the land, the land in the city at least. Now here are others doing the same thing to me, for the same or similar reasons. I hope that you like strong coffee."

"Yes, I do."

"It's Jamaican Blue Mountain: very hard to come by. One of the dubious advantages of urbanization is that there's now a place in town where we can buy this. There was a time when we had to order everything from Los Angeles that wasn't on the shelves of the Safeway in Indio."

He wanted to talk, to anyone I suppose, at least someone like me who was sympathetic. I was going to tell him that it might be better if I returned to the motel, better for his family if there were no outsider in the home. Listening to him, I decided to stay. Was it my curiosity, my willingness to meet his need for companionship -- from my observation, Miriam gave him all the emotional support he needed. I'm not sure why I held back. I suppose it was simply because I was content to remain there.

"What do you think of my son?"

"He's brilliant, but a little reserved. You get a different impression from his memoir than you do in person."

"It's the Indian blood. My first son, Arye, had more of the Mediterranean in him. He was very outward going, very friendly, everyone liked him." He was looking inward at some image as he said this. "I've always had a hard time reaching Zev. When he was a child, two years old, I even imagined that he might be a little autistic."

"Sometimes really smart people are that way only because they are living in their own world as much as in yours."

"He was always imaginative." Arin seemed to be looking into his past, riffling through a card catalogue of memories for something to tell me, an anecdote that he couldn't quite recall. At length, he skipped to the present and said with controlled emotion in his voice, "You'll never know what it feels like that your child respects you as a father, but doesn't really like you as a person."

"If you're talking about Zev, I think you're being too hard on him."

He poured some more coffee, looking injured and continued as if he hadn't heard what I said. "As he's the only one left, I should take whatever he gives me and be thankful that I have even him. Had he not come along when he did there would be no one at all. We had him rather late. We hadn't planned it. Maybe God knew something we didn't at the time. Do you believe that our fate is to some extent foreordained? I suppose that's an old-fashioned notion."

"I think that it's true, to some extent at least, but we always have the power to alter it,"

"Less so, when you're on top of this ancestral pile of expectations and possessions." He gestured with his outstretched palm at the books.

"I don't know, but it seems to me that we all have to define our own reality, whatever we come from, whatever our father believed. It's sort of what God said to Abraham, when he told him to get out of his father's house, not just physically but intellectually and spiritually as well."

"Zev has certainly taken that admonition to heart," Arin said. The rain had stopped, but water could be heard dripping from the gutters and the trees. Through the french window of the balcony, the waxing morning light appeared, still without a hint of the sun, more a diffusion of moonlight on the horizon over the still black silhouettes of the tree tops.

He got up, walked to the window, and stood there, a dark figure. "It always comes as a surprise, the dawn. Imagine, there were Native Americans somewhere who believed that it was their job to summon the sun every day or it wouldn't come. How's that for being self-centered?"

I walked over and joined him. "Maybe they were right." Above the trees, the morning light was pouring into the sky like an incoming tide, and I wondered how long before the morning stars would disappear.

"No matter how badly I felt the night before, somehow it goes away when I look at the morning sky," he said.

"Before the sun there's so much expectation."

"I expect I'll know about that strike today." Outside the birds were beginning to call to each other. He turned to me and said, "Thank you for seeing me through the dawn."

"No thanks are needed."

"I wanted to talk about something but it has somehow eluded me. And now I suppose that it's too late," he said.

"You know where to find me."

"Speaking of that, I want you to know that the whole place is at your disposal. So if you feel like riding just go down and saddle up. This is in fact a wonderful time to ride. I would go with you but I've got some things to attend to." With that, he left me. I stood by the window, opened it, breathed in the damp fragrance, then went to my room and dressed. All the while I thought of Arin, feeling friendship but not closeness, as though he were there to be appreciated but not touched, like some heirloom, like the artifact that was locked up in a cabinet in the library: talked about but unknown, a mystery like the face of God.

His suggestion was appealing. I decided to go for a ride in the desert, and I prepared for it with the anticipation of a child on the first day of summer camp. My enthusiasm filled me, filled the moment, and again I had to stand back and wonder at the return of feelings which I had thought were no longer a part of me. So I am still capable of a child's enthusiasm, I said to myself as I slipped the bridle over the horse's ears, having forced the bit between his teeth.

I mounted and, leaving the compound, saw what I had never before seen; the hills and mountains around the valley etched so clearly that if my eyes were capable of it, I could have made out the shape of a bird in a tree ten miles away. Never had the world been in sharper focus. Seldom had the air been so fresh and fragrant.

On that ride, I understood why people came to the desert and couldn't leave. Like the yellow flowers that were now opening on plants that had seemed dead, it was a place of secrets not willingly yielded up. I scanned the horizon and saw not simply the faint greening of the hills but the growing shape of the tower; alien, obtrusive, pointing its crooked finger at infinity. Beyond it, I could even see, clinging to the top of a cliff, the parapet of Francesca's father's aerie. Within a half a mile I came to another surprise for someone unfamiliar with the desert. What had been a ridged depression, a shallow stream bed, had been transformed by the night's rain into a roiling yellow torrent barely contained by its eroded banks.

Returning to the house I met Zev, also on a horse, a different person than the Zev of the night before. I had expected reserve; I met none, and he greeted me, smiling. He asked if I had enjoyed the ride. I told him about the flood, and he invited me to ride along with him. Feeling the residue of guilt, wanting to learn more about him, I willingly agreed. The ride was pleasant enough, but he spoke very little, other than to tell me about the plants that we encountered along the way. The last thing that I was about to do was raise his notebook, the tower, or Francesca. On the way back, I did manage to tell him that I admired his work with seeds. My compliment seemed to make him self-conscious, and so I didn't pursue it further.

Finally, when we were back at the stable rubbing down the horses with burlap sacks, without looking at me he said, "My father is glad you came to stay with us for a while. He's a lonely sort, without any close friends."

"I didn't know that."

He turned to me and for the first time opened up. He reached out with his eyes and said, "I wanted you to know that he needs the distraction. This tower has been driving him up the wall. It's a kind of obsession. You seem to be taking his mind off of it a little. I just wanted you to know that my mother appreciates it, although she probably won't say as much. And so do I."

"Thanks." I held back saying more.

"I'm sorry you had to see what happened last night." He paused and took a heavy breath as he searched for words.

"Well," I muttered feeling as though I was to blame.

He turned and led his horse down the stable.

Later that morning, Arin learned that the construction workers had gone out on strike. Pickets were already in place and a secondary boycott by the truckers was likely. He had been on the phone to the Defense Department and learned that their lawyers were considering an injunction on the ground that the strike threatened the national security.

"They must be expecting a war any month now," I said, trying to make light of it, but Arin wasn't in the mood for jokes. "Isn't the delay more the government's problem than yours? After all, it's their tower now, theirs and that church's."

He turned from his pacing and said, "As I said the other day, their payments to me are tied to the progress of the project, with the bulk of it coming on completion. They told me today that there will be no payments until this strike issue is settled," he said, running his hand through his hair.

"How bad is it?"

"I told you about the overdue notes. They're secured by the farm. If I default and can't sell the farm, we lose it. I called a real estate agent today to put it on the market."

"That's your only choice?"

He raised his eyes and shifted them around the room. "I could sell the library, these books. But that would take too long. Besides, I'd rather sell the farm. So now you know about as much as my lawyer."

"Have you told Zev?"

"Would it make any difference if I did? It would only lead to more recriminations."

"You might tell him." Just what prompted my candor with him, I don't know. Probably it was what Zev had said to me in the stable. Somehow I was feeling less a guest and more a counselor, so I counseled. He wrinkled his forehead and grumbled, "He'd only think me a bigger fool for getting so deeply into debt over the project. It's bad enough as it is."

"You'd better tell him about it."

"I'll think about it." He looked away, then, turning back to me, he added, "I appreciate your interest. Miriam and I have talked about it. She feels the way you do." Before he had a chance to tell Zev they experienced a collision of circumstances and will, which neither of them wanted.

Having seen Zev at the demonstration it came as no surprise to me when I interrupted a meeting of six or seven environmentalists, including Zev, in the library. I could tell that they were environmentalists by their sandwiches, natural grain bread and alfalfa sprouts. Not only that, there was a down-to-earth look about them, a faded glow as if they had showered in fresh rainwater, clothes and all, with a large bar of Ivory soap. I searched the group for Francesca, but she wasn't among them. As I expected, Zev had no objection to my working at the table throughout the meeting. Like his father, he must have wanted me to bear witness, although not in court, more likely to his family. Otherwise, with the wide desert around them, why would the snakes have a meeting in the mongoose hole?

I busied myself with the cataloguing, admittedly with one ear tuned to the discussion.

The gathering included a reddish blond beard, a fine profile, a woman who gestured with her hands as she talked, as though she were plucking imaginary oranges and someone who said nothing but took notes. With my peripheral vision and split attention, I saw yet another side of Zev's personality, an element of leadership still developing, but present. After all, even shy, reserved people sometimes become leaders.

As meetings go, it was quick and to the point. There was to be another march to the tower, this one by the church people on Friday of this week. More than a march, it was a reaffirmation of the world church broadcasting principle, and the meeting itself, complete with gospel singers, was to be broadcast on the church network of radio stations throughout the southwest. All of this had been planned before the strike. The discussion initially centered on the likelihood of a clash between the strikers and the Christians, or even other groups, since the Indians and the anti-war group wanted to bootstrap onto the publicity by staging their own simultaneous meetings. Whither the Halibut League: stay away, monitor, hold a press conference, or provide a buffer against violence? A rumor was afoot that a few radical Indians from South Dakota wanted to dramatize their own largely unheeded land claims by creating in incident which would provide them with some media attention. According to the blond beard, they hoped to be arrested for something.

They were discussing options when Arin came into the library looking as though he was about to step on a rattlesnake as he saw the group sitting near the window in a circle, some on chairs, some cross-legged on the floor. Considering his temperament he was remarkably restrained, although what passed for self-possession might have been simple confusion.

Seeing him they stopped talking and, except for the woman taking notes, they looked at him expecting him to say something. Zev stood up as Arin entered and said, "This is my father. I would like you to meet..."

Before he could finish the sentence, Arin interrupted with, "Yes, Zev, I'm sorry but can we save the introductions for later. Can I talk with you privately for a minute?"

I could see the uncertainty on Zev's face. With distaste showing, he said, "Be right back," and followed his father out the door. What went on between them, I couldn't say. Their voices were audible through the door, but I couldn't make out the words; the tone was intense and harsh, but muffled.

Seated at the far end of the room, the group probably didn't even hear that much. Their conversation was subdued and they looked ill at ease. By the time Zev returned, looking injured and withdrawn, the participants were getting up, having already decided to hold their own meeting on the same day at the tower. His attempts to keep them there were politely rebuffed.

Through all of this, I tried to find the biggest book that I could and close it around me. Despite my tendency to withdraw from a conflict not of my making, I felt compelled to intervene. After all, what did I have to lose besides a new friendship, and a place to stay? The risk was worth it. A drum beating in my head - or was it my pulse - I got up with resolution and approached Zev. I had resolved to tell him about his family's financial crisis.. From what I understood of his character, he would not close his heart to the news. He turned to face me, brooding and petulant. I swallowed, although there was no saliva, and said, "I'm sorry to have overheard. It makes me feel like I shouldn't be here."

"No problem," he said, watching me with suspicion.

"I've heard some things about your family's affairs that I feel you should know about.""Mr. Traig..."

"Call me Mendel."

"Whatever. My father and I don't need a translator. We both speak the same language."

"I'm not so sure about that."

"Please excuse me. I've got some things to take care of." He rushed past me, disturbing the motes of library dust as he cut through the sunlight on his way to the door. Before leaving the room he turned and said in a softer tone, "I'm sorry."

At least I tried, I said to myself, and for the second time I decided to leave, but not before lunch and a talk with Arin. Down the polished oak staircase I went, feeling like an executioner and a victim, if that is possible. Arin and Miriam were in the middle of a discussion when I entered the dining room, so engrossed in their conversation that they barely acknowledged my presence. All that I caught of it was the end of a sentence, "... and he simply turned and went back into the library, leaving me standing in the hall."

"Why didn't you simply follow him back into the room?" asked Miriam.

"Simply? What could I have said in front of all of those strangers that wouldn't have been ridiculous and made it worse?"

"I suppose you're right." Miriam looked down at her plate.

"You can't just repair a damaged wall with a handful of plaster."

They fell silent and I sat down and decided to speak my mind. "I know that as a stranger, it's wrong of me to talk to you about your problem," I began slowly, choosing my words.

"Not at all. If we didn't respect you, we wouldn't have invited you here in the first place," Arin said without enthusiasm.

"There's an old saying, 'Never give unasked-for advice,'" I said.

"Consider yourself asked," said Miriam. "You don't seem to be eating the marinated yucca salad. Would you like something else?"

"Always the good hostess. No, this is fine." To reassure her, I ate a piece of yucca. "Excellent," I said through the food. "I'll come right to the heart of it. In some way, both you and your son seem to be looking for an intermediary." They both looked at me. "It's not for me to analyze the history of your difficulties with Zev. I will say only that right now you've got to talk to him honestly about your financial problems at least. It won't stop him from hating the tower or even from trying to stop it, but you might improve your communication at least, and he might begin to understand you." Arin listened, his eyes not on me but on the table in front of him.

"He's right, Arin." Miriam looked across the table where a place had been set, no doubt for Zev. "He's our only one,

Arin," she said softly. With a look of pain he got up and left the room, saying nothing.

Once again I felt as though I shouldn't be here. "I hope that I haven't offended him," I said, breaking the silence.

She turned and showed me gentle sorrow. "He needed to hear it from somebody else."

"I thought because he left the table that I might have offended him." I paused. "I really should go back to the motel. You don't need a stranger getting into the middle of things. It just makes for awkwardness."

"You're wrong. Of course, if it's too unpleasant for you to be here, I would understand that. He hoped that you would ride with him to the meeting at the tower on Friday, and he was looking forward to *shabbat* with you. You know it's his day for philosophy. I know that this must be hard for you on a vacation." She said this with a sincere plea in her eyes. "As for his leaving the table," she continued, "he's probably gone up to talk to Zev."

"I hope so."

"So you see it was good that you spoke up."

Reassured, I went back to the salad, although I really didn't care for the yucca. "There's some rice pudding on the sideboard if you would like some," she said, breaking a silence.

"Thanks. Don't get up. I'll just help myself."

I was just spooning some into a bowl when Arin returned, slow moving, a piece of paper hanging from his right hand. He walked to Miriam and handed it to her, saying in a hurt voice, "He's gone."

She read the note and her face contorted with grief, then she shook it off and took his hand, saying, "He'll come back Arin; he's our son."

And he repeated, his voice hollow, "Our son."

I froze in my place, afraid that even the sound of the rice pudding falling onto the plate would disturb them. Still holding on to Arin's hand, she said, "Sit down, Arin. We'll have some coffee and figure out what to do."

13

ZEV AND FRANCESCA

Although Arin didn't come right out and say it, he must have blamed Francesca for Zev's open and hostile opposition to the tower. Everything but this in their relationship he could attribute to the loss of his first son and the way it had warped his tie to Zev. I didn't know it at the time and didn't find out until later when circumstances brought me closer to Zev and Francisca, but I suppose he was right, at least partly right. But there was more to it. Nothing is that simple.

It's funny the images that stay with you that keep coming back. Mostly it's the trauma. I still remember falling down the stairs into a fruit cellar when I was three, but I can't recall a single birthday party. Zev remembers his father looking all around him at the people getting on the San Francisco plane the day he left home for college. He remembers his mother trying not to cry. He remembers thinking that they must have had Arye on their minds, for it was still inconceivable to him that they might have been feeling his parting except in the context of the loss of their first son.

Once on the plane he thought not of leaving his parents' home but of Francesca who had gone to Boston to spend a week with her old roommate at L'Ecole Gallatine. He wasn't thinking about college. He was still doing his best not to face it. He hadn't even chosen a major, but the entrance examination had exempted him from the first year science courses.

When school started, he found the first semester courses easy enough to require little time outside the classroom. Nothing kindled his interest. Mostly he lived for the time that he and Francesca spent together, the hikes in the redwoods that covered the hills behind Palo Alto. She had a small one-bedroom apartment and a British racing green TR-4, giving them both privacy and mobility and insulating them from the fraternity/sorority rush. Although officially Zev had a dormitory room most of his clothes and books were kept at Francesca's.

For Francesca, the freshman socialization ritual was "forced and superficial." Not that she wasn't picking up friends of both sexes. But they were people of her choosing and caliber, like Marsh Feneman, a pianist, and Cory Metz, a woman who had an interest in poetry and who, like Francesca, was enrolled in pre-law. As for Zev, he neither sought out new friends nor encouraged any of the overtures of classmates. But at Francesca's urging he did go out for the swim team.

That first semester, San Francisco was Zev's classroom. After no more than a month, he found that he didn't even have to attend the lectures to stay on top of his courses, and with Francesca immersed in her studies, involved in freshman debate and a growing social life, he had lots of time to drive in her Triumph, or take the train to The City, as San Francisco was called. His first attraction was to North Beach, an Italian enclave decorated with transient artists, folk singers and what were called street people. There were coffee houses embellished with actual Italian espresso machines, head shops hung with Beatles posters and smelling of the resin of marijuana, Italian hardware stores with presses for pasta in the windows, and delicatessens festooned with yard-long salamis and selling foods he'd never heard of.

He sat in the window of Cafe Trieste, drinking coffee after coffee, sometimes even talking to someone across the table, but he never saw anyone twice. Once he came on some Indians with puffy brown faces, their eyes somewhere else, as they sucked wine from paper bags and pretended to watch the gulls bathing in the pool on the Civic Center. He tried to talk to them, but they rebuffed him.

He did eventually find someone to talk to, someone who taught him more than any of his courses that first year. He was a retired longshoreman named Stan Krakowsky, and they met over coffee at a table in Foster's Cafeteria. Krakowsky had a head stuck like a lump of clay on a bulky torso. Except for the small, grey, watery eyes, his face was as wrinkled as a leaf of dried tobacco. He had lost his eyebrows except for a few grey sprouts that marked the site, and red arterioles crazed the pale roundness of his cheeks. He lived in a small crowded room in the Tenderloin, among the bruised, staggering winos and male prostitutes in tight jeans. He had few wants other than an occasional fifth of vodka. Stan had been a Wobbly and remained a practicing anarchist.

Zev met Stan in a cafeteria line. About to pay for his coffee and apple pie, Zev found that he had no money in his wallet. Stan paid without being asked. It was, as Zev found out, nothing unusual for the man. He lent money to Tenderloin people almost daily, and nearly always got it back. He had three rules: "I keep no records. I loan no more than $10 at a time. I never give somebody who don't return the money a second chance." This he pronounced emphatically in his throaty voice, clicking his dentures, as they got acquainted at a table by the window.

Even as he sat there, he was approached by a stooped sparrow of a woman who, leaning on a cane, explained that she had broken her glasses. Without saying anything, he reached into his pocket, pulled out a crumpled $10 bill, and handed it to her. After she had left with a tearful thank-you, Zev asked, "Do you know her?"

"She's a human being. What more do I need to know?" was the reply.

"But you don't even have her name."

"She don't pay, she don't pay. She looks honest." Then a confidential smile and he touched Zev's arm and said quietly, "By the look of her, if she's a crook she's not so good at it."

So they got to be buddies meeting often for coffee. And sometimes Zev went with Stan to the Longshoremen's hiring hall, where he met others like Stan, colorful, vocal, political, sometimes drunken men. Once or twice he even went to a kind of clubhouse for anarchists, a dim smoky hall with worn wood floors and dark enameled folding chairs, lit by a few conspiratorial overhead globes. There he met worn-looking people in faded flannel shirts and baggy Sears basement work-pants who looked and sounded as out of place as the drunken Indians on the Civic Center Mall. They were fond of passion-ate speeches filled with clichés that none of the other people seemed to take seriously or even to hear.

One thing that Zev got out of this talk was the aware-ness that his family were anarchists, too, in that they existed as best they could outside of society. In fact, he concluded that we were a country of anarchists, of which John Wayne and Humphrey Bogart were the patron saints. At least this was what he told Francesca as they sat over a pizza at Thommaso's, their favorite three-steps-down Italian restaurant just off Broadway in North Beach.

"I would say that you're a good specimen," she said. "Lonely as a wolverine. Exposed to the best educational op-portunity that this country has to offer, you spend your time shuffling around the Tenderloin like a bindle stiff."

"Don't worry about it."

Her musical voice grew moist and she leaned toward him, her narrow blue eyes doing their best to look earnest, and said, "It's just that you have such a fine mind. But you seem to be debasing yourself."

"Not everybody springs from their father's head full grown. I'm just a freshman. The world is still my valedic-tory speech." She chuckled softly like a purring cat and her eyes narrowed even more. He could always deflect her with humor.

Francesca was single-minded. If she couldn't move Zev directly, she would try an oblique attack. One evening at a faculty tea, finding herself next to Professor Amesly Helvig, she seized the opportunity. Although Zev would never have admitted it, Helvig was as much as anything the reason why he had enrolled at Stanford. He was at the time to Botany what Fermi had been to physics or, even better, Salk to medicine. Having seen Francesca socially, it doesn't surprise me that she lost no time in getting and holding Helvig's attention. Even a forgetful, myopic professor looking at his watch and preparing to leave is not immune to a woman who is both intellectually acute and a pleasure to look at. So after about ten minutes of thoughtful questions drawing Helvig out on his subject, she told him about her friend who had discovered a new species of wild grape. And of course he took the bait. The classification of wild species of domesticated plants was his pot of tea, as the English say, for some reason.

"I would like to both see the study and meet the student," he said, in the languid way he spoke. "I may have some work that might interest him." And so, not even telling Zev, she personally delivered the Lost Miner Canyon study to Helvig and waited like a fisherman for a nibble. A whole week passed, and just when she was trying to figure out a way to discretely follow up without appearing pushy, she got a note in the mail from Helvig. He had read the study, found it impressive, and wanted to meet the author.

That night there were irises on the round cherry wood table in her apartment, and a bottle of Chateau Figeac, 1959 to go with the steak *au poivre* that she was preparing. It didn't take much prodding. She was surprised that he wasn't even offended when she told him that she had given the study to Helvig. In fact, she hadn't even explained it.

Before he could say more than "What's the occasion?" she handed him the note from Helvig. She didn't have to explain it. He understood what she had done. He looked at the note and back again at her, a silly incredulous smile on his face, and all he could say was, "I'll be damned." She pushed him into a chair, poured some wine from the Waterford crystal decanter that she had bought on impulse at an antique store next to the place where she had bought the wine, and she told him the story. He pretended reluctance, but it had all the sincerity of a hungry person politely refusing offered food.

Within a matter of days, Zev found himself standing in front of a cluttered desk in a small book-lined office, every surface of which was covered with periodicals and other papers. The sight of the disorder put him somewhat at ease. So did the unprepossessing appearance of Helvig. He was slight, with an oversized head appearing even larger because of the helmet of white disordered hair. Looking up at Zev with lively blue eyes and a yellow, toothy smile, he said, "Your study is a very impressive bit of scholarship for a high school student. If I hadn't known, I might even have assumed it to be an early draft of someone's doctoral thesis."

It didn't take much for Helvig to mesmerize Zev. As Zev put it, "I was like someone standing at a bus stop not knowing the schedule. The bus stopped and I got on." What Helvig offered was irresistible. He had just gotten funding of a project from the National Institutes of Science and UNESCO, to catalogue all of the cereal grasses in the world and to analyze their characteristics and potential as food sources. "There are, of course, many types of millet in Africa that are in cultivation today," Helvig explained. "But there are also strains that may be hardy, disease-resistant, even drought-resistant, that are potentially cultivable." He went on about seed banks, world hunger, climate and soil variations, tying together diverse facts and leaving Zev speechless, awed, and submissive. What most impressed Zev was the fact that Helvig was not engaging in a monologue with himself. He seemed to be talking to Zev and maintaining hypnotic eye contact. He concluded by offering Zev a job as a research assistant in the project and, provided he could pass some proficiency examinations, a waiver of second year botany requirements.

That night they celebrated at their favorite Chinatown second floor walk-up restaurant. Francesca was aglow in the changing yellow and green neon of the sign outside the window and, between bites of *Kuo Teh*, she kept humming some tune from "My Fair Lady."

Although Zev and Francesca lived together in her apartment for four years, their lives took on very different profiles. Zev worked on the Project thirty hours a week and had few friends. Francesca was a social magnet; her friends were always around her, dropping in for meetings or just for coffee. She was invited to parties and attended frequent committee meetings of environmental and peace organizations. According to Zev, she avoided a leadership role in any of these groups. Even then she functioned like a lawyer; supplying ideas, writing a piece for a newspaper, participating in programs but always maintaining her freedom.

Her freedom and where it would take her was in fact Zev's only concern at college, and that only in the last year as they each faced a choice of graduate schools. Francesca loved him, but she wouldn't simply follow him to Berkeley, where Helvig had arranged a substantial grant for him. He imagined her going east to law school and getting involved with someone more charming, more social, more Caucasian. There were always men tailing her. He often came home to find one of her male classmates nursing a beer. And many times he had momentarily wondered if there were more to the meeting than a discussion of ecology. So it was always with a sense of foreboding that he picked up the mail, looking at the envelopes for one from Harvard, Yale, or Oxford, where she had applied for a summer program.

Then one night as she tossed her bra into the corner laundry pile and momentarily turned toward him she said, "I forgot to tell you at dinner. I've gotten into both Harvard and Yale. The acceptances came the same day. Isn't that a coincidence?"

"I knew you would."

Her head popped out of the top of her white ribbon-bedizened nightgown, and as she adjusted the bodice over her breasts she said, "I really can't decide. I want to stay with you, but..."

"But. That's a typical lawyer's term."

"From the standpoint of my career, the East would probably be more useful."

"If we were married, you wouldn't think of it."

"But we're not married, Zev. And there's plenty of time for that."

"We could marry after graduation. We're as good as married now."

"Is that an offer?"

"Yes."

She was silent for a moment and she sat down on the edge of the bed and began to run a brush through her honey-colored hair making it rise and fall like mist. When at last she spoke, her musical voice was soft and shy. "Not now. We don't need it to be as we are. Do we?" Zev didn't know how to respond. He felt warmed and chilled at the same time.

Francesca just sat there brushing her hair, looking at him with a smiling perplexity in her narrow blue eyes. So they took it to bed with them. But Zev didn't drop it. It wasn't in his nature to press her. It wasn't in her nature to share what was her decision affecting her life. Zev thought about it from time to time and when he did it was with recurrent anxiety that he might lose her and never get her back.

Clara and I once talked of marriage and of separate plans. Clara was a promising pianist enrolled in a music conservatory in Vienna while I was already a student at the University in Warsaw. There was no reserve when we spoke of it that day in the languid summer twilight by the river. We knew then we would marry. But we never really know.

Uncertainty about the future was on Zev's mind on a spring day in their last semester as they sat together in a circle of redwoods with the knowledge that this could be their last visit to this favorite of places. This spot, a grove of second growth redwoods beside a shallow stream, was forty miles south of Palo Alto. It was reached by narrow roads that followed the folded contours of the deeply-cut terrain. They liked to drive with the top down up over the redwood-crowned ridges and down into the secretive stream-cut valleys.

Above them a chilling cloud had erased the tops of the trees and was throwing tendrils down through the lower branches. Somewhere the sun was doing its best to plumb the overcast, but form where they sat it was only a pale, diffuse white embolism leeching the deep red and green out of the trees. Francesca was sitting on a maroon and umber Navaho rug. She was sitting cat-like, her legs bent and tucked under her.

"You've become like your falcons, Francesca," Zev said.

She looked up, shivered a little and zipped her pale blue parka halfway up. "Not where you are concerned."

"I sometimes wonder about that."

"You shouldn't. It's true, I do a lot of different things and perhaps it's to avoid a commitment to any one of them. But I think that I have enough to give."

"You're so busy."

"No less than you are, Zev. You're always at the lab. You're like an electric typewriter when you're home giving off a little hum. I've become even a little jealous of Helvig. He sees you more than I do. I'm even a little sorry that I got you two together."

"No you aren't," he said, and he took out a pipe and began to fill it.

"Look at you--smoking a pipe now. Soon you'll begin to look like him, like a dog that looks like its master. And you should take the time to get a haircut. You look like Sitting Bull."

She has something on her mind, he thought. She always gets this way when something's bothering her. And he was right, for she said, "I've decided to accept that fellowship to Oxford this summer." She looked at him, waiting for his reaction. "Don't look so glum. It's only for three months. You'll be up to your knees in succotash. You'll never even miss me."

"I thought we were going to spend two weeks camping in the Sierras. I already told my father about it."

"We can do it next summer. It's such a fantastic opportunity. I just can't pass it by."

They had spent every summer together. One season shouldn't make any difference to either of them. Still, the news was disquieting to him. Even though he had worked full time on the family farm each summer and she had come and gone, visiting friends, even traveling to Europe, they had never been apart for more than three weeks at a time.

"What does that mean for this fall?" he asked her with trepidation.

"I'll go to Cal. We can be together and I can continue with my Sierra Club work. They've offered me an externship in their legal department. There are all of these questions concerning the Coastal Commission, developments that the Commission wants to stop. Of course, there's your father's tower."

Zev and Francesca didn't disagree on much, and they shared a common view of the tower. Francesca called it "technological idolatry." She had dazzled her environmentalist friends by weaning a substantial contribution to the Stop the Tower campaign from her Papa. Actually, it was as easy as getting money for a trip to Europe. When completed, the tower would thrust up just beyond the cliff between their house and Mount Har. She had also gathered some environmental data that was used in the lawsuit that had stopped construction. Zev liked what she was doing. To him, the tower was a repeat of the date grove. At the time, neither she nor Zev fully understood that the success of the case could bring about the financial ruin of Zev's family.

He leaned toward her and they kissed. He thought, it is so like her to tell me in this way, obliquely, in a sense dramatically. Why, she had even selected the site, totally Californian, and natural as well. She has control of her life, but of mine as well in a way. At least some good has come from my father's tower, he remembered thinking. But all that he said was, "I'm glad."

"Your father won't be very pleased." He kissed her again.

14

ONE PEOPLE

I woke up Friday more than a little curious about the meeting at the tower, especially in light of the threat of violence. The day was clear, but high trailing clouds foretold a weather change. I opened the window and breathed the morning fragrance of Arabian jasmine that grew along the wall under my window, the clusters of long pink and white blossoms giving off an almond-honey-spice scent. I dressed and went down to breakfast to find that Miriam and Arin had already eaten. Alone in the dining room, with strong coffee and freshly-baked rolls, my mind returned to Arin and to thoughts of my father. I imagined him in the marine twilight of his shop, lovingly examining a new acquisition. He had always found the time to be with me, talk to me, share his values with me, just as Arin had with his first son.

Mid-morning Arin found me in the library. By the look of him, he had shaken off yesterday's mood. "Miriam said that you wanted to come with me to the tower. It's a nice day for a long ride, and the horses are already saddled."

"Good. When do you want to leave?"

"In half an hour. Miriam is sending along a lunch. We'll even have a bottle of wine. We'll find someplace where we can watch the whole thing without getting involved if anything starts up."

"Then you aren't involved in it?"

"No. Why should I be? Like you said, it's the Government's problem. I got a call this morning about 6; it's 9 there. They are filing for an injunction against the strikers in Federal District Court in San Diego on Monday. So, we'll see. In the meantime, we have this event."

I took advantage of his light mood and asked, "What about your son? Have you heard anything?"

"No. But we've talked it over, Miriam and I. He's probably over there with Francesca. I'm sure he'll be at the demonstration."

"You're not apprehensive? There is a possibility of violence."

"I thought about it. In my grandfather's time, we'd have had a small army out there. My own father, given the same situation, probably wouldn't even have gone. I guess I'm someplace in between. I'm going and taking my rifle with me, although I'm sure I'll let the police do the shooting. If you're afraid, Mendel, you don't have to go. I can ride out there alone. I'll be back well before *shabbat*. That's one thing about a horse.

If we're late, we can always get off and walk the rest of the way home."

"I want to go."

We rode at a leisurely pace, side by side, breathing the aromatic desert air overlaid by the horses' smell. Arin was in a talkative mood; it might have been nervous anticipation. We fell into one of those chains of nostalgic association, like one old tune that recalls three or four others.

He told me about the lonely beauty of the desert when there was just one hotel in the valley; the peculiar *bar mitzvah* ritual which combined the Torah reading with a physical trial as well, although he didn't go into the details; the courtship of his wife; and a visit by President Roosevelt in 1933. I spoke of my very different boyhood: of a home often filled with artists and writers of the Jewish intellectual circles of the time -- my father had published a few poets, none of them of any lasting repute.

At one point, he looked at me and said, "I'm glad we got to know each other. We come from such different backgrounds and yet I felt from the beginning that we had much in common."

I wasn't sure what he meant but I said yes just to be agreeable. He continued, "You are the end of your line, and I guess that I could be the same, if not physically at least spiritually."

"Don't underestimate your son. Your grandfather might have said the same about your father, or your father might have said the same about you," I said.

"I know, but I'm sure they didn't. You see, we were linked together by a chain of traditions and common values. There was room for individual expression, but we were on the same road. Zev has the ability to fulfill himself in some way, when he matures, but it won't be in a way that would make his grandfather happy."

"But weren't they in agriculture, and isn't he as well?"

"Yes, but he'll go off to some university somewhere and do it in a laboratory. Whatever we did, we did it here on the land."

"His seed bank is here on your land."

"Yes."

We rode in silence for a while. "You've never been married, never had children?"

"No. Given different circumstances, I might have."

"You've missed some great joy and you've missed some great pain as well."

"If you had it to do over would you have done the same thing?"

"Oh yes. I don't even have to think about that one. Everything in my personal life, my wife, my children, none of the good things, can ever be taken from me. As for the bad, you must put it behind you and go on to something else. Like Lot's wife. You remember that passage."

"You mean in the Bible?"

"No, I mean in my ancestor's journal." He laughed.

We came over a rise and saw the tower, changed since even the last time. It had grown taller and was no longer alone. Near the base of the rock were five geometric, corrugated-metal houses, surrounded by a high chain-link fence. The place was beginning to resemble a concentration camp, I thought with a chill.

"What's that?" I asked.

"It's housing for the people who will operate the transmitter."

"So soon?"

"They want to have it operational in six months. You can see that they've been working around the clock."

"The boys in the submarines under the polar cap must be homesick." This one brought a small smile.

My eyes were caught by a few large, wheeling birds circling the top of the tower.   For the first time I saw the sandstone facade of the Palacio Beneveste on the summit of the cliff. It was squarely behind the tower, on a sort of ship's prow with the broken line of what I took to be Lost Miner Canyon on its right side.

Aside from the housing the area around the base of the rock looked like what Moses saw as he came down the mountain with the Ten Commandments. True, there was no Golden Calf, but more practically, several steers were turning on an enormous spit over a pit of hot charcoal large enough to serve as a forum for an ashram of firewalkers.

Near the fire pit, the people were mostly dressed in white. The program hadn't yet begun, and the crowd was still milling about or standing in groups, looking from a distance like a convention of seagulls. Near the crowd there were several trucks that I assumed to be radio and television equipment, and on the crown of the rock in front of the tower a small platform had been built with speakers on poles and metal folding chairs on risers. Workers were moving steadily between the trucks and the stage.

As expected, the church members were not alone. Distinguished by their placards on wooden stakes were the strikers, positioned along the side of the road below the rock and at the entrance to the work site on the summit. At the foot of the rock, across the road, the Native Americans, distinguished by their traditional brightly-beaded costumes and headdresses, were preparing their own rally. They had already begun some kind of ceremony and their resonant drumming and high nasal undulating chant was audible.

The third conclave, looking heterogeneous and Caucasian, a mélange of anti-war activists and environmentalists led by the Halibut League, was gathered somewhat behind the others. Beyond them were two police cars and an impromptu parking lot spilling out on both sides of the road. Aside from three or four excited dogs, there were some horses. I recognized Zev's horse standing near the environmentalists next to a white horse that I assumed belonged to Francesca. Arin must have seen the horses as well, for he was looking glum.

"Let's get a little closer. There's another rise on the other side of the wash," he said, as his horse moved forward. My horse followed and in a few minutes we reigned up and dismounted much closer to the scene but still able to get a balcony view, and none too soon. A trumpet blast magnified a thousand times by tall speakers exploded with the force of a sonic boom, causing the environmentalists to hold their ears, the Indian dancers to lose their beat, the horses to start and the disciples to gather at the base of the rock, except for the ones who were minding the fire pit. My eye returned to the platform in time to see that all of this noise was coming from only five trumpeters gathered in front of five microphones on the stage. Hearing this, I understood for the first time the prophecy that on the Day of Judgment the dead would awake at the sound of Gabriel's trumpet. With the advent of electronic amplification Judgment Day must surely be approaching. I shared this thought with Arin to cheer him up and drew a snort out of him.

As the last notes bounced off the hills and dropped silently to earth like loose feathers, a choir dressed in long satin robes, white with red sleeves, filed onto the stage and took seats on the risers. It was a segregated choir as all of the members were black. While the singers were still rustling in their seats, a slight woman enveloped in an organdy satin robe walked to the microphone. She had a pile of white hair and a pinched American Gothic face, and for a long time she said nothing at all. She simply looked out at the audience, ranging back and forth as though she wanted to make personal eye contact with each one of them. Before she could say anything, a spontaneous clapping began, like spattering grease, transformed into a hammer blow. The crowd was swaying in unison now to the rhythm of the clapping. Then someone began to chant and the whole crowd picked it up, although I couldn't make out the words. The woman on the platform continued to watch them. Arin passed me a pair of binoculars, and I focused on her face. She had the look of a mother watching her three-year-old recite a poem.

"That's the Reverend Linda Blaney, Collery-Matin's protégée."

"Is she going to say anything?"

"It looks like she doesn't need to."

She finally did speak, in a piccolo voice strangely magnified by the speakers, and the crowd stilled instantly. "Children of God," she began, hammering each word into granite. She had a funny way of pronouncing God, like the 'aw' in 'awful,' and she let the words descend on a vibrato. "Children... of... God," she repeated, letting each word stand by itself, as a whole thought. Then after a long pause she said it again, this time with the accent on 'children.' The next time it was the word 'of.' Finally, after a suspenseful delay, the single word 'God' exploded from her mouth and ran to all who would hear it. Again the stillness, before she said, enunciating each word, "We are all children of God." A silence. "Christ is the son of God." Silence. "Christ is our salvation." This last sentence quick and calm. With that she raised her arms in a crescent of benediction, her eyes to the heavens and she sat down as the crowd began a chant of "Praise the Lord."

"A woman of few words, but a powerful speaker," I said.

"Yes."

The choir stood and began to sing, their rhythm and chords enervating and complex. Even without the speakers, they were singing at full throttle, singing with all the physical strength and emotion that they were capable of concentrating in their voices, hard and sweet, riotous and sad.

They sang for a long time, ecstatic grace on their faces the physical, earth-rooted dimension of it flowing out from under the robes. Even the pickets stopped walking and leaned their signs on their shoulders to watch and listen. The sun was overhead now, and the shadows were all at one with their bodies. Even the tower's shadow was contained in a pool at its base. It was not hot but the sun made itself felt, blanching the colors and warming the bare skin. All the while, the Indians kept dancing and chanting and the environmentalists looked like they were enjoying the concert. About that time, we ate our lunch, cold chicken, corn salad, cold corn tortillas, and a bottle of Chenin Blanc thoughtfully wrapped in newspaper to hold some of its chill.

The sun, the wine, the food and the intermittent dry wind combined to make me drowsy, and despite the noise I lay down, my back pillowed against a worn sandstone rock, and dozed, for how long I don't know. The sound receded to a buzz until Arin bent over me to say that he wanted to go down into the crowd to hear what if anything was happening with the other groups. Regretting the wine, I picked myself up and rode with him to the edge of the Indian gathering. There was nothing to tie the horses' reins to but he told me that his horse would stay where he left him and mine would stay with his horse. In case we were separated we agreed to meet back on the rise in time to ride back before sundown.

I was glad that we had come close enough to really see and hear the Indians. About ten men and women were circling two drummers and a wrinkled old man with ebony hair was chanting, eyes closed, head tilted toward the sky. I asked one of the people standing in the crowd about the ceremony and he explained that it was to honor ancestors. "How long will it last?" I asked.

"No special time. When the old man there feels like he's in touch with Taquitz," he replied in a flat resonant voice. He was a Native American, by the looks of him a college student, wearing only a thong headband about his shoulder-length hair and a silver and turquoise belt to identify him with his culture.

"Who is Taquitz?"

"The old spirit who lives under the rock."

"Are you from here?" I asked.

"Santa Rosa Mountains."

I didn't know where that was but as he had turned back to the dancing I didn't pursue it further, except to speculate on whether the people had come from North Dakota as well. I found myself looking around for guns but could see none. The contrast between the Indian music, unamplified, singular, the quiet concentration of the crowd, and the expanded physical energy of the chorus and church crowd was grating, like discordant notes. Both shared tenacity and stamina having gone on for at least three hours judging by the shadow of the tower which had now enveloped the stage and was pointing down the rock toward the crowd. Arin had drifted away from me, and as I walked around the edge of the Indians, I saw him surrounded and engaged in an intense conversation.

My back was to the stage when the chorus finally stopped singing, with a final song that even I recognized, "Amazing Grace." In this they were joined by the entire group and the resulting sound was like those broadcasts of all the fans singing the National Anthem before the last game of the World Series, overlain in this case with a plaintive rendering by the chorus, still audible because of the sound system.

Gathered at a distance of perhaps fifty yards from me was the meeting of the Halibut League, now coalescing in front of a man who was standing above the crowd, apparently on a box or a chair, and holding a portable speaker in his hand. His voice came out of it compacted and yet projected, shrill and nasal. The amplification gave his every word a sense of urgency and irritability. The words themselves were not as provocative. He spoke of the "pristine desert" now scored by trail bikes and four-wheel drivers, of petro glyphs defaced, of a delicate landscape and ecology that would not recover in ten thousand years, just as the defacement of earlier times, the fire pits of 1,000 years ago, were still in place. Looking across the way at the ceremony he contrasted the gentle nomads of the past with the clear cutting of the world's forests and the commercial development of agricultural land, the oceans' pollution, the profligate waste of nonrenewable resources, the reluctance to commit sufficient funds to solar energy, bio-mass and so on.

A woman followed him to the box. The bullhorn made her sound as though she were being strangled, but she was exciting, deploring as she did the military pollution of the desert, not only by the tower, but by the corrugated sardine can housing and the prospect of nuclear targeting of the valley in the event of a war. I was standing at the rear of the crowd listening with one ear and letting my eye wander over faces when I was nudged on the shoulder. I turned to face Lieutenant Redo. By the look of him, I was the only person he'd seen who he didn't distrust. I suspect policemen feel that way all the time in crowds.

"I wouldn't have expected to see you out here," he said to me.

"Oh, I'm just a spectator. I came out with Mr. Binyan." That name registered, and he fluttered with respect.

"A friend of his, are you?"

"Yes, in fact I'm staying with him." Why did I have to tell him that?

"Quite a place he's supposed to have. I've never been there myself." His head shifted to take in the assemblage and he said, "Some carnival."

"I've never seen anything like it."

"That Reverend Matin always draws a crowd. I've got a cousin that belongs to his church. He's a real religious nut." As he talked, he continued to look about him.

"Are you expecting trouble, or are you out here just for crowd control?"

"A little of both. Some radical Indians from up north someplace are around with rifles. We don't want anything to happen to the holy folks."

"How's your son?"

"He's got himself a job, believe it or not--working at an auto parts place. He's nuts about cars. I only hope that in three months' time he doesn't steal enough parts to build himself one."

"Maybe he'll straighten out."

"I hope so. Well, I've got to be moving along. Let me give you some advice. If you hear any kind of popping that sounds like firecrackers, just fall flat on your face and hug the sand and rocks."

"Is there any chance of that?"

"You never know with these Indians. They could get high on Jimson weed and think they're Sitting Bull's ghost."

He walked toward the Indians, and I meandered toward the edge of the church rally, stopping someplace between the three groups. From where I stood, all three of them could be heard distinctly and yet scrambled. There at the vortex nothing was identifiable or comprehensible, neither the unamplified obscure voice of the past, nor the resounding voice of the present, let alone the austere voice of the future. Overhead, the sun was wheeling westward and the finger of the tower's shadow was stretching, pointing like the hand of a clock into the crowd. Someone announced something. I caught, "Collery-Matin," and I looked up to recognize the man who I had seen in the library, now wearing a white suit and looking down at all of us from the brow of the rock, the tower immediately behind and above him, almost as though it were giving birth to him.

I moved closer so as to hear him. He said no more than "Brethren," just that word before the sound system went out. He went on talking for a few seconds, but there were no words, and he stopped when the crowd began to shout, "Sound." Meantime he stood above them, deprived of the power to mesmerize them with his words, while the sound technicians ran here and there. Spontaneously, the crowd began to sing not one but several different songs. And this went on until someone gave Collery-Matin a portable speaker and he began again with much diminished authority.

"Brethren," he repeated, his voice tinny and crabbed like an old phonograph record, "Paul said, 'on this rock I shall build my church', and we shall do the same. On this rock we shall build our church, a church given to the word of God, not for us alone, but for all mankind." His voice rolled up and down, paused, slammed home, but the effect was dwarfed by his distance from the crowd. "We live in a time when Communism and Atheism threaten to stamp out Christianity and freedom." He stopped for a moment as someone walked up and said something to him. "As even now they tried to still my voice by cutting the wires that connect this rock with thousands of listeners in six states. But they will not still my voice, for I speak the words of Christ our Savior, and no conspiracy of godless men can still the divine truth."

"Praise the Lord," resounded from the crowd.

"Like a beacon, the word of the Lord will give light to the blind." At that moment his voice expanded and resonated as the sound system was restored and as I stood there he grew taller. "And the word of the Lord will beam to all the world from this very same tower that like the ram's horn of the Hebrews summons our hosts to do battle against Magog, in that final battle. Even as God smote the enemies of the Hebrews, so shall our enemies also be smitten..."

I caught a glimpse of the sun quickly fleeing the sky, plummeting toward the hills as though it had been shot down, and my thoughts shifted to Arin. The Sabbath had caught us unawares.

Then I saw Arin on horseback galloping up the road to the summit of the rock. He reached the top, dismounted, and began to climb the metal ladder which ascended one of the legs of the tower. Wondering what prompted him to do that, I suddenly remembered him standing on the roof of his home, that first *shabbat*, waiting for the sunset and the advent of Sabbath.

Then a dog not far from me, a mutt the color of the desert, began to howl, sensing, perhaps feeling, what none of us yet knew. I saw more than heard it, the stubby muzzle pointed skyward in supplication, its narrow black lips open and quivering.

I saw the running crack even before I heard the sound of it, heard it before I felt it. A long ragged fissure was running out of the canyon to the left of the rock and the tower. Then came a tremor much like the feel of an approaching passenger train and finally the sound of a high-speed freight roaring and tumbling toward me. The roar became a convulsion of the earth as though some gigantic animal sleeping under the earth's crust had suddenly stood up and shaken itself free, and I found myself snapped into the air like a cracking whip only to collide with the earth. Paralyzed with fear and helplessness I was again thrown up as a cat might toss a mouse into the air, and I had a jumbled view of others around me dancing and tumbling like drunken clowns. I smelled the dry dust of the earth, imagined it to be the smell of gunpowder, heard the clash of jackboots on cobbles, saw the death head and a pair of pale, unfeeling eyes.

I lay on the convulsed ground for what seemed like five minutes, feeling the ground under me move from side to side as though it were about to open under me. In and out, loud and soft came the sound of screams, a torrential grating roar and my lungs and nostrils filled with smothering alkaline clouds of dust.

Then the convulsion stopped and I lay still, touching the earth, grateful that it was no longer moving. I remember turning my head up and my first sight was the tower, grey and swaying against a swirling blue sky. Around me people were picking themselves up or moaning or crying for help. Faces moved like shadows, showing blank shock, fear, or pain, though some seemed calm and oriented. The trembling began again, but this time no more than that. As it came again I wanted to save myself, to hide, to hold on to something, and when it stopped I remember looking around with concern for those about me who were still or bleeding.

As the disorientation left me, I saw more and more and realized that now a fissure had opened in the earth, running from the left of the tower roughly across to where the fire pit had been; it had been swallowed up as though the earth had accepted it as a sacrifice. Fully ten feet across, the jagged, open wound divided the area in front of the rock so that what had been one field was now two.

I followed its course behind the tower with my eyes at the very instant that the point of the cliff began to shear away in a silent, slow floating collapse. The great house just dissolved into a billowing cloud of dust. It dissolved like the image in a dream, but the clashing, grinding cascade of shattering and striking rock was all too real. The sound swelled then faded, resounding up the canyon and far out into the desert like the end of a cadenza. For the moment nothing could be seen but a mobile cloud of yellow dust, already obscuring but not obliterating the tower. Then, except for the cries of the injured and the disembodied prayers, there was stunning silence.

Near me was a group of people on their knees in prayer. The Reverend too was on his knees, with his hands clasped. The sound system was out and I couldn't hear what he was saying; people were singing a hymn and that seemed surreal. The portable speaker of the environmentalists was still functioning and I heard someone telling people who were unhurt to gather in one place so that they could help the injured. I recognized Colonel Quinn, the man in the wheelchair at the demonstration, with a group around him. He was barking orders, his arms directing people this way and that. I saw two or three people trying to crawl out of the fissure and I realized for the first time that many must have fallen into it, some to be buried or crushed. Groups were already gathering on both sides and a few people were climbing down into it. A man walked up to me, asked me if I needed help, and I realized for the first time that I was bleeding from a gash on my cheek. I must have said something, for he went on to help someone nearby who was still lying on the ground.

I stood up shakily and looked about me as calm returned to my body. All around me people were sitting up or standing, looking dazed as though they had just awakened and found themselves in a strange place. Some were rubbing injuries or cuts. My eyes shifted to the cloud of dust around the tower and I suddenly remembered the sight of Arin climbing the ladder no more than a few minutes before the earthquake. I scanned the face of the tower but couldn't see him and it came to me that he might have fallen as the tower swayed.

I got up and ran, stumbling toward the road leading up the rock to the tower. I ran without thinking of my shock-induced weakness. I ran among people running in the other direction in terror, their eyes vacant, and among those who had fallen and lay injured on the ground. The dull thrumming of the Indian drum and the now-mournful chant of the old man came and went. I reached the base of the road only to be overtaken by Zev on horseback.

Without speaking -- he understood where I was going -- he helped me up behind him and we rode to the summit through small groups of the chorus. Everyone on the summit seemed to be either on the road or moving toward it, either out of fear of the collapse of the tower or simply to get away from the place altogether. As we went up, I had a better view of the crowd at the base of the rock. Some were standing singly or in small groups, talking or looking about. Others were bent over people who had been injured, while most were moving toward the parked cars. Among them I spotted Lieutenant Redo on his way to his car, and for the first time I wondered what it was like in Canyon Springs.

We reached the summit of the rock and dismounted. Zev dropped his reins and began to scan the area around the base of the tower. He ran a few steps, stopped, looked around him, ran again to another place, looking up into the superstructure. Feeling both weak and perplexed, I stayed where I was, letting my eyes wander.

I looked up and saw that the sun had still not quite left the sky, although it was little more than an orange skullcap poised on the hills. Then my eyes returned to the tower and I saw

Arin, dangling barely four feet below a catwalk wedged at his waist into the junction of two guy wires. Zev must have seen him too, for he was already running toward the ladder.

I followed close behind him. Looking up as I climbed, I saw hovering above the tower the sudden coming of the night like a cape hanging over us. It must be fatigue, I thought, like spots in front of my eyes, because as the sun disappeared completely the amorphous shape seemed to implode. We reached the platform and the vision passed. When I caught up with Zev he was standing at the edge of the platform looking down at the catwalk and beyond at Arin. Arin was not moving and it was just as well for any motion would have dislodged him and he would have plunged head first another 100 feet to the rock surface. He must have fallen from above, struck the edge of the platform, and literally careened off, catching in the guy wires that ran from stays to a point on the frame. As I stood there, Zev was already climbing down to the catwalk, no more than a beam without railings. Gripping the edge of the platform, I let myself down behind him, feeling the uncertainty of suspension in air for a moment before my feet touched the false security of its flat surface, barely eighteen inches wide. From where we stood, Arin was no more than four feet away, but to reach him one of us would have to lie down on the beam, hanging over it from the waist.

"We'd better get some help," I said. "I don't think that the two of us can get him off of those wires."

"But there's nobody down there," said Zev, his eyes ranging from the rock back to his father. Arin began to stir as if the sound of his son's voice had reached his consciousness; but his stirring, slight as it was, threatened to undo his precarious balance. A strange calmness in his voice Zev said, "Don't move, Father. Try not to move a muscle and we'll get you up from there in just a minute." Then, in a whisper, he said to me, "There's no time to get help now. We've got to try ourselves before it's too late."

From Arin a muffled, "I saw it." The phrase seemed unresponsive and confused, but he remained still.

"Look, there's someone coming up. They must have seen us," I said. But Zev was already crouching on his knees, hesitating while he planned the best way to reach Arin. Arin was lying across the two wires on his back, his legs and torso dangling over. He had to be at most semi-conscious or the awareness of his danger alone might have caused a fatal movement.

"We can't wait. At least we can try to secure him to the wire," Zev said taking off his belt. "If you can hang on to my legs I'll hang down and interlock my belt into his and one of the wires. The leather should hold him, even if he does fall off, and we can try to bring him up without endangering him." He looked up at me for confirmation and I nodded, at the same time crouching and feeling an immediate cramp of my knees. Fortunately just behind me was a diagonal member that secured the catwalk to the platform. Choking from the dust that was now falling over us, my eyes stinging and beginning to tear, I wrapped one arm around the diagonal and gripped Zev's leg just above the calf with my right hand, knowing that if he slipped he would either take me with him over the side or I would lose my grip and watch him fall right onto his father, dislodging him from his perch. I've never squeezed anything as hard as I did his leg as I watched him lower himself over the side like a gymnast, his belt clutched in his right hand. How long this took I can't say, in reality no more than 20 seconds. To me it seemed like an honest five minutes. I could feel my back muscles going into spasm as I stretched like a triangle. Zev reached his father's belt. Fortunately, it was thick saddle leather secured by a brass buckle. He made a pass at it, missed, then gently caught it with his left hand.

I looked down and saw that two men had reached the summit of the rock and were running toward the ladder. Zev had just worked the tongue of his own belt through the front of his father's belt when Arin turned suddenly, as though awaking from a bad dream. His torso moved up; to check the motion his legs moved up and he flipped over backwards. He hung for just an instant in Zev's loose belt before he fell toward the ground. As he left the cradle I felt my arm tearing out of its socket as Zev lunged toward him only to leave the catwalk and hang for an instant by my tenuous and slipping grip on his calf. His motion brought him in contact with the wires and with both free hands he gripped them as a gymnast might grip the handles of the horse. His leg slipped from my hand, but not before he could arrest his fall by suspending himself from the wires.

I withdrew, shaking all over, still gripping the diagonal. "If you can just hold on, the men are already on the ladder." Even as I said it, he was lifting himself to the point that one knee was already on the junction of the wires and his left hand was slipping back over the catwalk. I reached out and took his wrist with my free hand, holding him until I heard the clatter of boots on the platform above.

"Someone's almost here," I said to reassure him, and almost before I got the words out of my mouth a man straddling the catwalk and stabilized by the man behind him was extending both hands towards Zev. Only when he had Zev securely in his own grip did I let go. Reaching back trembling, I gripped the diagonal with my now free hand. Shaking, my teeth chattering, I leaned over to vomit, then slid down to the deck of the catwalk and rested my head against the diagonal, unable to move. I had the energy only to look at Zev.

"Can you come down on your own?" said one of the men.

"Yes, after a few minutes' rest. But stay with me. I feel weak," I said. We rested only for a moment looking down over the edge to see Arin lying still on the face of the rock. A deep visceral moan came out of Zev and he sobbed. With the hand that had gripped his wrist, I touched him. Reaching for his shoulder, I drew him toward me, and I wept with him.

15

DUST

Some things are too painful to talk about, because recounting them makes you relive the experience. There are such events in my life, more than one. I would have thought that the earthquake and its aftermath would be one of them. At the time I was too numb to record its full impact. Now, I sometimes dream about it and wake up in fear, my heart racing.

Zev went down to his father and knelt beside him, his face very close to Arin's head. For a long time Zev looked at him, then gently he closed his father's eyelids with his finger, bent down and kissed his forehead. I was standing nearby. He looked up at me and said in a level voice, "Help me get him on his horse. We'll take him home." I coughed and nodded. The cloud of dust had risen high over the canyon, and it was still settling around us like a sandy fog. We put his limp body over his saddle and tied it on. There was little visible sign of the impact, except for the back of his head, which was seeping blood. When we had secured him, I mounted behind Zev, at least until we could find my horse and Francesca.

We rode among the small groups of people, looking for her until Zev concluded that she had probably gone up a roundabout trail to her home. We passed among the survivors, some injured or in shock, others giving assistance or comfort. A column of cars was moving toward Canyon Springs like a funeral. Near the base of the rock about 20 people were kneeling together in prayer. The Indians had dispersed. The fire pit had been abandoned and the meat left to cook was already charred black.

We found my horse not far from where I had left him and we cantered in the waning dusk toward home wondering what we would find. I rode beside Zev, not speaking, not knowing what to say, like someone who sees a man severely wounded and is afraid that if he touches the injury he will only make it worse.

As the night closed around us, Zev said, "We'd better slow down. It's getting dark; besides, we've been working the horses pretty hard." I gladly reined in, feeling exhausted, sore, and chilled since the temperature had quickly fallen. By now we should have seen the glow from the lights of Canyon Springs but there was nothing and I began to speculate to myself about the destruction. Pompeii came to mind as did the ruined cities of Germany immediately after the War; block after block of shattered walls and piled rubble.

I looked at Zev's back wanting to say something to comfort him, knowing that he must be both fearing the worst effects of the earthquake; his mother's injury or even death, and the destruction of their home. I looked back at Arin's horse bearing him for the last time. Should I maintain the silence of a spectator, a stranger among the mourners, or would it be better to reach out to him with my memories and feelings, as I had done on the tower.

He didn't know it, but we were bound together by this common lesion in our memory, a lesion which might scarify but never disappear. I decided to speak. His letters to his brother came to me. His terse appreciation for my companionship with Arin moved me to think that I might console him a little, or at least make it easier for him to speak to his mother. The dread of that meeting must be oppressing him now. I caught up with him and rode silently beside him for a while before I said, "You did what you could, Zev."

"What?"

"You did the best you could back there. You risked your own life trying to save him. He knew that before he died. He could ask no more of you as a son than that."

There was no response for some time. Slowly and in a voice so soft that I had to strain to hear him, he said, "I wish I could believe it as easily as you said it."

"It's true, Zev. It was just a trick of fate that we had any chance at all to save him."

"If it were only that, only his death, but it's his life I'm remembering. Our life. He lost two of his children and was estranged from his third," he said with growing anguish and frustration.

"Maybe I shouldn't have spoken," I said softly.

He turned his head toward me for the first time. "No. It takes courage for you to talk with me about this."

"Whatever bad feeling passed between you and your father, I'm sure it was forgiven. It's no good to abuse yourself with it now. It won't do him any good, and it won't help you any. You loved him. That's what's important. You will honor him by living a decent life. That's the best you can do now."

"It's easy to say."

"You can blame yourself for your alienation, but you are both exaggerating it now in your mind and forgetting that it wasn't entirely of your making. A lot of it was his misplaced grief at the loss of your brother and sister. He was afraid to love you too much; afraid he would lose you too."

"I'm not much of a psychologist," he said, his voice thick.

"Neither am I, but it's obvious to me. It's just human nature to protect yourself from more pain. I know he was proud of you and loved you. I could tell by the way he talked about you."

"But he shut me out of his life."

"He didn't want to. He just didn't know how to bring you into it. He thought that you disapproved, and he couldn't penetrate your reserve. He took it to be disapproval."

"He was right in part. I did disapprove but I loved him no less for it."

"And I'm sure he loved you no less despite your disapproval. You didn't know that he had serious money problems. He felt himself to blame for them and was ashamed to discuss them with you. That was the biggest part of his hostility over your attitude toward the tower. He had finally brought himself to discuss them with you but you had already left."

"You know that for a fact?"

"I was there in the dining room when he went up to your room, and when he came back." He didn't respond and I simply listened to the scraping of the horses' hooves and shivered. There wasn't even the memory of the sun on the horizon and the temperature had again fallen. Somewhere a dog was barking. Otherwise there was silence, except for Zev's stifled sobbing. "I'm sorry," he said.

"Don't be sorry, not for mourning. It's better for you," I said, thinking how long it had been after my father's death that I had finally wept for him and for myself and what that had done to my capacity to feel anything. As if to keep from being numbed again by the memory I began to talk about it, less to console Zev than to get it out of me.

"My father died in front of my eyes as well. And not by accident," I began. "He was the proprietor of a rare book store. He also dealt in valuable Jewish artifacts. It was really an extension of his own collection. After the Germans invaded Poland anti-Semitic acts were encouraged. It wasn't hard. A mob sacked some Jewish shops. His was one of them. He was struggling with one of the looters when he was clubbed on the head. I was just coming up the street at the time. It seemed unreal to me, a dream. I saw him struck from behind. I saw him fall. I ran up the block to where he lay among the shards of glass from his window and a few relics that had been pulled out of it, smashed and scattered by the hoodlums. When I got there they were already moving up the street, chased by an indifferent Polish policeman. I was just a little kid. I couldn't have saved him." My words passed back into images in my mind: of my mother, of Clara, of all my losses, until my memory again covered them. "So you see...."

"I'm sorry. If anybody had said to me when this day began that it would come to this...." His voice trailed off.

The paralyzing horror of my father sprawled on the bricks of the street, blood oozing from his head, his eyes staring, empty, his face wearing a mask of anger, fear, brought back old tears, tears stored inside my heart for over forty years, and the memory of my childhood days in Poland.

My mother sent me to stay with Uncle Maier after my father's death. She thought it would be safer in the village, and it was for a while until the Germans came to get the Jews. I had been in a boat on the river fishing with Clara Boszawicz, the daughter of a farmer who worked for my uncle. We returned to find the Germans had taken my uncle and aunt and the other two Jewish families.

I spent the rest of the War with the Boszawicz family. I took the bed and place at the table of Roman, who had been killed in the German invasion. I passed for a refugee cousin from the city, went to church and school until the war was over. It was an out of the way place and the Germans seldom came through. Everyone in the village knew who I was. I was their resistance. After the War I left to find my mother. I never did although I learned years later from the fastidious records kept by the Germans that she, Uncle Maier, Aunt Hannah, every relative in fact but one were gone. Instead I found the

THE SEED APPLE 269

Joint Distribution Committee and an eventual sponsorship in America. I didn't tell that to Zev.

We rode on quietly until the horses quickened the pace on their own as we came within a quarter of a mile of the house. I could almost feel his anxiety as we approached the wall.

"At least the outer wall is intact," he said as we entered the back gate and rode between the fruit trees, breathing the scent of lemon and orange blossoms. The tile roof came in view, intact, and then, through a gap in the trees, we saw that the house and buildings were still standing. We left the orchard and approached the stables. Candles and kerosene lamps cast a pale circle of light on the windows of a few of the rooms of the house. The horses' hooves resounded on the cobbles, and as we were dismounting at the door of the stable, Miriam came out of the rear door of the house carrying a lantern.

"Arin?" she called out. "I've been so worried. I'm so glad that you're back." This made my heart rise into my throat, and I thought of my own mother when I reached home with news of my father's death. Zev dropped the reins of his horse and trotted toward her, to intercept her before she could reach us. I watched him stop in front of her. I heard her say, "Zev," with feeling and relief. What he said was inaudible, but I saw her collapse against his chest. He wrapped his arms around her and they remained so for a long time.

16

SECRET OF THE POMANDER

Both Zev and Miriam asked me independently to stay for the funeral, not only to help but to be part of the minion. It was not easy to be in the empty, silent house, but I remained without hesitation, doing what I could to break the tempo of their sadness and silence, at the table at least. Francesca was there as well. In fact, she moved in and stayed with Zev in his room. As I had seen, her family house had collapsed into the canyon. Her grandfather and the staff were buried at the foot of the canyon under tons of rock.

I came to admire Francesca even more and in a different way during those days. There was none of the feverish excitement of the dinner. Now her confidence expressed itself in calm strength and a gently caring manner toward both Zev and Miriam. She even had some warmth left over for me, transient though I was.

Once I sat with her for a time in a secluded corner of the garden, a semi-circle of benches facing a fountain. We talked largely about the earthquake and her relationship to Zev. It was twilight, after dinner, the night before the funeral.

"It seems that Miriam has taken Arin's death in stride," I said.

She didn't answer immediately, as though she were considering what I had said. "She's stoic. But the worst will probably come later, when Zev goes back to school and she is alone." Then she looked at me, her eyes full of feeling, and quite gravely said, "Do you have to go back to Bolton? I'm sure Zev and Miriam would be glad to have you stay on as long as you like."

"I'm sure that I could spend another six months in the library, but I must return in a week. What about you?"

"I'm going back to school in a few days, after I deal with some of my papa's lawyers." Her voice grew fluid as she said this. I thought back on that night when, two hours after we arrived at the house, she appeared, sober yet composed, her face yellow with caked dust except where the tears had washed it clean. She had been with Zev at the time of the earthquake and had ridden her horse up a back trail to the summit of the cliff, only to find a half-shell of the house looming over the cliff's edge. Despite her own loss, she reached out that night to Miriam and Zev with tenderness and courage. Seeing her then, I realized how much more there is to people than appears on the everyday surface. Not everyone of course. But I had seen before how profound tragedy reveals the substance of us all.

"Will you do something about a funeral for your grandfather?"

"I've thought about that. But he didn't practice his religion and under the circumstances I don't think he would have wanted it. As for a grave, he has a rather grand one. All the possessions he loved are buried there at the foot of the canyon with him. Sort of like the Pharaohs." She looked away from me and her hand went up to her face.

"What are you going to do when you finish school?"

"I think that I'll come back here, possibly set up a general practice in Indio. Do a little public interest work and otherwise go into trial law. I love New York and Europe, but fortunately I'm able to travel as much as and whenever I want to." She looked at me with what I took to be affection. She rearranged the skirt of the white Mexican embroidered blouse that fluted over her lap. Her hair was hanging free over her shoulders. I wanted to touch it. She turned and I saw her eyes expand as she watched Zev approach us. I turned toward the stone basin and watched the water overflow the brim, splash on the stone gutter and run in a channel toward the dense foliage surrounding us.

He bent over and kissed Francesca, greeted me and sat down on the other side of her. "Did you know that the earthquake reactivated this fountain?" he said. "It's spring-fed, but it's been dormant for years. We think that it's the site of the original pool that my ancestor described."

"Then you've come the full circle," I said.

"In many ways we have."

Within an hour after my conversation with Francesca beside the fountain she left unexpectedly for Los Angeles, promising to return the next day in time for the funeral. Her grandfather's lawyers wanted her to review some documents, she explained. Zev saw her off, then went through the motions of managing the farm, talking on the telephone to the straw boss, but he was clearly too restless and distraught to function.

As for Miriam, she was stolid. Two elderly cousins showed up, and the three of them spent time in the kitchen preparing the food for the funeral. They didn't talk very much. What they said was subdued. The sadness was very close to Miriam's surface but she simply did what had to be done.

I walked about, feeling unneeded and out of place. Zev noticed this and asked me to help; some busy work in the library to keep me off the streets, so to speak. I had already called Estelle Cantor to tell her I was well. She sounded very relieved and made me promise to come home soon. California was a dangerous place even though you couldn't get a heart attack shoveling out the driveway. I decided to write her a long letter, preserving as much as I could my recollection of the last days.

I was just finishing this letter when Zev came in and stood behind me radiating the feeling that, while he didn't want to disturb me, he really did. So I turned to him and he confessed that he had to give the eulogy and he was as immobilized by it as he had been before his first final exams. He had never seriously studied the family journals although he was familiar with them. He would be expected to incorporate the family history in some way. There was also the relic, the "pomander," to be opened. According to tradition, it was only opened at the death of the head of the family. The impression that he might make on the relatives and friends didn't much concern him. He had to do something that would have meaning to his mother.

I got the journals out for him and he was about to sit down when Arin's lawyer telephoned. He didn't have to deal with the matter; whatever it was. It surely could have waited a few days but he seemed relieved to be distracted from the task of preparing for the eulogy.

Zev didn't return until after supper. He ended up spending a long, sleepless night reading the journals and preparing the eulogy.

I was up much of the night looking over his shoulder sticking in my two cents whenever asked. I napped in the pre-dawn hours in the maroon chair in the living room. After talking with Zev again and giving him my own notes, I got some sleep in my bed. I awoke about 9:00, dressed, had some breakfast and looked around for Zev. Miriam hadn't seen him and assumed that he had finally gone to sleep.

It was 10 o'clock or so, and the funeral was less than two hours away when I saw him coming toward me in his pajama bottoms on the way to the bathroom.

"Did you finally get some sleep?" I asked.

His eyes were puffy and receded so that they hardly seemed open and he was bent as he looked at me and gave me a delayed response.

"A little. I ended up writing something for the funeral, but I wish someone else would do it. I'm no speaker, and...."
He stopped and looked vacant as if he had lost his train of

thought. "Francesca still hasn't come back from Los Angeles. I hope she makes it."

"Did you go through my notes?"

This produced a wry, weary smile. "I thought Europeans were supposed to have legible handwriting."

"I've been here too long."

"I scanned some parts, Mendel, but I was just too weary. I've only had two hours sleep. My head feels like it's full of crankcase sludge." He brought is hand to his forehead and grimaced.

"What about the box with the relic, did you get it open?" I asked with rising curiosity.

"I tried. But maybe I was just too tired by then. I couldn't figure it out. How are you with puzzles?"

"I used to enjoy them. Do you want me to have a look at it?"

"Please. I've got to open it."

I nodded and went to the library. The box was still on the table among the manuscripts, including my own. I picked it up, half-expecting my hand to tingle, feeling foolish at the thought. It was smooth dark wood and didn't appear to have an opening. I carried it to the balcony thinking that daylight might reveal something that the muted electric light had not. The sun was so bright that my eyes began to smart and I squinted as I turned it around. An image formed in my mind: my mother's dresser, the perfume bottles, one blue, the other clear with a yellow liquid, and beside it the round silver box, the pomander which held her rouge.

This was a pomander, I concluded, turning it in my hand. I looked closely and there it was, obvious when I wanted to see it; a fine horizontal line barely visible in the dark smooth surface. How simple, I thought, it pivots horizontally like my mother's rouge box. Grasping the top and the bottom, I turned each in different directions like a twist-off cap and nothing happened. I paused, turned it in the other direction and the top began to slide to the side. It would be improper for me to look at the contents, I thought, although Arin had offered to show it to me. Even so, Zev should be the one to open it.

I rushed inside, put the partly open box down on the table and rushed to the bathroom door. "Zev, I've got it started!"

He opened the door and looked at me quizzically, his face a mummer's mask of white on one side from the shaving cream, and he dried his hands on a towel. As we returned to the library I told him how I had managed to open it and he berated himself for not thinking of that.

He picked it up and carefully turned the top the rest of the way, revealing an old cloth bag no bigger than a golf ball, tightly woven, and of two colors, faded brown and faded red, reminding me of the color of old Persian rugs. Zev lifted the bag out of the little pocket and examined it. The red on it was an abstract design, a row of touching spheres each with a crown on the top. The cloth was very old but still supple. He pulled it open very patiently and looked inside to see what appeared to be three grape seeds, shrunken and dried, who knows how old.

"You're a botanist," I said, "what are they?"

The change in Zev was striking as he concentrated, looking from the bag to the seeds, rolling one of them gently between his fingertips, before he mumbled, almost to himself, "Pomegranate." There was discovery and wonder in his voice and in his eyes as he looked up at me and repeated it, "Pomegranate seeds. Look at the design on the pouch, pomegranates, see the calyx, the little spiked crown?"

We both fell silent for a moment as we stared at the three unobtrusive seeds, the dry old fabric of the bag, and the dark wood of the pomander, smelling vaguely of cedar.

Was it only the impact of suggestion on my pliant imagination? I sensed an evocation of the past. It was as if the dried seeds, the aromatic wood and sack, were imbued with the events that had surrounded them, and that my mind had become the medium of their story.

"Then Abraham's journal could be true!" I exclaimed. "These could be the seeds that King Solomon gave to your ancestor." I looked at Zev -- our faces were so close that my eyes blurred. He looked bemused, reflective, enjoying my enthusiasm but not sharing it. "Couldn't they be real?" I asked.

He shrugged and said, "The seeds could be any age, and the story could be true or false, whatever the age of the seeds." It was the botanist speaking, the expression of scientific logic.

The side of me that wanted to believe intuitively in the myth and its corroboration brushed his logic aside, but the part of me that lived in the time of laser technology and space shuttles won out for the moment at least, and I asked, "There must be a way to determine the age of the seeds?"

"It wouldn't prove anything, unless they are in fact 2,500 years old or at least 500 years old since the pomegranate isn't a native of this continent." He stopped, looked into space. "They could be that old. Grains keep in the desert. They found grain in Egyptian tombs, 2,500 years old. They could be descended from the original seeds. Or they could have been brought to the valley by Gabriel Cardozo in the seventeenth century." He put the seeds back in the bag. "Carbon 14 dating might give an idea." He rubbed his cheek and was surprised to find his fingers white with shaving lather.

Whatever the odds, it was thrilling to think that these seeds were possible proof of the earliest corroborated voyage across the Atlantic, a joint venture of King Priam of the Phoenicians and Solomon of the Jews, 2,000 years before Columbus. I raised my eyes out of my daydream to see Zev looking at me thoughtfully.

He raised his eyebrows and looked at the seeds. "One thing's certain. Whoever put them there was trying to say that life renews itself. You don't need Carbon 14 dating to come to that conclusion," he said as he slid the little box shut. "Do you know anything about the symbolism of the pomegranate?"

"Only something I read somewhere that the pomegranate was the real apple of the Garden of Eden, the forbidden fruit of the tree of knowledge."

"While I finish shaving would you mind digging around the library and see what else you turn up?

I watched him leave resenting that his logic had tarnished my belief, however romantic and naive. For me the little box had been filled with wonder. For him, it presented a problem of fact to be solved. And yet he hadn't denied the truth of the myth, only questioned it. Maybe I had been too quick to judge him.

With the pleasure that I've always felt searching books for information, the more obscure the better, I went through a half a dozen reference books, all of which were so happy to be remembered that they gave up their information, singing it in my ear.

Later, having dressed and showered, Zev found me sneezing over the displaced dust of the last treatise. I told him that according to several sources, the pomegranate was the fruit that Persephone ate, the fruit of death. Eating it had resulted in her banishment to the underworld. But it is also associated with fertility and renewal, as is any seed, and particularly with hope, the human state of mind without which there can be no renewal. He heard this, looking thoughtful.

When I had finished my little lecture, pointing out passages in the open reference works, he gave me a fond pat on the shoulder and said, "Thanks, Mendel," and without saying more, he left the room.

I remained in the library, musing on the possibility of a link between the Jewish Adam and Eve myth and the Greek story of Demeter and Persephone. All three had eaten pomegranate and been banished from a better world to a lesser world. Persephone came back from hers, at least part of the year, to renew life again and again. What about Adam and Eve? I walked out of the library, wondering what, if anything, Zev would make of it in the eulogy.

The funeral, like the first Sabbath ceremony, resembled nothing I had ever seen before and yet it was familiar. It was held in the patio between the wings of the house. Chairs had been arranged in a semi-circle around the coffin. Arin's body was in a simple wooden box on a raised platform. He was wrapped in a brightly striped cloth which might have been a prayer shawl and partly covered with dried pomegranates. The old men of the sabbath service were playing a monotonous melody on the flute and the drum as people gathered and took their seats. Zev was sitting in the front row between his mother and Francesca, who had arrived no more than twenty minutes earlier. He was wearing a loose white shirt over baggy white pants, and his bronze skin and black hair seemed even darker by contrast. The chanting stopped and he got up hesitantly and faced us.

Zev looked around at the familiar faces. Francesca looked up at him and offered silent encouragement, as did his mother. He unfolded a piece of paper with slightly trembling hands, looked at it blindly, took a deep breath and began in a rather tremulous voice.

"I never really knew my father and I don't think he knew me. I suppose we saw each other through the warped lenses of our expectations. That goes for everybody, I guess. For that matter, I doubt that many of us see ourselves, our society, very clearly either. Not that we don't have occasional insights." He looked around with uncertainty in his eyes, as though he thought he had said the wrong thing. "Since my father's death I've been sitting up there in the library trying to leach out of our history, out of his life, something to say about him, about all of us. Speaking isn't my best skill and to tell the truth I've never thought much about history. I'm more interested in biology, more interested in the present. I guess we all tend to take for granted the things that we inherit and that goes for cultural inheritance as well as biological. I'm sure I took my father for granted as I did the permanence of this house, this garden." His voice was beginning to smooth out, his frozen face was showing more feeling.

"To come closer to my point, what did I learn about my father these last few days? He was more than his biological and cultural heritage, but he never understood it. He was estranged from Abraham's God, he didn't expect miracles, he didn't expect God to intervene in his life or answer his prayers as Abraham did." He stopped for a moment, looking as though the thoughts were forming in his mind as he spoke. He shrugged a little and said, "Maybe Abraham's God died with Abraham.

"My father was no longer Anasazi, or Mayan, Toltec or Jew, but not yet an American either, if it is possible to be anything other than what you are personally. He came of age in the childhood of technology. He never really was comfortable with that either. He was like a man caught trying to cross a stream with one foot on one rock behind him and a foot on a rock in front of him and both rocks are slippery and loose. He never made it to the other side, but he didn't stop trying." He stopped for a long and painful time as if he had lost his way. Somewhere in the garden a bird began to sing and Zev began again.

"That striving is what ties him to all those other Binyans who are buried all around us in this garden. We Binyans don't just accept life. We've always tried to make it better in some concrete way. In that respect we're very American, the first Americans. Our name means building and we have always been builders, whether it was a stronger stone wall that would last a thousand years, or a more efficient way of watering our crops, or a tower to God. That's both a strength and a weakness. We've sometimes made life better for ourselves, a fire to cook our food and keep us warm and dry, but we've had to give up something else: innocence.

"Our earliest Jewish legend tells us that in the loss of innocence we were thrown out of the Garden of Eden. I don't agree. We never left the Garden. Life itself is the Garden. That's what I've learned these last few days. The Garden of Eden isn't a place, it's a state of being, and it exists as a seed in each one of us, capable of growing into a tree if we can find it and nurture it to maturity."

Zev was calm now his gaze was steady as he looked around the group, not mechanically but seeking personal contact with each of them. He was possessed in a way by his idea, and there was strength and authority in his voice. "In the mythical Garden of Eden, people were nude. The nudity wasn't physical, it was mental, spiritual nudity. In a word, an open, exposed mind, a mind not covered up with notions, preconceptions, or beliefs. A mind open to the many possibilities of the present and the always-changing future. That's what innocence is.

"In the Hebrew myth taking knowledge ended this state of innocence because when you think that you really know something you stop being able to accept something new that contradicts it. You stop believing that the future can be different from the present." His face looked radiant with this thought as he paused and looked around him. "It's a funny thing. We read about people of my age taking to eastern religions that are little more than this idea of open mind when here it is buried in their own lore. It seems nobody has ever told them that it was there. Why? Because we don't see it that way."

Again, he looked around him as if he were searching for doubt or indifference to what he was saying. "You probably think that I'm miles away from my father, but I'm not. My father was an honest man. He tried to be an innocent but couldn't be. His grace was that he was for the most part guileless. He had love, gave it to my mother, and shared it with his children. His fault was that his love carried the burden of judgment. It was not given without condition as my Great Grandmother Tamar gave it to Tyler Matthews.

"I suppose my view of my father will always be, not the times he comforted me when I had hurt myself, although he did that. Rather, it was his attempt to measure the coming of the Sabbath to observe the passing over of the Sabbath Bride." He paused and looked at me with affection.

"It was the newest member of our family, Mendel Traig, who finally helped me to understand the meaning of the Sabbath Bride. The Sabbath Bride comes to any spirit in repose, at peace with itself and the world. That's the simple meaning of Sabbath. My father never understood this. He was content with trying to observe her coming, like a spectator at a football game. It can't be done. You can't observe it, you can only experience it. Some people manage to experience it in their lives. In the end, she came to him as she comes to all of us at the moment of ultimate repose, our death. It's a small comfort then, but better than nothing."

Zev sighed as, no doubt, those moments on the tower passed through his mind. He looked up and said in a calm voice, "I went into this eulogy tradition of ours before the funeral with a skeptical mind. I've come out of it feeling that it was worthwhile. It's added a layer of meaning to my life: the importance of innocence, the truly open mind, and the importance of a hopeful outlook in everything you do. And it's even better because I got it right here at home from the tradition of my own family. I could even say that my father gave it to me."

He stopped talking, looked around him and I could see tears in his eyes. I had watched him, not the others. I have no notion if what he was saying made any lasting impression on them. I heard it.

Zev and five old men carried the coffin into the garden, following a labyrinthine path among trees and shrubs. Behind them walked Miriam, Francesca and the rest of us, no more than forty people. We came to a small opening in the trees in the middle of which was an open grave, the sandy earth piled to one side. The chanting resumed as the box was lowered by three ropes into the grave. Miriam, Zev and Francesca were standing next to the grave as the old men recited the *Kaddish*. Miriam was holding Zev's arm but not leaning on him. Their heads were bowed, looking into the open grave, their expressions solemn and inward-looking. The old man and woman who help around the house were standing just to the side of them. They too were looking into the grave but somehow beyond it. What could they see in that soil that they had lived on for so many years? The chanting ended, they formed into a procession, the drummer at the lead and all but Miriam left the grave walking slowly down the path. My place was at the end of the group and before losing sight of the clearing I looked back, but Miriam had disappeared. Ahead, the drum beat out a simple walking rhythm and in the trees birds were singing.

17

KNOWING GOOD AND EVIL

The day after the funeral, Sarah returned to Canyon Springs, thinner in body and, I imagine, spirit. She didn't contact me at first. Not finding me at the motel she assumed that I had already fled to the frost-firm ground of Western Pennsylvania after the quake (now I'm giving it a diminutive like they do in California). Enough digression. The subject after all is Sarah, and I am not a latter-day De Toqueville.

She had been around a day before she reached me. It seems that she had met Zev at the tower where she was making a survey of damage. After the meeting she casually asked after me. Zev told me about her reaction later that day.

"She seemed really happy to hear that you hadn't left."

"What do you mean, 'seemed'?"

"She was pretty grave at the meeting. It was probably just a carry-over of her mood."

"She must be worried about the tower."

"She gave the impression that there may be some damage."

"Does that mean that the tower might not be completed?"

"Maybe."

I looked at him and decided not to probe any further. One thing I can say; he didn't seem too worried. I went to the telephone and called the motel but she wasn't registered.

Later that afternoon, about four o'clock, Sarah called. My heart gave a little start as I heard her voice. She sounded tired and remote.

We didn't exchange more than a few sentences on the phone. Just enough to make dinner plans. I spent the hour or two before she came in a state of anticipation not unlike coffee nerves, looking forward to seeing her and wondering if it would be the same with us. After all, who knows what went on in Korea, or for that matter what I would feel when the time came.

There she was, dressed in a floral print and looking gaunt, for her at least. Even the car looked tired, with its thick coating of road dust on which some patriot had scrawled, "Bye American," either from illiteracy or a budding literary ambiguity.

Affection flooded her eyes as she looked me over. "I thought you'd gone."

"No, I'm still here. They wanted me to stay through the funeral."

"I heard." We faced each other muted by the common thought of death. "Get in," she finally commanded.

I obeyed, and before long we had left the Binyan garden and were speeding down that familiar road on which seemed to be located all the restaurants of the area. Perhaps in addition to the usual utilities, there is also a one inch pipe with soup stock running in it, the length of that road, I speculated. "So, where to?" I asked.

"Yugoslav, all right?"

"Depends," I said, "on which Yugoslav cuisine, Serbian, Croatian?"

She didn't have the answer, but we went anyway. Well, this isn't a restaurant guide. Suffice it to say that the food was tasty, the music authentic, and the wine robust. As for the company, we brought each other up to date. She talked about Korea and I told her about the earthquake and the funeral. She talked about her company and I listened. All negotiations of Alumaloy were suspended including the Korean deal until her report on the structural damage to the tower was completed and evaluated by management. The Korean deal was already closed but subject to review of the specifications and analysis by the builder's consulting engineers. Now I understood the visible tension. She was, as she had put it, the fall person. If she came through with a negative report it could be the end of her career with Alumaloy. If the report were positive she might get a promotion and the blame if anything went wrong.

"Any conclusions yet? That is, any conclusion that you are at liberty to share with me?"

"Not really. I've sent several components of the structure out to a metallurgical lab for microscopic examination, ultraviolet light and all that. I'm expecting the results tomorrow," she said, fatigue in her voice. Then, in a different tone, a soft tone, she said, "I'm so glad you're here. I'm getting used to having you around to see me over my crises."

"That's what friends are for."

"Do you feel like going someplace for a drink? Or would you like to go back to my room. I've got a bottle of cognac that I bought at the duty-free shop."

"We can't do better than that."

"Good. You don't have any curfew over there, do you?"

"Yes, they lock the gate and call roll at nine but I've got a 24-hour pass."

We returned to her room, not the same room, not even the same place. It was much more spacious, even with a table and two chairs, not to mention an original signed and numbered lithograph or two. She observed my expression and volunteered, "They made the arrangements for me. It's their way of putting me in a good mood."

"Does it?"

"I didn't go to engineering school to end up anybody's whore." She pulled the cork on the cognac and splashed a healthy two fingers in each of the snifters.

"Even the right kind of glasses. No detail omitted."

"For $150 a day what do you expect?"

Sarah sat down across from me and her expression changed from exasperation to an unspoken request for understanding, even support. I took a slosh of the cognac, waited for the warmth to channel down my throat, and asked, "What will you do if the report comes back showing damage?"

Exasperation again. "What would you do? Quit? Acknowledge it but understate its importance? Don't even mention it? Say that it's normal for an earthquake of this severity?"

"Are you asking my advice?"

"Sure."

"I'd give them my best professional judgment and wait for their reaction."

"And if they sack me I go back to being a secretary. No one else will have me."

"You think it's that bad, then?"

"I don't know, Mendel, but of late I've been wishing that I had taken a course in design instead. I've always liked the shape of coffee pots and coffee grinders." She downed her cognac, poured another and looked over my head.

I wanted to say, it's the sublimation of your desire to be a wife coming out, but I thought better of it. As my Uncle Heshie used to say, you get paid for your wit with shit or something like that. It sounded better in *Yiddish*.

We sat there quietly, drinking about a third of the bottle of cognac between us, the lights turned down thanks to the rheostat, blessed technology. Without talking about it we got undressed, or rather changed into our nightclothes; she into a diaphanous pale blue Grecian nightgown, and I into a pair of maroon silk pajamas that she had brought me as a present from Korea. What a pleasant surprise and much better than a postcard. Then we made love and it was as before with us, gentle release, like mother's milk to an infant, and we slept holding hands like two children.

The next morning, by the time we had both showered, room service had already produced breakfast, croissants even, on a balcony shaded with bougainvillea. The night had been good for her. She was fresh and calm as though she had passed on to some resolution or even resignation, I wasn't sure which and didn't want to discuss it. Fortunately the phone call from the laboratory didn't come until we had finished eating. The ringing startled her and I heard her quickened breath as she went to the phone. Someone on the other end did the talking and I couldn't tell from her response what she had heard, but I could see from her look as she hung up and turned to me that the news was anything but good. The color had gone out of her cheeks.

"What news?" I said, quoting MacBeth. She took no note of it.

"Bad news. Microscopic cracks in the surface of the metal. Not clear through, understand, but indicating weakness."

"So you could, if you wanted to, write an ambiguous report."

"Yes, I could. One that would build a lot of high-rises with Alumaloy and make me a very rich lady."

"The raise you were talking about?"

"More than that." She smiled a shallow smile. "They offered me a stock option before I came down here. I didn't mention it last night. Assuming that Alumaloy takes off, it could be worth, who knows, a half a million."

"That's both enviable and unenviable, if you understand my meaning."

"I'm afraid that I do," she replied, looking solemn. She looked around the room as though she were searching for something, then said, "Mendel, let me drop you back at the

Binyans'. I've got to go out to the tower and do a visual examination. I'll call you later."

I spent the whole day in the library, cataloguing and reading, not even leaving for lunch. There is no clock in the library, nothing to measure time but the length of the shadow on the floor and, as occasionally happens to me when I am totally absorbed in what I am doing, I suddenly find that I am very hungry and lunch time has come and gone. When I finally came up for air it was past four and the sandwich thoughtfully left for me in the dining room looked as though it had suffered from desiccation although not a fatal case. I ate part of it and thought about Sarah. Without returning to the library and with nothing better to do, it was too late to go for a ride - I might miss a call from her - I took a walk in the garden and instead of returning to my room decided to walk straight to her hotel and wait for her there.

My timing was good. She had just arrived and met me at the door to her room with a kiss. She smelled of perfume and sweat and her hair was dusty and disheveled. "I was just about to call you," she said. Her voice was gentle, but those eyes of hers were signaling disappointment, frustration, or both. I looked her up and down. Her beige pants were torn above the left knee and there were dirty smudges all over her cotton blouse, as though she had been crawling about in some cramped and dirty places.

"Sit down and order a couple of drinks, Mendel, while I shower. I'm exhausted. I feel like I've just climbed K-2 or whatever."

"You look like it too. What do you want to drink?"

"Gin and tonic," she called from the bathroom. "Double."

Before she was out of the bathroom someone was at the door with her double gin and my double orange juice. I've never adjusted to the cocktail hour. If I need some relaxation at the end of a hard day, I prefer a nap. She came out of the bathroom looking fresh and smelling of sandalwood, her hair tied up on her head. She went straight for the drink, her gauzy wrap parting as she walked. Turning a mischievous eye toward me, she said, "We're eating pasta tonight, Mendel; the way I feel, it's the only thing that'll help."

"And last night you were saying that I..."

"You're the sauce, Mendel, the sauce," she said, dropping the wrap at her feet and standing there like Eve as God made her; just for a moment before she covered up again.

"Sarah, you're looking more like Jane Fonda every day."

"It's my new diet, Mendel, better than Tarnower. I eat whatever I want and worry the fat off. Would you believe I lost four pounds yesterday?"

"You look like you had a bad day."

Waving her arm as though she were fighting me off, she said, "Not now, Mendel, let's make an agreement. We don't talk about it until after the main course. Let's pretend we're someplace else, someplace relaxing like Manhattan in the rush hour."

As always, my curiosity was gnawing away at me, but I shut up and watched her dress, a nice sight to see those fabrics layer themselves on the wonder of her form, clinging tightly here, billowing out or fluting there, concealing, enhancing, promising. I watched her, thinking for some funny reason of Rex

Harrison, and his nasal voice started playing in my head, "I've grown accustomed to her face..." and so forth. I was going all soft in the chest again and achy in the heart. I knew what was happening to me, but I couldn't believe it. I was falling in love with her, not just attracted to her sexually. More, much more than that, and at my age. Who knows, I mused, it may be just a symptom of precocious senility. Why take it apart, Mendel, I told myself, enjoy it while it lasts. You haven't felt this way about someone since... She turned from the mirror and looked at me with self-satisfaction. "I hope you like pasta?"

"Who doesn't," I replied, and off we went to the soup stock pipeline, in search of the one restaurant that hadn't yet imprinted our Visa.

As we reached the lobby Sarah realized that she'd left the address of the restaurant in the room and asked the desk clerk for the location. It proved to be somewhere between the steak and lobster and sushi. As we drove I remembered my father saying once that countries might save money and create more good will if embassies and consulates had restaurants serving inexpensive good food to the public instead of alcohol and propaganda to the diplomatic corps.

So dinner went as planned; high in calories and devoid of talk about the unmentionable at least through the main course. We were quite at ease with each other by then, Sarah and I. The small talk and the silences were natural and there were times when we simply looked at each other, no more than looked at each other. Those feelings of mine back at the room were still flitting around in my head like a giddy moth and I wasn't sure what to do with them or, for that matter, even whether to trust them. I was sure that they would pass, leaving me feeling foolish, like the morning after, or even feeling absurd. I couldn't imagine that she felt the same so there was nothing to do but keep it to myself and enjoy this holiday affair until the boat docks and we part for good.

Promptly after the coffee had been poured -- we passed on dessert, as the pastries looked as if they'd been prepared in a wax museum -- she went back to the tower with the question, apologetically framed, "Mendel, I'm sorry to get back to this, but I have to know something, something about the earthquake at the tower. Tell me exactly what happened to you?"

"Why do you want to know? Something about the damage?"

"Exactly."

"What did you find out there today? You can tell me now, I guess.,"

"What I was afraid of," she said, holding the coffee poised between the table and her lips. "A pattern of cracks, visible with a magnifying glass, at certain critical junctions of the structure. The reason I asked about the nature of the quake was to help me figure out how it happened."

"It was swaying."

"Yes, but what did it do when that first jolt hit it?"

"I didn't see that."

"You see, there's still a lot of ambiguity. Conflicting seismographic reports."

"It makes a big difference?"

"You bet. The increase is exponential. Any kind of structure is likely to suffer some damage, particularly one that's not built to the specifications of a building." She was looking through me and at me, reasoning out loud. "If the trembler was only in the fives, that means that the extent of the damage puts in much more doubt the resistance of Alumaloy under stress, especially since the tower is built on a big rock, which reduces the stress."

"Are you trying to say that you still don't know what to put in the report?"

She moved her head from one side to the other, and said, "There isn't any building that can be built economically to be indestructible, or more properly, damage-proof."

"Have you called your office to tell them about your findings?"

"Yep."

"And the reaction?"

"Dead silence," she said as she fell into one of her thoughtful moods, absorbed again by the weight of her, as yet unresolved, decision. She looked into her coffee cup. Finding no answer there, she picked up and peeled a sugar cube, then took to stacking cubes and alternately shaking and pounding the table, observing the reaction. I couldn't tell if this was simply a game or ratiocination. For all I know Einstein used sugar cubes as well. She looked up to see someone she recognized and didn't want to see, judging by her expression. He came right up behind me, a tall athletic-looking man with a swarthy, heavily lined face and thick straight hair, about my age by the looks of him.

"Jerry!" she said, sounding both surprised and annoyed.

"Sorry to hunt you down like this at dinner, Sarah. Prescott asked me to come down tonight after I told him about your call. You can understand why. The desk clerk told me where you probably were. I was going to wait at the hotel, but I wasn't sure when you'd come back," he said, looking at me.

"It's all right," she said with resignation. Then she introduced us. Jerry Colfath was Vice President, Sales-Engineering. "Sit down, Jerry," she said casually. "Let me buy you a drink, on Alumaloy, of course." She caught the waiter's eye and ordered three cognacs. First came the small talk: the trip down, somebody's automobile accident, office gossip, nothing about the subject at hand. Sarah continued to play with the sugar for the most part avoiding Jerry's eyes. Finally, after watching her with an expression of mild irritation, he said, "That going to form the basis of your report?"

"It might just as well," she replied, a half-smile twisting her lips momentarily.

"Then you're still not sure how to deal with it?"

"That must have come through loud and clear."

"With all this uncertainty, I would think that you could write a report that wouldn't really hurt, recommend using heavier joints, possibly even taking the suggestion of additional tungsten in the alloy. Isn't that what the R&D lab is talking about, Alumaloy II, I think they called it."

"We've been through all that before, Jerry. In simple English, tampering with the formulation of the alloy is likely to create other problems, like making it too brittle."

"That's just a guess, though."

"It's not a guess. We tried it," she said irritably.

"Sarah," I said, "maybe you two want to talk about this privately."

"Yes, that might be better," said Jerry, looking at Sarah.

"No, I don't really want to prolong this tonight. I've had a long, hard day...."

"Prescott asked me to call him, at any time in the night or the morning, Sarah. He wants some assurances. He doesn't want to wait for months while the consultants screw around. Rumor will kill the whole sales program if that happens. You know how Prescott thinks...."

Her voice was controlled but barely so as she looked at him defiantly, and said, "Jerry, if Prescott wants an answer tonight, just tell him one word, tell him it's negative. Because with the preliminary data, I'm not going to flatly exonerate the product from any hazard. And consultants and more tests is just what I'm going to recommend. And if he thinks that I'm going to spend the next ten years of my life waiting for a building to collapse in Rio or Seoul, just tell him he can sit on his tower. So you don't have to wake him up. Call him now and tell him that. He's probably watching the movie on T.V." She was bristling like an angry cat.

"Now calm down, Sarah, watch that Irish temper."

"It's not temper, it's indignation, righteous indignation."

"Whatever, you're swimming out beyond the breakwater, you should know that."

"Don't you think that I've thought of the consequences? I've been around that shop long enough to know how the game is played."

"Nothing like that, Sarah."

"OK, Jerry, I don't think we have any more to talk about. Sorry I got pissy. But it's my ass that's on the line, not yours."

"It's the whole company's, Sarah. We'll all be affected," Jerry said, getting up and standing over her, looking grave.

"It's more than the company, Jerry, much more, and that's what Prescott will never understand. For him the company is everything, for me it's just a way to get what I want out of life."

"Sarah, I'll call you tomorrow, before breakfast. I've got a room at the same hotel. Nice meeting you, Mendel." She watched his long strides and gave a long, long sigh. Then she looked at me and said, "I guess that's that." A self pitying smile. "Could you use an assistant?"

"Why not?"

She paid the check with plastic and we drove back to the hotel. The only thing that I said on the way back was, "I want you to know, Sarah, as one of the occupants of the world, that I admire your integrity."

She looked at me as though she wanted to say something bitter, but she changed her mind and her features softened. "Thanks, Mendel, it means something to me that you said it."

Back in the room we had a silent nightcap. She was looking like the defeated candidate on election night that at least has the satisfaction of having run a clean campaign. Once again my feelings for her returned, not only in the head but the heart. I sat there sipping the cognac, wondering what, if anything, to say about it. Do you tell a woman who has just fallen in the mud that she's pretty? We got in bed and she turned on the late show, I suppose so as not to have to talk. It proved to be a vintage John Wayne film, the last thing she wanted to see. Off it went at the first deodorant commercial. Off went the lights as well and we warmed up to each other slowly. Holding her in my arms she reminded me of a wounded hawk, not a very romantic image I confess, but I have no control over what comes to my mind. She calmed down after a time, that and some more cognac - and I should give myself a little credit. I could feel her letting go after I massaged her neck a little. All the time we lay there silently. I wondered what, if anything, I should say to her about my feelings.

We made love about three A.M. And afterwards she said it to me, "I love you, Mendel," softly, almost a murmur, but with conviction.

"And I love you, Sarah." Just like that it was out, a relief to have said it, to have opened myself to her as she had to me. Not since Clara had I heard those words, and not since Clara had I spoken them, and it felt like the first warm spring day when you take off the storm windows and let the outside in.

I can't tell you what she was thinking as we clung to each other in that anonymous hotel room with the two signed lithographs. We clung to each other and we were not alone anymore and that was enough. Touching from ankle to shoulder, breathing with sssanother person is also making love. Later we slept.

The next morning, we were already up and about when the telephone rang. It was Jerry, telling her to return to Los Angeles for a luncheon meeting and that moreover she shouldn't plan on returning to Palm Springs. Her face and body were taut as she hung up the phone and told me that she would be packing up. We looked at each other, searching for a measure of our feelings. What I felt was a loss as she said this, but I tried not to show it. This was after all a mobile society and love did not guaranty a life together.

We had another continental breakfast on the balcony, not speaking much. She was preoccupied, fretful, apprehensive about the coming meeting. About all she said, between the fresh orange juice and the second cup of coffee, was "Shit." Expletive is a word that fits the way it came out. For whatever reason, the word was cathartic for her. She brightened up after she said it, looked at me with that open light-filled gaze and said more philosophically, "So, here I go again. How much longer will you be here? I could come down on the week-end or you could come to L.A. You can stay at my place of course. You'll like the view." There was a gentle entreaty in her voice.

"That's all you need, with all that's going on, to have to put up with a tourist. You'll want some peace and quiet."

She didn't respond at first. She just looked at me and smiled, as much with her eyes as with the rest of her face. Then she said, "You're not just a tourist, Mendel." As she spoke these last words, her voice grew fluid until it melted.

I must have flushed, I know I did, and I said, "I somehow thought that we were just a shipboard romance, something that glows like a Fourth of July sparkler and then goes out."

She looked hurt when I said this. "It doesn't have to be that way, Mendel."

"Don't misunderstand me, Sarah. What I said last night I meant, with my soul I meant it. I had felt it before."

"Then why didn't you say it?"

"I was afraid it would sound foolish, coming from me."

"Loving another person is one of the few things we do that isn't foolish, even when it's not returned." Again, the feeling kindled in her eyes.

"There was another reason." She waited. "I couldn't really trust my feelings, or know yours. It's been so long for me…." My words choked off.

"It's been long for me too, Mendel. Too long for both of us."

18

THE MANY DIFFERENT TREES OF THE GARDEN

When, on the morning of my departure, Zev gave me the choice of their old station wagon or the horses, I chose the horses. It was a grand day for a ride, we had plenty of time, and it somehow seemed the right way to go.

I took my time that morning, packing, walking around in the gardens, sitting near the fountain, and in the library. One part of me didn't want to leave this little Eden, this arcane library with its obscure books, the heady fragrances, the curving paths, the worn tiles and dark polished oak of the cool shadowed house, the sharp-edged mountains and empty blue sky. All of this I had grown accustomed to, begun to see with now-familiar eyes, and finally even taken for granted as if it were mine. I would miss them all.

When the time finally came I faced Miriam, stout and erect, in front of the door. I put my arms around her embraced her stolidity and kissed her on the cheek.

Gently holding my arms, she said, "Are you sure you won't stay a while longer, Mendel? The library is up there calling to you. Can't you hear it?"

"I hear it."

Disappointment showing, she said, "I just have to tell it that you will be back someday."

"I will try to return, Miriam."

"You are always welcome." She stood up on her toes and kissed my cheek, then she handed me a basket. "Some lunch for the trip. The airplane food isn't real, I've been told."

We mounted, and I waved to her as we rode out of the courtyard. I took a last look at the house before it disappeared behind the trees. On one wall some scaffolding had been erected, and several workmen were patching cracks from the earthquake.

"I still can't understand why the quake did so little damage," I said as I shifted in the saddle to steady myself against the spine jarring trot.

"They still know so little about earthquakes. Sometimes a quake strikes a certain place while, due to the character of the substructure, a place five or ten miles away hardly has any damage. I don't know much about it. It's not my field, you know."

"I'm sorry that Francesca wasn't there when I left."

"The quarter started a week ago and she was already late."

"I like her very much."

"She likes you, too."

We were riding on a trail skirting the town but in sight of walled subdivisions.

"You never did get into the canyons, did you? Too bad."

"I'm sorry I didn't get to see your personal canyon."

"It was beautiful. I was out there the other day. The stream is already beginning to cut a new course through the debris. Given enough time, it will restore itself."

"Surely, not in your lifetime."

"No, but we've got to take a longer view of things." He pointed toward the serrated ridge of San Jacinto peak. "If you think that the canyon is a mess, think what this place looked like when that mountain came pitching up out of the ground."

"But that wild grape of yours."

He shrugged. "It's still there, probably. And if it isn't, it's not the first species that has disappeared, and it won't be the last."

"You're pretty philosophical."

"Not really. It's just that I can accept natural change a little easier than I can accept things we do to the earth."

"I suppose I'm prying, but what about your father's finances? Will you be able to deal with his debts?"

"You're not prying, Mendel; after all, you knew how bad it was even before I did. I've talked to his accountant and gotten a summary of our situation. He had a lot of life insurance. That will take care of the immediate problems. And if we need any more, we'll just sell off half of our Indio farm land. It's not part of the original holdings and 640 acres is too much for any family anyhow. We'll be fine. Everybody should be in our shape." We rode on and he added, "Thanks for caring."

"Francesca told me she was planning to come back here after law school," I said.

"Yes, she is."

"What about you?"

"I guess I'm bound to the land now."

What he was saying was drowned out by the roar of a plane taking off. We watched it climb trailing a plume of black smoke.

"What did you say?"

"I started to mention my plans, that's all. I've been doing this research on food sources from desert plants, or at least plants requiring very little water. I want to start an institute down here, put together some grant money from international sources, foundations, the U.N., hopefully even government sources."

"Sounds like a novel idea."

"Not really. It's even selfish. You see, I'd like to commute to my job on foot or on horseback, and come home for lunch. Riding a horse it seems is becoming a tradition in my family and I suppose I should honor a few of the traditions."

We tethered the horses on a Hertz rent-a-car sign, undoubtedly creating an impression on arriving tourists. As I tied my horse using the knot Uncle Maier had shown me in another world I thought back on my first day as a tourist. Now here I was looking at the tourists coming and going with mild disdain.

We divided the baggage between us and entered the air-conditioned lobby. As before, I felt the chill and discomfort. "Sure you won't stay a while longer?" he asked as I stood in the line.

"I can't I've got to return to my life, to my own reality. Besides, my friends back in Bolton miss me."

"This could become your life, Mendel."

I could see that what he was saying was more than politeness. He meant it. I realized how far I had come with him and it touched me.

"Thanks Zev," I said as he walked me to the gate, past bright illuminated plastic signs advertising hotels and rental cards.

We walked past the gate for the Chicago-New York flight, and Zev said, "We're passing your gate, Mendel."

"No, we're not. It's Gate 3, see?" I said, showing him the boarding pass.

"You're connecting through Los Angeles, then?"

"Yes, with an overnight stop over."

"Good for you." I could see from his expression that he knew why.

"Well, Zev, you'd better get back to those horses. You forgot to lock the ignition and some tourist might think one of them is the Mustang he's just rented."

"If he does, he'll have a hard time finding the air conditioning switch."

I thrust my hand out and he took it. "Good-bye, Zev."

"Come back to us, Mendel. You're almost one of us now."

"What do you mean, 'almost'? Your mother initiated me. And, for that matter, so did you with the pomegranate seeds."

He nodded. "Then you must come back for sure for our wedding."

I thought to myself, Abraham's descendant and Messer's descendant, the last in the line of each are joining together, perhaps to make a new people for the Valley. The lesion that has festered will be healed. I wondered what the children would be like.

"You and Francesca have set a date?"

"More or less. Sometime this year."

"So send me an announcement. And one thing more. Let me know the results of the carbon whatever test of the pomegranate seed." I heard them call my flight, but it was a small airport and I wasn't concerned.

"I'm not going to test it, Mendel."

"Why not? You a man of science, and a botanist to boot. Think of the splash it would make if it turned out to be as old as Solomon."

He looked down at the package he was carrying, shifted on his feet, and said, "I've decided that it's not important to me how old it is."

"So what is important?" I pressed him as he showed no sign of saying anything else.

"Well, for others, it's that they believe, and what it means to them as people. If it gives meaning to their lives, it makes no difference whether it's true or false."

"And as for you?"

"As a botanist, what's important to me is that my ancestors thought that their most important possession wasn't gold, or something like that, but a few seeds. That's a statement that connects me to my past in a way I would never have thought possible."

So he had taken something out of the eulogy, I thought. "I've thought a lot about what you said about the Garden of Eden, innocence and the open mind. Maybe you missed your calling; you should have been a philosopher or a theologian."

"Scientists should be philosophers, I guess."

"But you know there's a flaw in your Garden of Eden analogy, a worm in the apple, so to speak."

"You'll miss your plane, Mendel." He took me by the arm. "I'll walk with you and you can tell me about the worm."

"It's this. Why is the tree of knowledge both in the Garden, the consciousness, and at the same time forbidden?"

"Good question," he said. "Knowledge had to be there because humans are fitted out with a knowledge factory. We have memory, reason and intuition; the machinery to synthesize experience, turn it into discovery by some spontaneous process in the mind."

"So why was knowledge forbidden?"

"Only the fruit was forbidden, the byproduct. Because a byproduct stops the process. It's finished, so it's not knowledge. Knowledge itself is a tree, always changing, putting out new branches and new roots. Knowledge is never an absolute because when something is repeated a piece is always missing and another piece is always added, like the dead branches on a tree and the new branches."

He may have reinvented some philosopher's ideas, for all I knew, but it was original for me and appealing as well. We both heard the plane called and he turned to me and handed me the brown paper package he'd been carrying all along, saying, "Open it."

It was, as I expected, a book with an old leather binding, dark brown, split at the corners, a memento from the library. I opened to the first printed page and recognized it with a reverent shock.

"I can't accept this. It's the most valuable book in your library." I handed it back to him, but he put his hands behind his back.

"Mother and I want you to have it and I know father would have felt the same. You came into our lives at a critical time and your being here has meant a lot to us. You're not the first to drop in on the Binyan family like that. You know. You've read about it."

"An old book, maybe, would be a fine present, but this is priceless. Do you have any idea what it's worth?"

"A good friend is worth more, Mendel, whatever its value. Besides, what with your notes you might be our next Gabriel Cardozo. You might bring the story up to date."

I drew close to him, he wrapped his arms around me and I kissed him on the cheek.

"Sir, you'll miss the plane," said the ticket taker, and I hurried on to the tarmac. Missing it was the last thing I wanted, because Sarah would be waiting for me at the airport and I was already looking forward to seeing her.

I took a seat by the window to get one last view of the valley from the air. The plane took off, circled and headed north.

I searched the ground for the large square of green with the U-shaped orange tile-roofed house in its center, but I couldn't locate it. Except for the fact that I was carrying an incunabula, a first printed edition of the Old Testament, it might never have existed at all.

Opening the basket, I found the lunch Miriam had packed for me, and I recognized some of the food we had eaten after the funeral. I had asked Miriam about the custom of burial in the wooden box, the body covered with pomegranates, thinking that the fruit was some kind of preservative. "In a way it is," she had told me. "You see, the seeds in time produce trees and fruit, fertilized by the body."

"But how could they, several feet down under a wood lid?" I asked.

"We don't leave all of the pomegranates in the box, just some of them. Others get taken out after the funeral and planted. And the lid is no more than a fourth of an inch thick."

"Is that what you were doing when you stayed behind?"

"Yes. It's our way of saying good-bye," she had said.

"Then some of the trees in the garden are rooted in your ancestor's graves?"

She had looked past me, an odd, secret smile on her face, and said, "A lot of them are. Especially the fruit and nut trees. The olive and fig trees as well. I think they might be the oldest."

I peered again into the lunch basket and had that familiar feeling that comes when you've left something undone and know that you can't do a thing about it, like leaving the house and forgetting to close the window on a day that portends rain. What had I forgotten?

19

LOOSE ENDS

Sarah met me at the airport, and what a place--traffic going round and round like a giant modern carousel. As I waited at the curb in the shadow of a ziggurat-turned-parking garage I saw the same buses and jitneys over and over again. It struck me that there was no exit. Eventually she got there and took me to her "place". It had a smoggy view stretching toward what she claimed was the Pacific Ocean. I couldn't tell.

Sarah had written a negative report on the tower and her bosses weren't happy about it. We had a good night together, concentrated like vanilla extract, for we both knew that we might never see each other again. She certainly wasn't going to come to Bolton and, having made my choice when I could have gone to Israel some years back, I wasn't going to leave. So there was this inevitability, this beginning and end to the night and the parting again at the cacophonous, frantic airport.

When I got home there were the old friends glad to see me, Nudelman, Estelle, Dr. Zucker pronouncing me cured, the pile of magazines and solicitations, the dinner parties, the old and deep warmth and comfort, even if the weather was rotten. Sarah and I kept up contact, we talked on the phone, we wrote, but as time went on our ossified passion began to feel like those plastic meals in front of Japanese restaurants. Oh, the love had been real enough, but only for a few nights and days, it was shallow, a kind of ship-board romance. So we became precocious old friends, the kind you send holiday greetings to with an end-of-year report, and when you lick the envelope the sweetness of the memory comes back as well.

At least Zev and Francesca married. Of course I got an invitation with a personal note but I didn't go. I sent a nice present, an antique majolica plate showing two young people obviously in love. The woman looked like Francesca, which is why I bought it.

Francesca kept her promise to open a law practice in the Valley. She's got plenty of money and is devoting herself to environmental law, all of it *"pro bono,"* which means for the public good, I guess.

The tower didn't get finished, thanks to the earthquake and Sarah's bad report. Zev tells me it's become a tourist site. He's deeded it to the County Park District to put an end to any prospect of commercial development. His seed project is occupying him and he has several grants. He's been planting some of his own seed too for the last I heard Francesca was pregnant.

I've tried to get Zev to send me a copy of Tamar Binyan's Journal, the one I never read, but he refuses. He tells me that it will be waiting for me when I return for a visit.

I'm back in my familiar trench, complacent as an old house cat. I often think about Binyan Valley. Someday, I'll go back. In the meantime, there's the Synagogue budget and a good cup of coffee with Estelle Cantor on a rainy day.

Sheldon Greene